The Prisoner's Cross

The Prisoner's Cross

Peter B. Unger

RESOURCE *Publications* · Eugene, Oregon

THE PRISONER'S CROSS

Resource Publications
An Imprint of Wipf and Stock Publishers
199 W. 8th Ave., Suite 3
Eugene, OR 97401

www.wipfandstock.com

PAPERBACK ISBN: 978-1-5326-9613-8
HARDCOVER ISBN: 978-1-5326-9614-5
EBOOK ISBN: 978-1-5326-9615-2

05/10/22

For my father whose life and ministry enriched
so many lives, and whose war time journal and
iron cross made made this work possible.

A special thanks to Don Seagreaves whose friendship, support, and imput, inspired me to undertake this work.

Contents

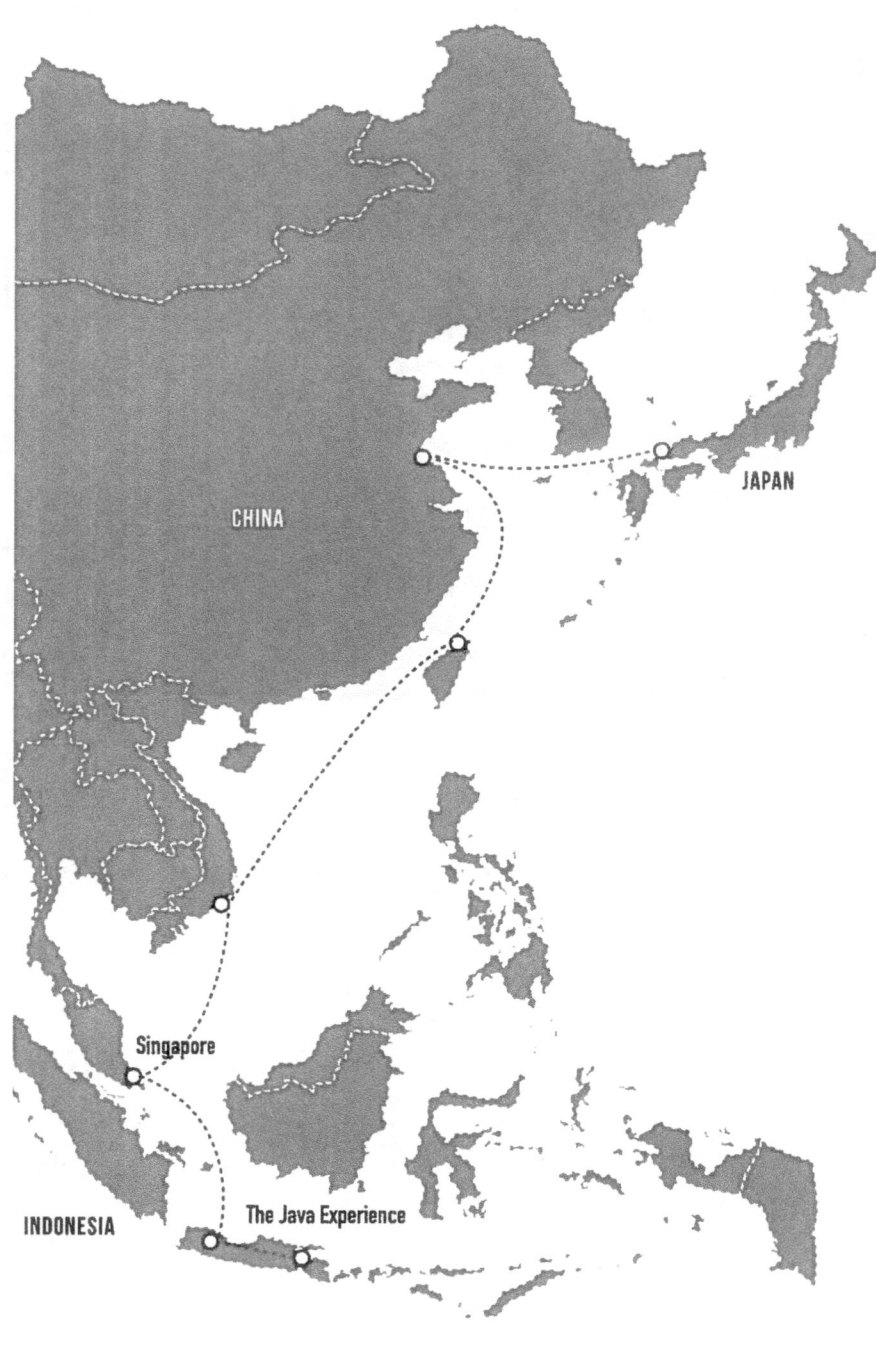

CHINA

JAPAN

Singapore

INDONESIA   The Java Experience

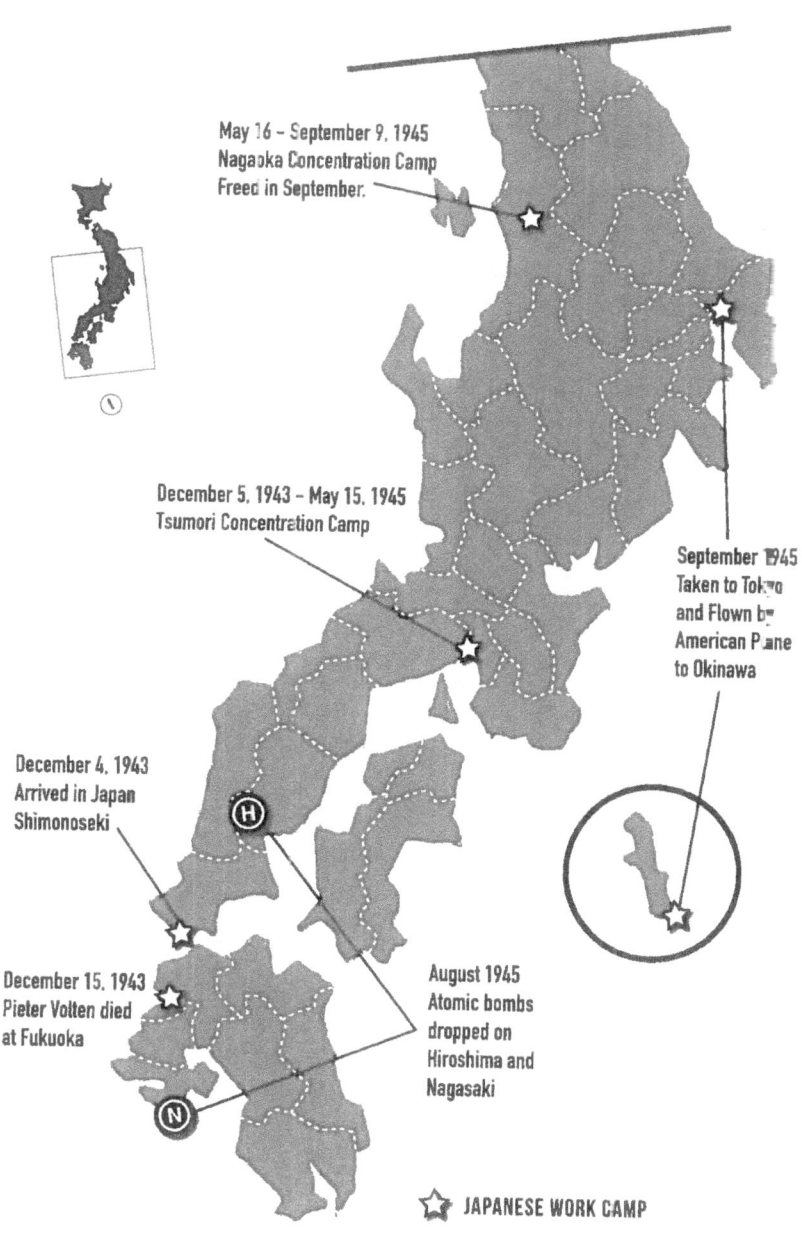

May 16 – September 9, 1945
Nagaoka Concentration Camp
Freed in September.

December 5, 1943 – May 15, 1945
Tsumori Concentration Camp

September 1945
Taken to Tokyo
and Flown by
American Plane
to Okinawa

December 4, 1943
Arrived in Japan
Shimonoseki

December 15, 1943
Pieter Volten died
at Fukuoka

August 1945
Atomic bombs
dropped on
Hiroshima and
Nagasaki

☆ JAPANESE WORK CAMP

The Call

It was the worst phone call of his life. The date May 12, 1993, the time 4:30 in the afternoon were seared onto his heart and mind. Don had just come home from his summer job, a daytime shift at the local Ford plant. His father, Jim Campbell, had worked at the plant, just outside of Boden, Kentucky, for decades. Don had grabbed milk from the fridge and drunk directly from the carton. His mother would teasingly chastise him whenever she caught him in the act, but she was not home. Alberta, or Berta, as everyone called her, often picked up her fifteen-year-old daughter from school, and was usually home by now. "She must be running some errands," Don thought.

Both Berta and Jim were products of a working-class background. Berta's father had worked for many years as an auto mechanic. His last job, as he neared retirement, had been at the newly opened Ford plant. Berta's mother had worked mainly as a homemaker. She had a natural intelligence and reflective nature that she had passed on to her daughter. Berta's father was a kindly affable man. Alberta had inherited the best of both her parents' traits. A warm, loving person with a quick smile and an easy, gentle laugh, Berta was also a natural nurturer. Don was close to his mother. The two would often sit and talk at the kitchen table for long periods. Their conversations started with Berta asking about his day. More recently Berta had been asking Don how his studies were going at the local community college, where he was nearing the end of his first year. Their conversations would then naturally flow in a variety of directions. The big questions of life held an interest for both Berta and her son. For Berta this had always been framed by her deep faith and involvement at the First Baptist Church off Main Street in the center of town. Berta had an open-mindedness to hearing ideas that others from her background might find threatening.

Don had taken Intro to Philo his first semester and Intro to Comparative Religion his second semester. What he had learned had both challenged his faith and broadened it. In his comparative religion study he had seen parallels between all the world religions, such as the common values they all seemed to espouse. He had also discovered big differences. He found himself wondering, "Could the same God be at work in all these religions." If so, he had thought, how would this account for the Buddhist lack of belief in any God. He had shared these thoughts and questions with his mother. Berta would lean forward, cupping her head in her hands as she listened to him. She seemed to eagerly soak up all Don was sharing as if learning vicariously through him. Typical of her responses were remarks like, "Don, God is much greater than we can imagine, and we should not put him in a box," and, "I am okay with other folks' beliefs as long as they're okay with mine."

Berta had recognized Don's intellectual and academic ability during his high school years. She had urged him to consider seminary as an option down the road. Don had grown up in Boden's First Baptist Church, attended Sunday School there, and been active in the youth group. More telling was that he had continued to attend the church each Sunday with his mother and sister throughout his teen years after finishing Sunday School. Although as a young man he did not feel he was ready for adult baptism. During his teenage years Berta had seen him reading his Bible regularly, which he kept on the table by his bed.

Through most of Don's growing-up years his father, Jim, had worked the day shift at the local Ford manufacturing plant. He would often come home from work, walk into the kitchen of their small ranch house, and grab a couple beers out of the fridge. Ignoring his wife and son, Jim would then retreat to the living room where he would flick on the TV, usually to a cop show or a Western, and sit back and watch TV until dinner time. He would repeat this ritual after dinner, making return raids to the fridge for more beer. Jim remained incapable of understanding the close bond mother and son shared and was jealous of it. By early evening, while Berta was cleaning up in the kitchen, Jim had drunk himself into a stupor. Jim and Berta had met in high school in their junior year. They had dated throughout their junior and senior years. In the two years following graduation they had broken up and gotten back together a few times before deciding they would stay together. Soon thereafter Jim decided to join the National Guard and before enlisting Berta and Jim had gotten married. Fertility problems had delayed their having children and accounted for the nearly five-year difference between Don and his sister, Sue. Don had often wondered what his mother had ever seen in his father. Their essential natures stood in stark contrast to each other. Where she was warm and loving, he was often sullen and indifferent. Raised in a working-class family, Jim hardly ever talked about his parents and two brothers, one of whom had done some time in prison.

His father had been an alcoholic ever since Don could remember, and he had learned from his mother that Jim's father had also been a "drunk," as she put it, and could be physically abusive. Don knew even as a teenager that his father's decline was due to his dysfunctional family background, and alcoholism and had little to do with his job or working-class background. He knew of too many families from the same economic class as his whose home life was functional and happy. Given a small town's tendency for bad news to travel fast, he knew some of the wealthiest families in town had had more than their share of tragedy and scandal. A son of one of the executives at the plant had been arrested for dealing drugs while away at college. The unfolding drama of his trial and prison sentence had made the local papers.

Jim, when drunk, while never physically abusive, had often been verbally abusive. A bad day at work was all it took to bring out the worst in Jim. By mid-evening the target of this abuse was Berta, who by this time was usually sitting quietly on the coach knitting. His slurred verbal attacks most often focused on some dust or dirt he had spotted somewhere in the living room. Rising to his feet and then stumbling around he would tell her that "she was a lousy housekeeper, that this was her only job, and she couldn't even do that right." Don and his sister, knowing such scenes were almost routine, had by this time retreated to their bedrooms. They could still hear the muffled sounds of their parents arguing behind their closed doors. The arguments always seemed to wind down in the same way, with Berta repeatedly telling Jim to calm down, and go to bed, and with Jim finally waiving his hand dismissively at her as he stumbled off toward their bedroom. The answer Berta had given to Don, whenever he asked what she had ever seen in his father, was that "he was not the man then that he is now," and that "life had worn him down."

Perhaps, Don thought, but the cruel streak his father often exhibited was something he could not forgive. One of his earliest memories painfully reminded him of his father's cruel streak. Don was only four or five. He had been jumping up and down on the couch in their small living room. His father had come over to scold him. In his childish exuberance, Don hadn't realized his father's intent. Then the memory comes sharply into focus. As his father stood in front of him, Don had yelled several times, "Daddy, catch me," and then with the impulsive energy of a young child Don had leaped toward his father's arms inches away. His child's trust yet unbroken, Don was sure his father would catch him. Instead, his arms still at his sides, Jim took a step back and let Don fall to the ground. The thick shag carpet broke his fall. As tears flowed, Don's mother came running from another part of the house. Shrugging, Jim walked away, muttering under his breath, "It's better he learn now, that the only one you can trust in life is yourself." Don had no recollection of the physical pain, but this early childhood experience had scorched an emotional scar onto his psyche. The experience became emblematic of many experiences to come where his father exhibited a lack of caring, often combined with cruel comments and actions. Jim's bitterness toward life most often manifested itself as resentment and anger toward those closest to him. Whatever feelings of love that still stirred within him threatened to weaken the anger and resentment he felt toward life. On some level these emotions were all that Jim felt stood between him and utter defeat in the face of life's injustices.

Don loved his mother despite her denial of his father's alcoholism, but hated his father for the way he verbally abused her. His relationship with his father, apart from an occasional exchange about sports or cars, was devoid of any depth or outward signs of affection, much less love. When Don was younger his father had never taken advantage of these common interests to build a closer relationship. He had never invited Don to join him when he worked on his car, or taken him to a regional minor league baseball game, or participated with Don in any of the father-son activities common at that place and time.

Don had adored his younger sister ever since Berta brought her home from the hospital. He loved playing the role of big brother. When he was in high school, and Susie, as the family called her, had been in middle school, she would most often come into his room, throw herself across his bed, and ask what he was doing. She of course could see that he was studying at the desk next to his bed, but this was her teasing way of interrupting his studies to get his attention. Don would smile, turn toward her, and say, "Not much, how is my baby sis doing?" or some variation of this counter inquiry. Susie would then most often tell him about some incident that had happened at school. Many of these had to do with a teacher she didn't like, or some social interaction among her girlfriends, most of whom Don knew. Susie steered clear of sharing any interest she had in a boy, as she knew she would automatically get a mini lecture from him. He would start by telling her, echoing their parents, that she was too young to date. Depending on whether he knew and liked the boy or not, Don might also threaten to tell their parents. He would then often add for good measure that if he heard of any boy mistreating her "he'll wish he was dead." Even though Susie did not tell Don very often about her latest boy crush, she did so occasionally just to tease Don, and because she secretly enjoyed her big brother's protectiveness. Susie had not inherited her mother's more reflective nature. Nor did she share Don's academic aptitude. Neither had she inherited the sullen emotionally detached nature of her father, vivacious and socially extroverted she got along well with everybody.

Don had heard the phone ring, in its loud slightly jarring way. He slowly started to lay down the newspaper he had been reading at the kitchen table and began to turn in his chair to get up and answer the phone. Before he could stand up, he heard the footsteps of his father coming from the living room. Due to a shake-up at the plant his father had recently been put on night shift, and had to be at work in an hour. Jim came around the corner from the living room into the kitchen and grabbed the phone off the wall. "Campbell residence," he barked in his usual flat affect businesslike tone. A long silence followed as Jim listened to what the caller was saying. Don looked up at his father, the blood had drained from his face. His expression was one of stunned horror. "What's wrong, Dad?" he asked with a growing sense of dread in the pit of his stomach. Jim, who now appeared to be in a state of frozen shock, ignored his son. "O dear God," Don then heard his father say in an anguished tone. Another briefer period of silence followed. "I'll be right there," Don's father then said in a hushed tone his voice breaking. Jim hung up the phone and turned slowly toward Don with a look of horrified disbelief. "What's going on, Dad?" Don said with an increasing tone of urgency and dread. Jim fixed his gaze on Don and the horrified shock on his face softened a little. With an expression of depthless despair, he softly said, "Your mother and sister were just in a bad car accident." "Are they okay, Dad?" Don asked, terrified to hear the answer. Jim spoke haltingly, "A young man, he was driving very fast, ran a stop sign just outside of town, he T-boned your mother's car. Don, your mother and sister were killed instantly." His father's words threw him into a state of shock. He had heard his father's words, but his mind couldn't process what he had just said. The whole thing seemed surrealistic to Don. He stared at his father with a look of disbelieving horror. What Jim said next hit Don like a second massive knock-out punch. "I have to go and identify . . . ," he said, his voice trailing off. Then standing in frozen silence, his back to Don, Jim remarked, "It would be best if you stayed here."

After his father left, Don remained seated for a time. He remained unable to absorb the news he had just heard. To do so would be to admit that he would never again see the two people he loved most in the world, who made his life worth living. Time seemed to stand still as Don sat frozen at the kitchen table, his head in his hands. Finally forcing himself to take some action, any action, he called the pastor of his church to alert him. The pastor's wife answered. Clutching the phone and speaking in an obviously traumatized tone, Don asked to speak to Pastor Tim. Sensing how upset Don was she responded in a gentle caring way, "I am so sorry, Don, Tim is not in right now, I will have him call you as soon as he gets home." The pastor did call a short time later, but Don was in no condition to answer the phone call. His father later made the phone call to the pastor to make the necessary arrangements. Don had mumbled, "Thank you," to the pastor's wife, and then said, "I am sorry I have to go." He had only a blurred, hazy recollection of what he did after hanging up the phone. He vaguely recalled stumbling into the living room, grabbing a bottle of Jack Daniels out of his parents' liquor cabinet, and then stumbling back to his room. He drank until he passed out, wanting to escape the nightmare his life had just become. Don awoke in the middle of the night feeling extremely nauseous. He stumbled into the bathroom and began to throw up violently.

The shock and numbness Don continued to feel allowed him to function on autopilot through the memorial service at the church and in the days and weeks that followed. During the week after the accident he saw his father cry for the first time. Sitting at the kitchen table, head in his hands, his father had sobbed in a convulsive, uncontrollable way. The emotional distance that separated Don and his father had prevented him from approaching or offering his father any comfort. He too had felt the full reality of the loss hit him a couple of times during the weeks following the accident. Still he did not allow himself to break down until he was alone in his bedroom at night. When he did, he threw himself onto his bed and muffled his sobs by sinking his face into his pillow. Pills the family doctor had prescribed for Don dulled the pain and deepened the numbness and zombie-like behavior that lasted most of the summer.

With only a month left before Don's second year at the community college was due to start he had seriously considered dropping out and just working at the plant. Deep down, though, he feared that if he did this he would just end up like his father. This would not have been because of the job, but because of any inherent tendencies Don too might have toward depression and alcoholism. He felt a deep anger toward his father not for having these tendencies but for his denial of them and the destructive consequences this wrought. It was his resentment of his father that finally drove him, still in a shocked haze, to make the decision to continue his education. As the beginning of the fall semester approached, and the harsh reality of the accident came crashing down on him, Don's shock and numbness slowly began to give way to a raw anger. Don began to feel a deepening anger, even rage, toward the young man who had walked away nearly uninjured. He felt a growing anger toward the senseless injustice of the accident, and the God who had seemingly allowed it to happen. Before long he began to feel an anger toward a world that seemed to be filled with so much senseless suffering, loss, and injustice. Somewhere, though, too, in the back of his mind, Don knew that anger, turned inward, had caused his father to spiral into a bitter shell of a man.

Don was already aware he had an anger problem. It had its roots in middle school when a group of boys had singled him out as a target for bullying. For most of seventh grade he had been pushed, shoved, and hit from behind.

The boys had sought him out and harassed him in the hallway, at recess on the playground, and after school. In groups of three or four they would surround him and begin pushing him around. "Hey faggot, you want to fight," one would say. Another would then say, "He's not going to fight because he's chicken," in a mocking disdainful tone. The abuse would only end when a teacher would approach, or the school bell would ring. Don would then take advantage of this to push his way through the circle of bullies.

Don, who was now a wiry, muscular five foot ten, with chiseled good looks and sandy blond hair, had, in his middle school years, been small for his age. Later, trying to understand why he had been singled out he suspected it was due to his more sensitive nature, inherited from his mother, and his studious ways. His academic ability had placed him in the "A Track" classes that offered college preparatory courses. Both Don and the bullies came from the same working-class background, but the boys that had bullied him were all in the "B Track." This was the track for the students less academically inclined, who were expected to graduate high school but then pursue working-class jobs. Many would no doubt end up working for the town's largest employer, the Ford plant. Others would work at a variety of skilled-labor jobs. Jobs that involved intelligence and ability but were often not given the respect they deserved by schools that prized academic achievement above all else. Don came to dislike the academic tracking system, for while it might be a good fit for some students, it could also pigeon-hole other students who might not realize their full academic potential until later on, sometimes not until college. He had often wondered, given that he and the bullies came from the same background, if there had not been some jealousy or resentment of his placement in the academic track. Never fully understanding why he had been singled out for bullying left Don with a deep underlying insecurity about what had made him different. Had he in some way brought the bullying on himself? What had made him different and so vulnerable to such abuse and ridicule. The feelings of guilt and shame over his inability to fight back, were issues he would struggle with for years to come. His mother, finding bruises on Don's back and realizing what was going on, wanted to go straight to the principal. "That will only make things worse," Jim had said. "The only way for this to stop is for Don to stand up for himself." "But Jim," Berta had responded, "they always attack him as a group, he'll just get beat up." "Maybe that's what needs to happen," Jim would retort in a discussion-ending way. Berta had then whispered to her son to "tell the teachers," but Don's father, by this time, had already indoctrinated him into his narrow view of how a man should act, or at least what led to becoming a man.

Don did not tell his teachers about the bullying, nor did he fight back during the rest of middle school. He just endured the abuse as best he could by avoiding the bullies in whatever way he could. By his second year of high school Don had shot up seven inches, and he had grown a thick skin over the insecurity that had arisen in him because of the bullying. Much of this thick skin arose because of a decision he had made soon after his growth spurt began, to never let anyone bully him again. By his sophomore year of high school this resolve had become fully internalized. The thick skin that had developed around his insecurity took the form of anger, and at times rage. When one of the former bullies during his sophomore year passed him in the hallway, shoved him and then said "excuse me" in a mocking tone, Don had shoved him back. When the bully turned back around and said, "Do you want me to put you six feet under," Don stood toe to toe with him, and in a rage cursed him out. The other boy, caught off guard by his behavior muttered, "You're crazy," and walked away. Another altercation occurred later that year when two former bullies began harassing him after school in the hallway as he was walking to the busses waiting outside. One shoved him from behind toward the other bully who was facing Don. A rage instantly welled up in Don that caused him to turn around, run at, and tackle the bully who had just shoved him. Then, as a crowd of students gathered round, he straddled the bully and rained down punches on him, mostly to his face. A teacher, seeing the commotion, raced over and pulled Don off the boy. The principal suspended all three boys for a couple weeks. From that time on the bullies left Don alone. He justified his rage by telling himself that his father was right, that this was the only way to handle people that tried to bully him now, or in the future. Deep down, though, Don knew that he had overreacted and that the rage he had felt would create more problems for him in the future than it would solve. He also knew that what had made it possible for him to fight back was a leveling of the playing field, essentially his growth spurt, and the fact that only two of the former group had bullied him in this case.

Now another layer of anger had been added. His anger at the world and God for the senseless loss of his mother and sister had expanded the cauldron of anger that roiled just beneath the surface. Without realizing it he had also begun developing a secondary defense. Don increasingly projected a cool, detached persona. If others shared in conversation something of their personal life, he remained serious, cautious, and guarded, and would not reciprocate by sharing anything personal, particularly about his past. It kept people at an emotional distance, and could also be used in an amplified way to chill out people he wanted nothing to do with. This defense was a double-edged sword as well. It was making him into something of a loner, which again, deep down, Don knew was not who he was. He also knew that while his cool reserve might limit interactions that aroused the rage within him, it could not prevent such instances from arising altogether. Once such a provocation occurred the cauldron of anger seething, then erupting from within Don could easily overwhelm any self-control. Two such provocations had happened toward the end of his summer job at the plant. On one occasion, when Don had arrived five minutes late. A normally brash coworker had chided him for being late. Don had immediately gone toe to toe with him and screamed into his face, telling him to "shut the hell up." Fortunately, three other nearby coworkers were able to separate the two before their conflict escalated. In another instance, a coworker, not knowing of Don's loss, had teasingly said, "Why don't you smile once in a while." This had prompted Don to tell him to "leave me the hell alone." Fortunately, in this case, the man had backed off, saying repeatedly, "Chill out man, I didn't mean anything by it." By summer's end Don had already begun shunning friends from high school. He didn't consider this to be much of a loss as they had primarily just been drinking buddies. He simply told himself that he had outgrown them.

All through his second year at the community college Don stayed increasingly to himself. He submerged himself in his studies as a way to distract himself from the raw grief that lay suppressed just beneath the surface of his consciousness. Despite this, some memory would occasionally be sparked that tapped into these feelings, bringing them to the surface and causing him to spiral into depression. What Don could not have known at the time was that his grieving process had stalled out. The feelings of vulnerability, helplessness, and the worthlessness, of no longer feeling loved, were so painful that any distraction was preferable, be it his studies or, when a provocation arose, anger. Not being able to come to any understanding of the injustices in his life, his anger, not unlike his father's, was being used to project the negative energy that consumed him out onto others and the world. Don had found some consolation, though, in the two higher-level philosophy courses he took in his second year. The ethics course he took in the spring semester had enabled him to wrestle with questions about suffering and injustice, even if they didn't offer him any ready answers.

Midway through the fall semester Don made the decision to apply to the seminary. He came to believe that his mother and sister had become like guardian angels, their spirits watching over him. This helped him to recapture something the of the unconditional love his mother had given him in life, and offered some much-needed comfort. He had applied to seminary as much to please his mother's spirit as any other motive. Don couldn't imagine himself as a pastor. He was too broken, too angry, his faith had been shaken to the core. Perhaps, he told himself, given his academic aptitude, he could use the seminary degree to teach, to help others wrestle with the deeper questions of life. He did not want to apply to any conservative Christian seminaries. The comfort Pastor Tim had offered him had been peppered with religious platitudes: "It was God's will, Don," "You just have to trust God at this time," and "They're with the Lord now." He knew that there might be some spiritual wisdom in these words, but at the time, he was not ready to hear it. The emotions he was feeling, that were seething just beneath the surface, needed to be affirmed and expressed, even if he wasn't ready to have this happen yet. Don also wanted the freedom to ask deeper questions and seek deeper answers than he thought his tradition could offer. He had applied to a prominent seminary in the northeast, a mainline Protestant seminary in New England. Don had reviewed the application materials they had sent him. They promised an academically rigorous curriculum and counted top-notch biblical scholars among their faculty. At the time this appealed to the side of him that hoped to find rational biblical and theological explanations for the sufferings and sense of injustice he was experiencing. The seminary was also connected to a major university and presented itself, in the application materials, as both a seminary which trained its students for the pastorate and one of the university's graduate schools, which appealed to students who hoped to become college or seminary professors.

In early spring Don had received a letter in the mail from the seminary. He had been accepted despite the bold gamble of applying. Don had not thought his chances of acceptance were very good. While the school's minimal educational requirement was two years of college, the application materials indicated that consideration here was contingent on compensatory life experience. Don knew this usually referred to students older than him with more life experience. The seminary generally preferred student applicants with a four-year college degree. His essay had, he assumed, turned the tide with the admissions committee. Don had fabricated his reason for attending the seminary. Citing the accident, he had written that he now had deep empathy for all who suffered. He explained his call as a desire to utilize that empathy through ministry.

Once the school year was finished, Don had once again worked over the summer at the plant. The cauldron of anger within him had settled down somewhat, although this was largely due to the wide berth his co-workers now gave him. He had, in the past, owned a couple of beat-up old cars that he continually had to fix up to keep on the road. He had bought the latest one, a 1979 Pontiac Catalina, off a friend for a few hundred dollars. Its suspension was shot, and it belched smoke, but it still got him from point A to point B. It would now take him to the seminary, where he was due to start in early September. Soon after, it would break down again.

The Incident

As Don drove his Pontiac Catalina through main street of the university town, he was amazed at how manicured the town appeared. As he passed the main gate of the campus on his left the lush green lawns of the campus in front of the administration buildings came into view. He saw students sitting on blankets studying. He noticed a couple on a blanket. The young man was sitting with the arms of a sweater tied around his neck, the sweater behind his back. The young woman with him was laying on her back next to him with a book resting on her stomach. The architecture of the buildings appeared colonial and they were built largely of stone. Don had also noticed that most of the cars lining the street were expensive models. There were BMWs, Mercedes, even Porches in the mix. He suddenly felt self-conscious driving his beat-up old beast of a car through town. Almost on cue it belched smoke out the tailpipe just as he passed the main gate to the campus. Main Street was lined on both sides by upscale stores. It was the epitome of a quaint college town.

The graduate schools, including the seminary, were on the north end of town, the direction Don was headed. He had received his room assignment with the acceptance letter. Once he had arrived at the seminary, he grabbed his suitcase and duffel bag, and made his way to Whitney Hall, the dorm he would be staying in. Don soon found his room and with the door unlocked he opened it and walked in. Two neatly made up beds lined the walls on either side of the room with desks at the head end of the beds, facing the back wall. A large window, in between the two desks, divided the room and let sunlight flood the room in the morning.

On the left side of the room his roommate sat in a recliner he had positioned at the foot end of the bed next to a bookcase. Don tried to smile congenially as he put his things down beside his bed, but he sensed intuitively that David and he could not have been more different. As he turned back toward David, and smiled once again, he saw that David did not smile back, but simply puffed on the pipe that he held up to his mouth with one hand. Don extended his hand and introduced himself. "Hi, I'm Don

Campbell." David, without taking the pipe out of his mouth, extended the hand that had been holding it and in a formal tone said, "Good to meet you, I'm David Martin Edwards the Third." Don suppressed a spontaneous urge to smirk. Who tacks a number onto the end of their name? He knew that in some high-society circles this might be the norm, but otherwise thought this a custom of an elite minority in a former era. Don also thought he had detected a slight English accent when David introduced himself. Don broke the awkward silence, "I'm from Kentucky, where are you from, David?" David spoke slowly and deliberately in what sounded faintly like an upper-class English accent. "I am originally from Houston, Texas, but more recently I lived in England and studied at Oxford University. As he spoke, Don had noticed that he seemed to be wearing a slight sneer of a smile on his horn-rimmed bespectacled face. Don initially thought that David had spent some years studying in England. He was later to find out that David had spent nine months studying at Oxford after college, in some special overseas study program. This of course begged the question as to how the English accent had developed in such a short period of a time, and even more mystifying was what had happened to David's Southern drawl. Don was also to find out that David was indeed from a very wealthy Texas family, and the nephew of a US senator. At the time, though, Don's follow-up impressions confirmed his intuitive hunch that David could not have been more different from him. As he busied himself putting his things away, out of the corner of his eye he saw David sit back in his chair. Don turned his head sideways, smiled at David and looked again at the chair David was sitting in. It was a leather recliner that he had obviously brought into the room. He also noticed that David's side of the room was immaculate, with all his books neatly lining the shelves of the bookcase at the foot of his bed.

As David went back to reading the book that lay across his lap, he continued to puff on the pipe he once again held to his mouth. A Harris Tweed jacket with elbow patches that David was wearing completed the ensemble. Don didn't want to be judgmental, but there was something about David's whole manner and persona that seemed fake and pretentious. David seemed to be playing a role. His academic elitist demeanor was so over the top it almost came off as satire. Still Don was determined at this stage to make the best of the situation. Don finished putting away his things and then sat down on his bed. "So David, have you bought your books yet?" he asked. "Yes, I have already purchased all my books, I like to get a head start on the readings for my courses." Don had found the slightly patronizing tone with which David had answered him annoying, and whatever further conversations he would have to have with his roommate, for now, he just wanted to make a hasty exit. "Well I think I'll head over to the bookstore and see what books I will need." Don had applied and been approved for a student loan in the months following his acceptance letter, that covered his room and board, as well as an additional allotment for books. Don paused and looked over at David waiting for a response. When he did not respond and kept on reading his book, Don got up and left.

The bookstore was in the basement of a large building that housed classrooms and sat diagonally across the quadrangle from his dorm, and next to the seminary chapel. As he passed the growing numbers of students walking across the campus, Don found that he had a hard time making eye contact with most of them to say hi. Many seemed to be walking and talking in small groups and he was unsure of how they had struck up their relationships so quickly. He also began to realize that his baseball cap, worn backwards, along with the hooded jacket and jeans he was wearing, set him apart from how most everyone else was dressed. Most of the men were wearing khakis or dress slacks and shirts, and most of the women were dressed in a more formal way than the female students at the community college back home. As Don descended the stairs that led down to the bookstore in the building's basement, he was now feeling more and more like he didn't fit in here. Walking into the bookstore bustling with students, he steeled himself. He was here, and no matter what, he would give it the best shot he could. He knew from orientation materials sent him soon after his acceptance letter that he would be taking intro classes in Old Testament, New Testament, theology, and church history. Don began looking at the piles of books on tables throughout the center of the store. Amid the book-filled bookshelves that lined the walls were labels that designated the different classes. He also found them taped to the edge of the tables right below the different piles of books for each course. Don quickly picked up the required texts for three of his four courses but was having trouble finding the books for his last course on theology. He finally found the course label on one end of a table toward the front of the bookstore. He then began to check the piles for the required books for the course. He soon found the first one and as he picked up the textbook off the top of the pile, out of the corner of his eye, he saw a pretty brunette across the table from him. She was already holding several books in one hand, and appeared to be looking for another book among the piles. Don had looked at her a second too long and felt his face redden as she looked back at him. "Which textbook are you looking for?" he asked, hoping to move past the awkwardness of the moment. "Oh," she replied, "I still have to buy one text book for the intro class to theology, and I just can't find It." Don had put all the books he had bought into a basket he had picked up at the door. "That's the only course I need to buy books for as well," he said, seeing an opening to further the conversation. She smiled back at Don and then lowered her head to continue her search for the book. Don walked over to her side of the table, extended his hand and introduced himself. The young woman looked up at him, smiled, and said, "I am Wendy Bowman, it's good to meet you." As they exchanged introductions he noticed just how cute Wendy was. With dark brown eyes, dark shoulder-length hair, bangs, a petite build, and fine features, Don found her exceedingly attractive. As they continued looking through the piles of books together, he looked sideways at her. "So where are you from, Wendy?" Don asked. "I grew up in Texas, but my family moved to the Midwest when I was in high school," she answered. This explained, Don thought, the slight Southern accent he had detected. "How about you?" Wendy asked. "I am from Kentucky, I've lived there my whole life. I mean up until now." he replied, realizing that what he had just said sounded like a bad joke. This made him feel momentarily awkward and inarticulate. "Well Don, I think I have all the books I need, so I am going to head back to my room." As Wendy headed toward the cashier, he grabbed the two remaining books he needed for the theology course and went to pay for them. Wendy and Don traded glances and smiles as he stood behind her in the cashier line. When it came Don's turn to pay he noticed Wendy talking to another female student in the hallway just outside the door to the bookstore. Finishing his purchase, he walked out the door just as Wendy was climbing the stairs ahead of him. Catching up with her he asked her what she thought of the seminary so far. "It's pretty much what I expected. I had an uncle who went here about twenty years ago. He helped prepare me and told me what to expect."

As they walked outside and down the steps of the building together, Don suddenly felt confused. He was strongly attracted to Wendy, and perhaps, if the attraction proved mutual, it was time for him to risk opening himself up to a relationship. Still, while she had been one of the first people on campus that had seemed open, and friendly, she also seemed to be out of his league. She appeared to be from the same middle- and upper-middle-class backgrounds as many of the other students. Don didn't want to appear pushy, so at the bottom of the stairs he turned to her and said, "Well it was good to meet you, Wendy, I hope we run into each other again." "It was good to meet you too, Don Campbell. I am sure we'll see each other around, as well as in class." Her tone had a slightly teasing quality to it. She also seemed to have a mix of both down-to-earth and formal ways about her.

As Don headed back to his room, he was uncertain of whether she would become a friend, much less be someone he could ask out on a date. At least he had broken the ice with her. For now, though, he too would head back to his room and skim through the books he had just bought. He would soon be receiving the syllabi in the classes, with the reading schedules, but he could at least familiarize himself with the different course textbooks. Don would have his first class, Intro to the New Testament, the following morning, and these were the textbooks he would skim through first. He only wished his roommate was someone he felt more relaxed around.

Don's first week of classes went by uneventfully. Each professor seemed to have their own unique lecture style. His church history professor was a tall, thin, grey-haired man named Canfield, whose monotone lecturing style had many students bringing the largest cups of coffee they could to class. The subject matter had been somewhat disappointing as it was more of a history of Christian thought and theology than a course on the history of the church. A better title for the course, Don thought, might have been "Intro to a History of Long-Dead Theologians." His Old Testament professor was a short, stocky man in his fifties, who wore wire-rimmed glasses, and always had on a "Raiders of the Lost Ark" type hat. Overall, though, he seemed to Don to be more scholarly than adventuresome. His theology professor, a middle-aged man named Wallace, was of medium height and build. At first glance, Wallace, who wore glasses and, as most of Don's professors did, a suit and tie, also appeared scholarly and aloof. He would soon learn that this was a misleading first impression, as Wallace often flashed a warm, welcoming smile that made him more approachable than his other professors.

Wallace was the only one of his instructors who had been a pastor for over a decade before earning a doctorate and beginning his seminary teaching career. His pastoral experience was evident in the many illustrations he brought into the lectures from his ministry days. One illustration in particular had caught Don's attention and had resonated with him. The lecture topic dealt with the theme of suffering in theology, one which he was specifically interested in. As a young pastor in his first church, Wallace had learned that a couple had just lost their only child, a teenage girl, in a car accident. Wallace immediately headed over to the parent's house. The wife greeted him at the door, her face distorted by grief. "Helen, I just heard the news, I am so sorry," Wallace said, knowing how insufficient words were at a time like this. "I am really worried about my husband, I have never seen him so angry. He is in the back, chopping wood, I don't know if he will even talk to you," she had replied. Wallace nodded his head trying to convey a look of understanding. In reality, given his inexperience, he had no idea what he could possibly say that would be meaningful given the depth of this man's grief. Wallace made his way around the side of the house, and came into the backyard just in time to see the father violently swing an axe down on a piece of wood sitting on a tree stump. As Wallace approached, he knew the husband had to know he was there but he kept splitting wood, ignoring the young pastor even when he came to stand on the other side of the stump. An awkward silence followed. Without looking up, the father, in an angry, defiant voice, said, "Pastor, if you have just come to offer a bunch of religious platitudes you can turn around and go back the way you came." Wallace prayed silently for guidance from the Holy Spirit, and then started speaking, only intuiting what he shouldn't say. The words that came out were, "I can't imagine what you're feeling. All I know is that whatever it is, it is completely understandable." Wallace continued to stand there for another few minutes, as the father continued to split wood, and then before turning around to leave, bowed his head and said a prayer, lifting up the father's grief and anger to God for validation, and help. As Wallace turned around to leave and began walking away, he suddenly heard the words, "Thank you, Pastor." When Wallace turned back to respond he noticed that the man had said these words while continuing to split wood and without looking up. Wallace stayed in touch with the parents, but was sure it was by not trying to fix anything, but merely affirming the nightmare they were experiencing as well as God's presence, that he was able to minister to them. Wallace did not explain the story except to use it as an illustration for a theological understanding of the ministry of Christian presence. It would be one of many critical insights Don would gain over his first year at the seminary.

Other than Wallace, though, Don's other instructors approached their subject as an academic discipline with little or none of the ministry references that he assumed would be an integral part of a seminary education. By the end of his second New Testament class Don's professor seemed to take this teaching style to an extreme. His primary focus in the class, other than lecturing on the different types of writings in the New Testament, was to teach about a set of methods he called the "biblical criticisms." The students were to use these in their exegetical assignments or papers where they interpreted designated New Testament texts. Don understood these criticisms to be a discipline that studies textual, compositional, and historical questions regarding Scripture. To Don, Wilson seemed to enjoy analyzing texts that had to do with the mission and deeds of Jesus in ways that questioned any possible supernatural interpretation. This also had the effect of reducing Jesus to a teacher of religious ethics who was merely human. As a matter of course, Jesus' divine mission and incarnation were also brought into question. In lectures Wilson utilized the criticisms the way a pathologist dissects a cadaver. By the time Wilson was done analyzing a text in a lecture he had systematically undermined any traditional faith basis for it. He had peeled away the layers of the text like an onion until there was nothing left for those who clung to the essential truths of the faith.

Wilson had often referenced Rudolf Bultmann, a theologian and New Testament professor from the earlier half of the twentieth century, who heavily influenced the development of form criticism. Don came to understand form criticism as a literary or textual analysis of Scripture, used to discern a text's original form, and it's literary historical setting. Wilson, referencing Bultmann, had instructed that since we can't know anything for sure about the historical Christ, all we can do is extrapolate the most essential meanings of texts, regarding his life and mission, for our current existence and lives. Don did not understand Bultmann in any depth, but the high regard with which Wilson seemed to hold him was at odds with his enthusiasm for biblical historical criticism with which he sought to discover something of the historical Jesus. Although Bultmann's biblical theology and Wilson's overzealous scholarly use of the historical criticisms had served common cause by undermining any historical basis for supernatural occurrences in the Gospels, including Jesus' miracles and the resurrection. They also both claimed that little of Jesus mission and ministry could claim historical validity.

The fact that Matthew, Mark, and John had based their writings or dictations on memories of, and as witnesses to, Jesus' mission and ministry seemed to hold little weight with either camp. And while Paul had not known Jesus he was continually in direct contact with those that had. Wilson had also lectured that the diverse agendas of the New Testament writers, evident in both the Gospels and Paul's epistles, had cast doubt on their historical validity. As for NT author agendas, Don questioned, why could each writer not have been divinely inspired to relate historical facts through a variety of lenses so as to bring the fullest understanding of Christ's mission to the world.

Don not only found himself repulsed by Wilson's use of biblical criticisms as the only way to study Scripture, and by implication to prepare for a sermon, he also felt an anger slowly rising within him. He had decided to go to seminary partly to gain theological and biblical insights on which he could rebuild his faith. Instead this professor seemed intent on undermining what little faith he had left.

By his third class, in the second week of the semester, as Don listened to Wilson employ these criticisms on a variety of Gospel texts, he began to feel an edgy restlessness. He knew it was a warning sign when he felt this way. Don knew, his anger could more easily rise to the surface, and that he was more apt to lash out impulsively. It had happened enough times before with fellow high school students, coworkers, and the occasional stranger who all had picked the wrong day and time to be critical, abrupt, or rude to him. Still Don knew he had to go to class and wanted to get off to a good start academically. To calm down he tried telling himself that he would avoid taking another class with Wilson in the future. After all, he reasoned, there were other New Testament professors at the seminary who most likely did not hold Wilson's narrow liberal views. He had just had the bad luck of the draw this time around. Still these self-reassurances did little to ease Don's growing frustration with Wilson given his emotional state at the time.

By the third week of the NT class Wilson turned his scalpel to the resurrection narratives. The overall thrust of the lecture was already predictable. "There is much evidence to suggest that these narratives are a creation of the early church and so we should be careful not to regard them as historical fact," Wilson had stated at one point. He then went on to reference a group of scholars called the "Jesus Seminar" to back his assertion.

The Jesus Seminar was composed of a group of liberal scholars and lay persons who used their own biblical critical methods, and other anthropological and historical tools, to examine the historicity of the mission and ministry of Jesus Christ. Using colored scriptural highlights, after discussion and then a vote, they determined, from the most likely to the least likely, which texts depicted Jesus' teaching and ministry with historical authenticity. The votes were cast using beads of four colors, red, pink, grey, and black, the same colors later used to highlight Bibles utilizing their rankings. The color red was used to indicate which texts could most authentically be traced back to Jesus. Texts involving supernatural occurrences, including the resurrection, were assigned to the least likely category, the black color code. The seminar had been greatly influenced by the quest for the historical Jesus, initiated by Albert Schweitzer, who wrote a book of the same name, and was largely a product of the emerging scientific worldview. A teaching document of the early church, which is not extant, called "Q," from the German word *Quelle*, for "source," was relied on heavily by the seminar members in making their determinations. As was the "Gospel of Thomas," an early Gnostic gospel, which contains the purported sayings of Jesus and which some scholars believe was written in a similar form, a collection of Jesus' sayings, as that of "Q." The disproportionate reliance by seminar members on these two resources has been hotly debated in the broader scholarly arena. Their authorship, date of origin, and agenda cannot be accurately verified—seminar members assume an earlier date for both Q and the Gospel of Thomas than that of Mark, the earliest Gospel—despite seminar assumptions.

The end result of the seminar's determinations was that the figure of Jesus had been reduced to a one-dimensional figure that was totally a product of Jewish-Hellenistic culture and the early church. One who was seen as incapable of original thought if he had just been a product of his provincial, Galilean, Jewish culture. Don, partly in reaction to Wilson's assertions, had read articles that reflected the growing critical reaction against the conclusions of the seminar in the greater scholarly community and included well-respected biblical scholars such as the Anglican N. T. Wright and New Testament professor Luke Timothy Johnson. Questions had been raised about the self-fulfilling selection criteria of the seminar members, and that a significant number of seminar members were scientists, and laypersons, and not Christian scholars. Don worried that a pseudoscientific mindset could be creeping into some of the more liberal seminaries, and that the generation of pastors they produced might be susceptible to unbalanced biblical perspectives. This influence, he thought, contained a bias which assumes a foundational premise that rules out the possibility of any supernatural explanation. Don also wondered how much their biblical perspectives might in turn undermine the faith of parishioners of the church traditions they served.

While the accident had shaken Don's faith down to its foundation, he had still clung to his belief in the resurrection. Don felt the anger within him growing, and knew it could overflow any minute. He had applied to a more liberal seminary hoping they would be more open-minded, and help him to arrive at deeper insights about suffering and injustice. He had never thought that liberal, in a seminary context, meant questioning everything about the faith, including its most essential truths like the resurrection. Hadn't Paul in his first letter to the church at Corinth said that without the resurrection the whole faith would fall apart? Part of Don knew he was projecting his anger at Wilson onto the seminary, and other theologically liberal seminaries, and that this was unfair. Given his limited classroom experiences in biblical studies Don had seen little evidence, as yet, of the broader biblical and theological perspectives that he knew must be represented in such seminaries.

It was with his anger primed that Wilson decided, as he occasionally did, to break up the lectures by asking if "anyone had any questions." Don's hand shot up quickly, he felt his face redden and tighten into a rigid grimace that registered the mounting anger he felt inside. "Yes," Wilson said, nodding his head in Don's direction. "With all due respect, Dr. Wilson, if you question the resurrection won't the whole faith begin to fall apart?" Don asserted in a defiant tone. Wilson was startled by his challenging tone and caught off guard by the impertinence of the question. Looking down from the lecture platform, and over his reading glasses, he fixed his gaze firmly on Don. After a few seconds of awkward silence Wilson responded, "I am only calling its historicity into question, not the meaning of the resurrection for our lives as inspired by the Holy Spirit." Wilson then turned his head and was about to ask if there were any more questions when Don, without raising his hand, spoke out again. "But if Christ didn't really die on the cross and pay the price for our sins and salvation isn't that meaning just an illusion?" Wilson re-fixed his gaze on Don with a disapproving scowl. "Your name please?" Wilson demanded. "My name is Don Campbell, Dr. Wilson." "Well Don," Wilson said in a patronizing tone, "is it not enough that the early church believed so fully in the transformative meaning of the resurrection for their lives that this faith phenomenon, imparted through the Holy Spirit, has been at work ever since through the body of Christ, we call the church." Don, with a tone of defiance and disdain, then blurted out, "how can there be such a Spirit if Christ was just a dead man, wouldn't all his claims then just be that of a crazy man." Wilson tried to regain control of what had become a growing argumentative exchange between Don and him. "I would be glad to discuss this further with you, Don, after class, but we need to move on now." No sooner had Wilson finished the sentence than Don, whose anger was overwhelming his ability to reason, blurted out accusingly, "Excuse me, Dr. Wilson, how is what you're teaching us in any way preparing us to be pastors? I have only been a student here for a few weeks, but I already feel like the rug is being pulled out from beneath my faith." "Don, I do not permit such outbursts in my class," Wilson responded in an irate tone. Resting his forearms on the lectern Wilson leaned forward and fixing a stern gaze on Don that clearly indicated he had enough "You do not have to remain in this class if you don't want to, but I will determine the material covered in class, and while you may not agree with it, you cannot impose your view on the class or me." By this time, one could hear a pin drop in the classroom, and the rest of the students were now staring at Don. Knowing that his anger had once again escaped his control, and that this time it was in a setting where it had left him, in a way he had not experienced before, vulnerable and exposed, Don felt he had only one out. He slowly picked up his books and walked down the aisle between the seats toward the door. Then motivated only by raw emotion and impulse, he turned and before exiting shouted at Wilson, "I am not sure how you can call my belief in the reality of the resurrection a view and still call yourself a Christian." With Wilson's disparaging gaze again fixed on him, the whole class turning around to stare at him, and feeling like he had nothing to lose, Don then got personal. "I think you are more into being a scholar than a Christian, Dr. Wilson, and would rather give a lecture on the resurrection than actually believe in it." He did not wait for a response from Wilson but wheeled around and walked out the door. The sudden release of his anger had felt cathartic, but now that it was spent, Don began to feel the shame and embarrassment his behavior now aroused within him. He also began to fear the consequences that were sure to result.

As Don left, walked down from the second floor where the classroom was, and out the door, it dawned on him fully how foolish his public display of anger had been. He was sure to be reprimanded by the administration.

Even worse he had now established, for himself, a bad reputation among his classmates, one that was sure to spread across the campus where he already felt like an outsider. On his walk across the quadrangle back to his dorm room Don felt like a doomed man. He was relieved not to find his roommate there when he entered the room. Flopping face down onto his bed he managed after awhile to fall into a fitful sleep. When he awoke, he checked his wristwatch for the time, and realized he had slept through dinner. Trudging off to the library he resolved to salvage what little he could of the day; besides, he thought to himself maybe nothing too terrible will come of his classroom outburst. Arriving at his room later that night, David greeted him in his usual stiff, overly formal, and impersonal way. It was hard to tell if he had heard anything about the incident.

To relax before going to bed Don picked up a sports magazine laying on the floor next to his bed, and laying down on his side began to leaf through it. He soon felt sleepy and called it a night. When he awoke in the morning he scrambled to get to the cafeteria for breakfast. Swinging by the in-house student mailboxes near the dorm's front doors, he grabbed a couple flyers and one letter from his mailbox. As he read the words across the front of the letter, Don suddenly felt a cold clammy feeling come over him. In neat handwriting were the words "Dean's Office."

The Reprimand

D on opened the letter gingerly and read it. "Dear Student, the dean has requested that you meet with him in his office Wedneday morning at 11:30. Please be on time." The dean's signature made the letter look even more official. Any hope that his professor might let the incident pass was now gone. He wasn't sure how much trouble he was in, but he would soon find out. Later that morning Don found his way to the door marked *Dean's Office* in the administration building. He walked in and found himself in the dean's secretary's office. The door to the dean's office lay behind and to one side of her desk, and had the words "Dean Mitchell" inscribed on a plaque on the door. The secretary, a woman who appeared to be in her fifties, wore her hair in a '60s-style beehive on top of her head and had on ornate glasses that curved up on the ends. She reminded him of a no-nonsense librarian. As Don approached her desk, she looked up at him with a businesslike expression and said, "Can I help you," in an authoritarian tone that lacked warmth or personality. "I am Don Campbell, I am here to see the dean," he responded. Without answering him, the secretary leaned forward and pushed a button on an intercom and said, "Dean, Don Campbell is here to see you." Don could not make out the dean's response, but as the secretary released the button, she looked back at him, and in the same manner and tone told him, "Take a seat, the dean will let you know when he is ready to see you."

Five minutes later Don could hear the dean's voice through the intercom, and the secretary told him he could now go into the dean's office. Don opened the door to the dean's office and walked in. The dean, who was still sitting behind his desk, started to rise when he saw him come in. "Have a seat, Don," the dean said, nodding to one of two leather armchairs on the other side of his desk. The dean waited for him to be seated and then sat down himself again. Don then noticed that as Mitchell reclined back in his chair, he was looking him over, trying to size up what kind of unstable troublemaker he had in front of him. Such disciplinary meetings between the dean and a student were fairly rare, and the dean was particularly unaccustomed to dealing with a student like Don, who had been blatantly disrespectful to a professor during class. After a momentary pause the dean leaned forward in his chair and said, "Don, I am sure you know why you're here, don't you?" "Yes, sir," he responded. "What on earth caused you to challenge Dr. Wilson in class in such an inappropriate way?" The dean's authoritarian judgmental tone made it clear that Don's side of things would hold no merit with him. He also was not about to share any personal information about his past that might make the dean more sympathetic. More importantly, even given the dean's patronizing judgmental tone, Don knew that he had handled the whole situation horribly, and had wished a hundred times over that he had taken Wilson up on his offer to talk more with him after class. It would have given him a chance to cool down and he would, most likely, have taken a more respectful tone with Wilson. Still there was something about Mitchell's overall demeanor that had annoyed him. Don knew if he lost it with the dean he could be kicked out of the seminary. His stark awareness of this reality helped him to keep his anger in check. Even so, he felt driven to say something, in a calmer way, about the shock he had felt when Wilson questioned the resurrection. Don quickly figured that if he was going to register this concern in a more legitimate way he had better apologize first for his in-class behavior. "Dean Mitchell, I now realize I was out of line in the way I behaved in Dr. Wilson's class," he started out, "but I hadn't realized that belief in the resurrection would be questioned at any seminary, including here." Don knew he was qualifying his behavior in Wilson's class, but felt that, although it might have been better to state it separately, he had a valid point here.

The dean paused as if to weigh his words very carefully then said, "Don, we take academics very seriously here, and that means offering students the latest scholarship of some of the top Biblical scholars." Don knew intuitively it would be better for him to hold his tongue, and say something like, "Yes sir, I understand." But there was something about the dean's patronizing authoritarianism that had struck a nerve. Don felt that the dean's statement held a clear bias toward one liberal school of Christian scholarship. He also obviously believed that the seminary's heavy reliance on its academic reputation to attract students made the undermining of what some at the seminary regarded as naïve faith beliefs of less consequence. Don, again aiming for a calm respectful tone, responded, "But Dean, if the seminary is also about preparing students to be pastors isn't it possible that some scholarship, if presented, particularly by NT professors, as the predominant view might undermine this goal which is equally important?" Mitchell leaned forward, extended his arms, and placed them on his desk, hands down in a looming imposing way. "Don, you are not here to do a replay of your argument with Wilson." The dean was obviously going to sidestep Don's question no matter how respectfully he tried to raise it here. "For you," the dean continued, "to have caused this much of a disruption this early in the semester concerns me, Don. I don't know what your issues are, but I strongly suspect controlling your temper is one of them. We expect, as is clearly indicated in your student handbook, that our seminary students will act in mature and responsible ways. Therefore"—Don knew Mitchell was about to lower the boon—"if you disrupt another class, and do so in a way that is personally disrespectful to one of our instructors, we will have to put you on disciplinary probation." Don had read the handbook, and knew this meant a three-month period where any other infraction meant a permanent expulsion from the school.

Don met Mitchell's stare with his own. He tried not to look angry, or sullen, but could feel his jaw tightening, and his face redden. He felt his anger rising. With as blank an expression as he could muster, and trying not to sound impertinent, he said, "If that's it, Dean, I have a class to get ready for." Although Don knew his words alone conveyed a certain uncowed defiance. "Do you understand how probation works?" the dean responded, not quite ready to let him off the hook. "Yes," he responded in a monosyllabic tone. "Well, I think we have reached an understanding, Don, haven't we?" Don, still refusing to be patronized, grinned, and looking straight at the dean said in a slightly mocking way, "Loud and clear." He then turned and slowly exited the dean's office. As he walked through the secretary's office and passed her, he said sarcastically, "Have a nice day." Don walked slowly back to his dorm room oblivious to anything around him and lost in thought.

Don knew he was out of line, and that his temper was still getting the best of him. It also disturbed him that he had vented his anger in the same smug, formal, sarcastic way he suspected was the convention among the more status-oriented. The last thing he wanted to do was become like a stereotype he despised, and had encountered in David, and the dean. Neither did Don feel this was a more valid way to express anger than the way he had been able to back home, at least before the accident. Back then if he had an issue, particularly if it was between guys, his friends, a coworker, or with strangers, you just bluntly told the person face to face what it was that had irritated you, and let the chips fall where they may. The problem was, and Don knew it, since the accident he did have an anger problem, and it was coming out in ways he couldn't really justify. But he was not ready yet to deal with his raw grief or the emotions of shame and humiliation that were now all roiling just beneath the surface of his consciousness. His anger was fast becoming a fixed perimeter around these deeper overwhelming emotions. It protected him from dealing with what was really bothering him, but he knew it would create many other problems for him in the future, perhaps the near future. And as for the old code on how to handle anger as a kid, it had worked well in the working-class circles he had grown up in, but he knew, even if he could resolve his deeper anger issue, the old way of venting his anger would not work here.

As he walked into the dorm Don continued to ruminate. Back home, before the accident, even with his anger issue, he had a better chance of regaining control of his temper. Expressing anger there was seen as an acceptable emotion within certain boundaries. If one stayed within those boundaries, of no physical violence and refraining from hurling personal insults, one could clear the air with an old friend, or even set the stage for making a new friend. The stifling formal and disingenuous atmosphere he had experienced at the seminary might give the appearance of more self-control, but in reality it was just a more insidious, often premeditated form of anger expression. One thing Don knew for sure was that he was out of his element here. Even after the accident he had not been tempted to act out this way in any of his classes at the community college. He began to doubt, particularly with his anger issue, that he would be able to survive in such an environment. He now felt thoroughly exposed for the working-class, Southern redneck he was. What could he have had in mind enrolling in a prestigious Eastern school? What troubled him even more was that he had begun to doubt that any plan that God might have for his life could work here.

As Don entered his dorm room his heart sank, there was David reclining in his easy chair, wearing a bow tie, dress shirt, and slacks with matching brown dress shoes and puffing on his pipe in full scholarly mode. He was staring directly at him while holding his pipe to his mouth. Don threw him an annoyed, weary glance. He was about to fling himself on his bed when to his chagrin he noticed that he had left the letter from the dean's office open and on his bed. Had David lowered himself to the point of reading it? Don tried to reassure himself with the thought that, that would be inconsistent with the scholarly elitist affectation David worked so hard to project. He failed to convince himself of this, however. David didn't have a genuine bone in his body, and whatever insecurity had led him to assume such an extreme affectation probably also prevented him from developing a healthy conscience. David, watching Don with the same imperious stare, waited until Don picked up the letter, put it back in the envelop, placed it in a book on the desk, and then lay down on his bed. Then, after clearing his throat, with as English a sounding harrumph as he could muster, proceeded to question him about his day. His overly formal, impersonal, and obviously disingenuous tone grated on Don's already frayed nerves. He felt anger flaring within him. "So, Don, how was your day?" David asked. "Fine, David, just fine," Don responded in weary, slightly irate tone. "You look upset, did something happen?" David persisted in asking. After a long pause, Don, in a weary, dismissive voice, replied, "I am fine, David, I just need to be left alone right now." "I see," David answered in a slightly bemused way that to Don suggested he knew more than he was letting on.

Don lay on his back for some time, his emotions swirling around inside him. He tried to keep the mixture of worthlessness, anger, and growing depression he was feeling at bay. Did he even want to continue at the seminary, he kept asking himself. After laying there for some time, another emotion arose within him, one that had, since his sophomore year of high school, resulted in the habituated behavior of fighting back no matter the odds. It was an emotion best summed up as defiant rage, the utter defiance of a cornered animal whose self-preservation was on the line. He would not let them win, whatever that meant. He would not let them chase him out. Don wasn't sure how to fight back against something that was nothing like the bullies he had encountered in middle school. There was no simple fight-or-flight choice here. In fact if he continued to fight back, especially given the intensified anger he had felt since the accident, he would give them the fodder, the excuse they needed to throw him out. He wasn't sure will power would be enough, but he would try. Each day after all, he told himself, is a new day, but this sounded cliché, even Pollyannish, and rang hollow to Don even as it sprang to mind. No matter, he reasoned, I will just have to figure it out as I go along. He would start by trying to get himself in a better state of mind.

Although Don would try to keep his anger in check, he would not sacrifice his pride. His pride was all he felt he had left, but he also had to find a way to stand up for himself, or at least handle himself with dignity when insulted or provoked. Don realized that these two resolutions might work against each other in this current environment with its subtle and disingenuous rules of engagement. Suddenly some long-ago advice of his mother on how to stand up for yourself came to mind: "Don't yield your position, don't bluster either, but maintain with dignity a position you hold dear." It hadn't worked with bullies, but maybe it would here if he could bring his anger under control. Deep down Don suspected only a transformational experience, hopefully involving his faith, would liberate him from the anger that imprisoned him. Despite his ruminations he had not succeeded in motivating himself to get up and go to his next class. Don then recalled that the girl he had met in the bookstore was in his Intro to Church History class that met the following morning. Perhaps he could find an opportunity to talk to her again. He knew he needed to be low key and not appear too needy or he would scare her away. He had decided to skip that afternoon's class to give himself time to calm down. Still the prospect of running into her gave him the motivation he needed to resume going to class the next day.

Friends and Would-Be Lovers

D on's mother knew he had something of an anger problem after middle school. She had taught him to count to ten, when angry, before reacting and if that didn't help to pray as well. He had discovered this didn't work for him, particularly if he felt bullied. His anger rose within him too quickly. He had to be prepared for those occasions that provoked his anger. Don resolved to come up with his own strategies. When around anyone who might potentially give him a hard time, he had taught himself to look serious and detached from his feelings. A certain intensity he naturally projected at school and in new social situations also helped to keep anyone from getting too close to him that he didn't want to get to know. The only thing that had worried him was that the image he projected at such times came too easily, and too closely reminded him of his father's behavior with everyone, including the family. His father lived by what he considered to be the manly maxim of "don't complain, don't explain." It had worked for him in situations where complaining was not constructive. Don's father, however, had conflated it to mean don't share feelings and you won't feel vulnerable. Don had grown more generally reserved with people since the accident. He knew, though, that it could impede healthy relationships with those he chose to develop or maintain close ties with.

Don resolved to never act that way around those he let into his inner circle. Nor would he ever let alcohol become an additional coping mechanism. Although a negative motivation for him, Don did not want to become the abusive alcoholic his father had been. He would use emotional detachment as long as it worked for him, and had assumed as a teenager that he would naturally outgrow this behavior as an adult. Don came to realize later that such behavior can be modified over time, but once it had become habituated behavior it was hard to shed entirely. During high school, and even into college, it had worked well in defusing loud obnoxious wise asses. Less nobly he had used such behavior to end relationships with girls with whom he had only been semiserious. He was just waking up to the realization that such past behavior while not patronizing or elitist had been every bit as disingenuous, and could be cruel as well.

The last girl he had dated back in Kentucky, a girl named Jill, had been taken with Don enough to continue pursuing him despite his melancholy, a behavior that after the accident had compounded his chilling out behavior. He knew there was much of the lost little boy about him, and suspected Jill had been drawn to him by a desire to save him. The problem was Don did not want to be saved. Unwilling to share his deeper personal feelings, their time together, usually spent at Jill's house watching TV on the couch in the family room, inevitably ended the same way. After Jill had made repeated attempts to get him to open up, and told him how good a listener she was, Don would find an excuse to leave. Eventually he just stopped taking Jill's phone calls. Don had not consciously been cruel. It would take a long time before he realized that while keeping people at a distance lessoned the chance of an angry confrontation, it also prevented anyone who might cause him to expose feelings he was not ready to deal with from getting too close.

But Don was in a very different environment and set of circumstances now. He had come to the seminary seeking answers, albeit rational ones, for the questions he had stemming from the accident about injustice and suffering. He now sensed that the kind of callousness he had shown toward former friends and girlfriends would only worsen his precarious status here at the seminary. Somehow despite his tendency to keep people at a distance emotionally Don knew he would have to open himself up enough to make some friends, or at least a friend, and possibly a girlfriend if he was to survive psychologically in this place. Even if it consisted of only a few individuals Don knew he needed emotional support to survive in an environment where he felt like such a misfit. Considering this prospect scared him, and went against what felt natural to him, but for the first time, in some small way, it felt alluring too.

The next morning Don headed out to his church history class. He was determined to keep a low profile and his nose to the academic grindstone. Still smoldering from the dean's dressing down, he had become even more determined not to let him win by forcing him out of the seminary. Don entered the classroom, which was on the ground floor of the same building where he had his unfortunate exchange, on the second floor, with Wilson. As he walked into the classroom, students were milling around looking for seats. Don quickly found his seat toward the middle of the room. He leaned over sideways to take his textbook and notebook out of his backpack. Out of the corner of his eye he saw Wendy sitting a couple rows over. He paused just long enough to stare at her. Sensing that someone was looking at her, she turned her head sideways briefly and smiled shyly in his direction. Don suddenly felt his face flush red. He smiled back and averted his gaze as he sat back up. For the rest of the class he kept glancing over at Wendy, only to have Wendy sense this each time and return a friendly, but fleeting smile. Don was sure this was a sign she was interested in him and would not be doing this if she was trying to discourage his attention. Wouldn't she then just ignore him? Neither, he suspected, was she going to get caught up in some in ongoing class flirtation. Her looks and smiles were friendly but discreet.

Sensing this, Don tried hard to return his focus to the lecture, but try as he might he kept finding himself distracted by Wendy. It didn't help that Canfield had a monotone delivery that rivaled that of Ben Stein. A tall, thin man, he had the peculiar habit of grasping the sides of the lectern with his hands, then with elbows turned out he would lurch forward as he lectured, pushing his head and neck out to the edge of the podium. This had earned him the nickname of "the vulture." About an hour into the lecture another sight began to distract Don. At the very front of the class a student named Fred had fallen asleep in the center front row of the classroom just below the lecture podium. He looked like a kill the vulture had just dropped. Fred had fallen asleep so soundly that he had planted his forehead on the desk, with his arms hanging by his sides. This was not the first time he had fallen asleep in class. Fred was almost always one of the last to enter class. The seats up front were usually the last seats filled, and this helped set up the worst possible scenario with somnolent Fred having to listen to the school's most monotonous lecturer in the worst possible location. It had been apparent to most of the class that this is what had led to Fred's semicomatose state. Over the last few classes Don had seen a few students snicker when five minutes into the lecture Fred could be seen getting the nods. His head doing a good imitation of a pigeon feeding. In Fred's defense Don had noticed numerous students at the front of the class also getting the nods, which then resembled a group of pigeons feeding, but Fred was the only one who ended up looking like his forehead was glued to his desk.

Meanwhile the vulture, oblivious to the impact his lecture was having on poor Fred, had just kept droning on. Don glanced sideways at Wendy again and sensing his look she turned toward him and smiled. Don smiled back and nodded in Fred's direction. At first Wendy gave him a puzzled look, but when Don nodded, and motioned his head in Fred's direction again, Wendy looked and seeing Fred in uninhibited deep sleep glanced back at Don with an acknowledging smile. After what seemed like an interminable period of time the bell rang, signaling the end of the class. Don gathered his textbooks and notebooks and began to walk slowly toward the door. He saw Wendy ahead of him and hoped to catch up to her in the hallway or on the steps. Once in the hallway Don saw Wendy starting down the stairs, and he quickened his walk to catch up to her. About halfway down the stairs and trying to appear like he was passing her and had just noticed her, Don turned toward Wendy and said, "That guy sure was sound sleep." "I can't believe the professor never noticed him," Wendy replied, shaking her head and smiling. Don, continuing the small talk, said, "I am amazed more people don't fall asleep in his class." But then, not wanting to sound too critical, he added, "He obviously knows his stuff, it's just the way he delivers his lectures." Wendy smiled in agreement but said nothing. Don, not wanting to waste the opportunity, said, "I don't know if you remember me, we met at the bookstore the first week, my name is Don Campbell." "I remember," Wendy said, adding, "I can't believe we're nearly a month into the semester already." As they reached the bottom of the building's front steps, Don, knowing many were headed to the cafeteria for lunch, turned to face Wendy and asked, "Are you headed to the cafeteria?" "Oh," Wendy replied, "I am sorry, I am headed over to the library to catch up on some reading for my 1:30 class." He felt his heart sink, this seemed to be a clear signal that Wendy was not interested in getting to know him better. An impulsive part of him wanted to agree that getting in some extra study time was a good idea, and then offer to walk with her to the library. After a moment's reflection, he knew this would come off forced and too needy, and if she wasn't interested in him at all, clueless. "Of course, I understand, see you around," Don responded. While she probably wasn't interested in any kind of relationship, he knew there would be other informal opportunities where he would run into her, where he could be more certain of this. He was just too attracted to her to not leave the door open to the possibility she might still show an interest.

Don had applied weeks earlier for a work-study position. He had just received a letter in his mailbox directing him to talk to the manager of the seminary cafeteria. At dinner that night, instead of going through the cafeteria line, he walked directly into the kitchen located on the side of the large dinning area. The kitchen was bustling with activity. One student was pushing a tall cart full of trays with large pans of food toward the serving line. In one corner of the kitchen was what appeared to be an Asian international seminary student up to his armpits in a sink full of pots and pans. There were a number of students from Taiwan at the seminary, and Don thought it likely he was Taiwanese. A mix of students and staff, all with aprons on, were milling about while performing various duties. Don stopped and asked one older lady, stirring a large pot of soup, if the kitchen manager was there. "He's not here right now, but you can talk to the assistant manager. His name is Tom," the woman responded, pointing toward a young man in a white chef's coat and hat.

Don walked over to what appeared to be a young man roughly the same age as him. Tom was about five foot nine, and like him had sandy blond hair. "Hi, are you Tom?" Don asked. Tom took a break from chopping carrots, which Don had noted he had been doing with amazing speed and dexterity. "Whose asking?" Tom said with a big friendly smile as he wiped his brow. "I am Don Campbell, I just got a letter that there might be a work-study position available in the kitchen." "Well, Don, today is your lucky day. As you can see, John Hu over there is washing pots and I think he's losing the battle. How would you like to work with him three nights a week?" "No problem," Don responded. "There are two sets of sinks over there and you can work alongside each other," Tom continued. "I had a restaurant job awhile back washing pots and didn't mind it," Don shared. "When can I start?" He then asked? "Actually, I think John could use some help right now," Tom said, as one pot atop the growing pile next to the sink came crashing down. "I am free right now," Don replied, nodding in agreement as he watched a second pan come tumbling down. "Great," Tom responded, "let me show you where the aprons are," leading him over to a large metal drawer. Don instinctively liked and felt a kinship with Tom. Here finally, although it was a seminary employee and not a student, was somebody who seemed open and friendly in a down-to-earth way. He was later to learn that Tom had started working at the seminary right out of high school. With an intelligent, quick mind and a real interest in learning to cook he had worked his up way to assistant manager of the kitchen.

"By the way Don," Tom said in the same friendly voice and manner, "the kitchen crew usually eats after their shift is done." "No problem," Don said as he put the apron on and walked over toward John Hu. John, seeing him coming, wiped his brow, and with a thick accent but in a friendly way said, "Oh, good, I could use the help." After exchanging introductions, Don filled up his sink with soap and water and started grabbing pans and washing them. Within a week he had settled into a routine. Once done with his shift Don would grab his tray of food and sit down to eat at the staff table in one corner of the dining room next to the cafeteria. Within a short time Tom would join him, and the two, discovering they had common interests, struck up an easy friendship. It wasn't just their working-class backgrounds and sensibilities, but also the innate intelligence and the broader interest they shared. Where Don loved philosophy and theology, Tom loved literature and poetry. Most would never guess that either one, upon first meeting them, had such varied interests. Philosophy and theology helped Don to question and grapple with the big questions of life, and particularly those related to suffering and injustice. For Tom it was, first and foremost, poetry that gave his rich inner emotional life an outlet. He had a special fondness for the American poet Robert Frost and the Scottish poet Robert Burns. Soon Tom had invited Don over to his apartment for dinner, where he was introduced to Tom's fiancée, Sarah. Tom had cooked a wonderful Italian meal, chicken marsala, for the three, and with wine flowing conversation went on well into the night.

Don still had hopes that he might build a relationship with Wendy. What he could not have known of course was that the reason Wendy was only open and friendly to a certain point, was that she had romantic ties with another man on campus. As Don would find out, the seriousness, however off and on again of that relationship, and the comfort level Wendy felt with someone from her own regional upper middle-class background, would in the end make any relationship between them difficult if not impossible. Meanwhile, deep down he knew it was only a matter of time before some other incident might tap into the reservoir of anger flowing just beneath the surface of the defenses he had worked so hard to maintain. Events of the last year and a half had taught Don that just when he thought he had begun to feel more centered and was gaining a more positive outlook, certain chords, if struck, could arouse an anger within him that he had a hard time controlling; an anger he now felt toward the unfairness of life itself. Feeling bullied or condescended to seemed to top the list of catalysts.

Calm Before the Storm

Don's friendship with Tom continued to grow stronger. Invitations to Tom and Sarah's apartment became a regular event. Don and Tom could be seen sitting together after all three dinner shifts Don worked. In fact he would come late to lunch just so he could sit and eat with Tom at the staff table. Don continued working his three evening shifts washing pots. As their friendship grew, they found they shared even more things in common. Both took a certain pride in manual labor and working with their hands. They also, at times, shared a certain juvenile sense of humor. Both shared a disdain for political correctness, particularly when it masked an elitist, patronizing, and even prejudiced attitude. As they got to know each other better they were able to share something of their respective dysfunctional family backgrounds. Tom's mother, like Don's father, had been an alcoholic and had at times been emotionally abusive. Both found outlets for their reflective side in ways that enabled them to wrestle with their deeper emotional issues. Don loved the works of C. S. Lewis. As a child he had read the "Narnia Chronicles" his mother had bought for him. In college he had an English teacher who encouraged him to read Lewis's *The Great Divorce* and *The Problem of Pain*. These and numerous other books that dealt with theological and philosophical issues offered Don insight, and touched on the emotional issues he struggled with. Overall, though, they spoke more to the intellectual side of his nature and less to the strong emotions his rational side tried so hard to suppress. Tom's love of poetry had also offered him an intellectual outlet, but he had found that reading and writing poetry had helped him to process his emotions as well.

Tom had shared some of his poems with Don. He had been surprised by their sophistication. The poems had a confessional theme but were also optimistic. In Tom's poems pain and trial gave way to hope and grace in a non-doctrinal Christian way. Tom's faith understandings had been broadened by other friends he had made at the seminary. His unchurched background had helped him maintain an open-ended faith perspective. This freed Tom to explore spiritual issues in his poetry unhindered by narrow Christian beliefs. In

reading Tom's poetry Don got glimpses into some of Tom's emotional struggles, and the way he sought the balm of grace to help heal them. Ironically
it was Tom's poetry more than any seminary course that offered Don some
initial insight into the emotional pain he was struggling with. In contrast to
his intellectual pursuits this insight dealt with becoming more open to grace
as an experience and not just an intellectual insight.

Don pondered on what was obviously more of an experience of grace
for Tom. Emotionally he was not sure he was ready for such an experience,
and sensed that his anger, some of which he felt toward God, would impede
him from having such an experience. Still he felt hope that, if in some way
he could work through his anger he might avail himself of such an experience. Don even began to wonder, by opening himself to the prospect of
experiencing that grace, if he might have turned a corner, or made some
forward progress, in dealing with the demon of his anger.

Don's friendship with Tom, and some weeks of calm that fall, gave
him enough confidence to attempt to make more friends on campus.
These attempts would leave him feeling rejected, and even more discon-
nected from the greater seminary community. On one occasion Don accepted an invitation from a student named Doug to stop by his room at the
other end of the first-floor dorm hallway. One Sunday afternoon, taking
a break from his studies, he went to Doug's room. The door was partly
open, and after knocking Don heard Doug yell, "Come on in." Doug and
two other male students were huddled together on chairs watching a small
TV perched on the end of Doug's desk at the head of his bed. They were
watching a well-known televangelist his mother used to watch and making
fun of him. "Come on in, Don, you can have a seat on my roommate's
bed, he's not here. Listen to this bozo," Doug then added, "He's preaching
on Revelation, and trying to match up the symbolism with some actual
historical timeline." Don was suspicious of such speculative literalism, but
his mother had always liked this evangelist so Don found their mocking
humor hard to stomach. He also wondered, given that it was a Sunday
on a seminary campus, why they could not find a more positive religious
focus. The fact that he was sitting behind and off to one side of the three
of them, and didn't feel like joining in, left Don feeling like the odd man
out. Eventually Doug, noticing how quiet and serious he was, glanced back
at him and teasingly remarked, "Don, you look worried that the end of
time really is about to come." "No," he said forcing a smile, "just stayed
up too late last night studying." As the other three went back to mocking
the evangelist, Don felt increasingly uncomfortable. Finally realizing the
situation's futility, he got up and remarked, "I think I am going to catch up
on some reading, I will see you guys later." Without turning around Doug

yelled after him, "See you, Don." Even though Don suspected there were other students on campus that he might have more in common with, this experience reinforced the feeling Don had that he was a misfit on campus. he would not visit Doug's room again.

November and December of that fall semester had passed without incident and the Christmas holidays were fast approaching. Don had opted to remain on campus over the holidays. The new semester started mid-January. Not feeling like he fit in at the seminary, or back home anymore, Don wondered if he would fit in anywhere. Trying to focus on the positive, or at least the constructive, he decided in preparation for two of his spring semester's courses, Philosophy of Religion and Systematic Theology, to buy the textbooks for the courses and start reading them.

A small minority of students, mostly international students, also remained on campus over the break. Tom's grandparents had invited Don over for Christmas dinner. He felt some guilt over leaving his father alone during the holidays, but took comfort in the fact that even if he had been with his father, they would have interacted very little. His father's primary focus would be, as usual, the TV and the beer he would be guzzling. Don had run into Wendy numerous times on campus: at the library, in the cafeteria, walking across the quadrangle. She always seemed to be open to talking with him, but did so in a slightly flirty teasing way that seemed to show interest in Don while keeping him at a distance at the same time. Don resolved to ask her out on a date to test the matter, but before he could work up the courage, she always, perhaps sensing his next move, hinted that she was in a rush to get somewhere. Still he felt strongly attracted to her and rationalized that her academic drive and discipline left her little time to invest in any relationship.

The break went by quickly. Don had gone to the university bookstore and bought a few best-selling historical biographies. He ended up, for the most part, reading them in place of the textbooks for his upcoming classes in theology and philosophy. The break had become a time to indulge his introverted side, which, coupled with his increasing tendency to withdraw since the accident, made for even longer periods where he either watched TV or read. At one point he was watching the serial TV drama *Dallas* in the first-floor student lounge when three Eastern Orthodox students from Eastern Europe came in and joined him. They had full beards, wore conical black hats, and long flowing black gowns. Their laughing, friendly manner put Don at ease. Though their thick accents made it difficult for Don to understand much of what they said, he had no trouble understanding them when in a burst of laughter, they would turn to Don and say, pointing at the TV, "This is JR."

Don had also run into what appeared to be one very quiet young Asian woman in the library vending room, whose vending machines offered coffee, as well as an assortment of snacks. The room also had a number of small tables, with chairs around them, where students taking a break could sit. The young woman always seemed to be sitting by herself and seemed to interact with other students even less than himself. Don had said hello to her as he waited behind her to put money into the coffee machine. He had slowly become a coffee addict during his first year at the community college, and was drinking up to six or seven cups a day. After saying hello to her he had joked about his addiction. She had flashed a shy smile his way as she glanced back at him. At the time Don assumed she was an international student. She must know English, he told himself, or she wouldn't have been able to study at the seminary, but maybe, he speculated, she has low confidence in her ability to speak it fluently, or a thick accent makes her hard to understand.

With fewer students on campus during the break, particularly at the library and in the vending room, Don had taken more notice of her. She always seemed to be by herself, but he had been reluctant to initiate any further contact given what he had assumed would be communication difficulties. Don had noticed that even when she sat with other students at the cafeteria, she did not seem to be engaged much in the conversations. He began to wonder if language and cultural barriers had made her feel like an outsider at the seminary. He felt a strange empathy for her despite their very different backgrounds. He would always smile and nod at her when he saw her, and she would smile back in the same shy way. Don continued to think of Wendy and hoped to find just the right future time and occasion to work up the courage to ask her out. As the holiday break passed and the new semester began new opportunities would be presenting themselves.

The Date

As Don had noticed numerous times there was something about Wendy's teasing flirtatious manner which conveyed an interest him while at the same time kept him at a distance. Did she see him as a kind of bad boy, the only redneck on campus who somehow attracted her and repelled her at the same time. Don still hoped, however conflicted she might be, that on some level she was attracted to him. By the way she spoke and carried herself he suspected she came from a middle- or upper-middle-class background. Her speech had none of the Southern colloquialisms he so commonly heard in many of the people he had known from more working-class backgrounds. Her tastefully casual dress made her look as if she could appear at a semiformal event, including worship, on short notice as is.

Don by contrast most often wore jeans with a shredded hole in one knee, and during the winter, a leather wool-insulated coat with a hoodie underneath. Through spring, summer, and fall, he wore a baseball cap, which he often wore backwards. This was a habit formed in high school which now had the unintended effect of making him look somewhat juvenile. When they would walk down the steps together from class, or approach each other from opposite directions on the quadrangle slowly and greet each other, the sheer contrast in their manner and appearance occasionally drew attention. Even knowing how different they were Don could not help himself, he had to make an effort to find out once and for all if Wendy had any interest in him.

One foggy morning, early in the new semester, Don was walking across the quadrangle toward the cafeteria and spotted Wendy walking with another young woman ahead of him on the sidewalk. He walked quietly behind them, so as not to draw attention, without a plan in his head of what he would say. As the young women approached the steps to the cafeteria building Don impulsively called out to her, "Wendy, wait up." Wendy, looking mildly startled, turned around and seeing him smiled, but not quite as warmly as she usually had. She then whispered something to her companion, and the other girl headed up the stairs into the cafeteria by herself.

Wendy appeared to wait patiently, but with a certain lack of antici-pation, as Don approached. "Good morning," Don said as he greeted her. "Good morning, Don," she said with her usual polite pleasant Southern drawl. He drew a deep breath and took the plunge. "Wendy, we keep run-ning into each other, and seem to hit it off." As Don spoke these words, he thought to himself surely there must be a better way to get out what he was trying to say. He plowed ahead, "Anyway, I wondered if we could grab a bite in town, and maybe catch a movie afterword sometime?" There, Don had said it, done it, for better or worse. Wendy gave him a serious searching look for a few seconds, but for what seemed to him like forever. She then said, "Sure, I guess that would be okay." Although Don was relieved, there was something about her response that seemed less than enthusiastic. "How about this Friday? We could walk into town together and grab a bite at the local diner. I think *Star Wars* is playing at the theater up the street." "Yes, Don, that would be fine," Wendy replied. "We can meet here in front of the cafeteria at six if you like," he suggested. "Sounds like a plan," Wendy responded, quickly adding, "I promised my friend I would have breakfast with her, I'd better join her." "Of course, I understand," Don replied as he walked up the steps with her. As they parted ways, Wendy glanced sideways at Don and gave him a congenial smile.

Tom was working the early shift. Don loaded up his plate at the serv-ing line and then carried his tray back to the corner staff table. Now that the deed was done he was worried that he had totally misread Wendy. This was beginning to feel like a pity date. The girls he had dated back home had been more down to earth and unsophisticated than Wendy, but had a more unaffected and honest way about them. While Don had been attracted to Wendy's high-class sophisticated manner, he was also begin-ning to realize that, at least with her, such a persona made it harder to read where she was coming from. This left him feeling like his normal radar for such situations was not working, which left him feeling particularly vulnerable with a girl like Wendy.

They met by the seminary steps that Friday at six as planned. Wendy was her usual polite but formal self. On their walk into town Don was deter-mined to learn something more about her even, though, unfair as it might be, he knew he would remain somewhat guarded about his past, or at least the more traumatic elements of his past. If this was a pity date he in no way wanted to play off that. As they walked toward town, he asked her, "So I detect something of a Southern accent, where are you from?" Don knew he had asked her this before but could not recollect her answer. "Cleveland, Ohio," Wendy responded. "I was actually born in Texas, but my Dad's job took him to the Midwest when I was a teenager." Wendy then proceeded to politely inquire, "And where are you from again, Don?" "I am from a little town in central Kentucky called Boden," he replied. "I could tell you have a Southern accent as well," Wendy followed up. After an awkward pause in the conversation Don asked, "You're a year ahead of me, how are your studies going?" "I have an uncle who attended the seminary over a decade ago, he told me that the academics here were rigorous, so, I came prepared to study hard." As they approached the diner in the center of town Wendy remarked, "So Don, how are you adjusting at the seminary, you seemed like you might have had some trouble at first?" Don was taken aback by the question. Had she heard about the incident in Wilson's class, or had he appeared to be more of a loner, and misfit than he had thought? With a slightly defensive tone Don replied, "Well I guess, I mean, I am not from the same background as many of the students here." "What background are you from?" Wendy asked. Don was getting uncomfortable with the direction the conversation was going, afraid that it might lead down a path and to topics he did not want discuss. Fortunately, they had arrived at the restaurant, and Don deflected the question by saying, "Well we're here." He then held the door for Wendy as she walked in. After being seated, and ordering drinks, Wendy a diet coke and Don a coffee, they perused their menus. Don remarked, "Well I know what I am going to have, how about you?" In a quiet voice Wendy responded, "I think I know too."

After the waitress took their orders and was walking away Don veered the topic of conversation in a different direction. "So Wendy, you have one year left after this one, are you thinking of going into parish ministry?" "I hope too, although it can be hard for a woman to get a church, even in our tradition. I may have to start as an associate in a larger church. How about you?' Wendy reciprocated politely. "I am not sure yet, but I am leaning more in the direction of teaching," he responded. Don continued to ask Wendy questions about her background and interests. Frustratingly she never seemed to offer him more information than the question required. Nor did she ask him any more questions about his background. The information Don did garner from his questions indicated, not surprisingly, that Wendy was from an upper-middle-class background, and that her father was some kind of corporate executive. Her parents had been Episcopalian but had joined the Presbyterian tradition when their children were small.

The movie theater was only a few blocks up the street from the restaurant and on the same side of the street. So as the 6:30 show time neared both agreed they should head out. Taking their seats in the crowded movie theater he helped Wendy take her coat off. Don's radar had begun to function again, and he had already decided not to attempt to hold Wendy's hand, or make any other moves that could be construed as romantic on the date.

They watched the movie, eyes straight ahead, throughout. Fortunately, it was a great movie and enjoyable in and of itself. When they came out of the theater the evening had grown colder, and on the walk back to the campus they walked a little closer together. They made polite conversation about the movie, talked about how good it was, and shared their favorite parts. Don walked Wendy to the front of her dorm. She thanked him for the evening. Then Don, even though his radar, which now seemed to be working and was instinctually warning him about pursuing the relationship any further, impulsively asked, "Would you like to go out again sometime?" "Don," Wendy replied in a serious, concerned tone that he sensed in the pit of his stomach would end in rejection, "you're a nice guy and I needed an evening out, but until recently I have been in a serious relationship with another student on the campus I met last year. We were even considering becoming engaged. I am just not sure where things are with that relationship, and it would not be fair to you, or anyone else, to date again until I know where things stand with this relationship." Don swallowed hard. Even though he knew she was letting him down easy, he had just lost all hope of having a relationship with Wendy, and it hurt to hear her confirm it out loud. Don smiled weakly, and said that he understood, and then thanked her for the evening. As he walked slowly across the quadrangle back to his dorm, he felt a dark cloud of depression descending on him once more. He wondered if this depression would lift enough for him to continue to maintain a positive attitude toward his studies and life on campus.

When Don entered his dorm room, David, as usual, was reading in his armchair and smoking his pipe. He greeted him with a cold politeness. In hindsight, Don began to see something of the same disingenuousness in Wendy, although nowhere near as blatant or cold as with David. He clearly saw how the formality of that politeness and friendliness could be used to create a wall between them and others. Don realized too that he did not know David any better now than the first day they had met, and he suspected David preferred it that way. Don too had walled people out, but he had done this to protect himself from feelings stemming from traumatic experiences. With them such behavior seemed normative and socially conventional in varying degrees depending on the type of relationship.

A couple of weeks passed by quickly as Don, more through a force of will than anything else, immersed himself in his studies. His theology classes focused heavily on the great thinkers of the Middle Ages, like Augustine and Aquinas. This did not interest Don as much as the more contemporary theologians Soren Kierkegaard and Paul Tillich. He had also hoped to learn more about the secular atheistic writings of Nietzsche and Sartre but knew they would not be covered in any seminary theology class. Fortunately, his

Philosophy of Religion class focused on relevant philosophers and theologians from the enlightenment era to the modern era. The syllabus had indicated that the course would touch on these philosophers as well as Soren Kierkegaard, many of whom Don had been introduced to in his college philosophy course. The secular and atheistic writings of Nietzsche and Sartre, and the non-doctrinal theological writings of Tillich and Kierkegaard, had freed him to ask the deeper questions about the pain and suffering with which he was struggling.

These authors, in different ways, offered Don new ways of thinking about these questions even if they didn't offer him any ready emotional resolutions. Don liked his Philosophy of Religion professor, who like himself seemed to be something of a rebel, or just a free spirit. His teacher would entertain questions even if they challenged the status quo, including those that challenged narrow liberal theological Christian understandings. Even his appearance was different from that of most of the other professors. Younger, with longer hair and a beard, he wore jeans, like Don. While he too, like most of the seminary faculty, had a more scholarly air about him, Don felt more comfortable with him. Despite his erudition there was a lack of pretentiousness about him, and he seemed oblivious to the academic posturing many students and professors seemed to be invested in. Don soon found himself spending more time reading non-required philosophy books than he did the textbooks for his philosophy course, or any other course. On his own he bought Kierkegaard's *Fear and Trembling*, a work that dealt, in a personal subjective way, with the radical cost of faith. He had also bought Nietzsche's *Beyond Good and Evil*, which critiqued the nature of Christian doctrine and and morality, and how they had been used to perpetuate a master slave morality in Christendom. Kierkegaard and Nietzsche could be dark, and even though Don did not agree overall with their philosophical and theological positions, parts of their critiques of the Christian tradition had resonated with him. Tillich, a contemporary theologian whose books offered a whole new set of theological terms, such as "ground of being" for the Divine, for older doctrinally laden terms, freed Don from language that too often for him had been weighed down by narrowly understood antiquated religious language. With new fresh and broader theological terms and concepts he felt liberated to wrestle with the deeper questions that troubled him most. Tillich's *Courage to Be* exhorted the reader to have courage, not in denying the anxiety that nonbeing or death and meaningless arouse within us, but in the face of them. Tillich wrote about an existential courage that affirmed being in the face of nonbeing. Tillich used the terminology "Ground of Being" for God as a new way of expressing the antidote for our fear and anxiety in the face of nonbeing.

Tillich, in particular for Don, seemed to affirm the doubts and questions his mother and sister's death had raised, while at the same time affirming his search, at least intellectually, for answers and hope.

Looking at the clock in the library and seeing that it was nearing eleven, Don decided to head back to his dorm room where he would read further in bed. It had been a little over two weeks since he had last talked to Wendy. Now when they passed each other on the quadrangle or in the classroom they would both smile weakly at each other. As Don headed back to his room, despite the hurt Wendy's rejection had caused, and the mild depression that followed, he once again felt himself regaining some emotional stability. The fact that Don still had trouble connecting with other students, be it because of his more provincial ways and Baptist roots, or the loner persona he projected, no longer seemed to bother him as much. He was just as happy to ignore them as they were, Don assumed, to ignore him. He had begun to accept, as he had been able to keep his anger under control for a longer period, that he too was part of the problem, with the possible of exception of David. Don realized that the key to his success at the seminary was to keep his anger in check. He knew as well that there had been lulls before where it seemed like his anger was less of an issue. But he also knew that he was not yet a dormant volcano, and that given the right set of circumstances his anger could erupt again with a new fury. Little did Don know that just such a set of circumstances was about to cause an eruption that would make his expulsion from seminary almost certain, and leave him in a darker place than any since the accident.

The Tripwire

The semester had started smoothly enough. Don had gotten off to a good start. His student loan had come through in a timely way, for a change, permitting him to get all his required textbooks ahead of time. He liked his courses better, particularly his Philosophy of Religion course. By the middle of February he finally felt like his darkest days were behind him. He still wrestled with his anger at times. In addition to his philosophy of religion and theology courses Don had also signed up for a course on the New Testament book of Acts, Luke's history of the early church. Typically, higher-level courses at the seminary broke classes into smaller groups called precepts, which met at a separate time during the week from the lectures. The leader of each group, not surprisingly, was called a preceptor. Preceptors were drawn from the PhD ranks and were paid a small stipend. Don's group of ten or twelve students had a preceptor by the name of Fowler. Don had instinctively not liked him from the first class. Fowler had a stiff formal teaching style and seemed to carry a disdain for his students. The attitude he projected in class, Don had decided, could best be described as weary impatience. He also shared a similar theology with Wilson, Don's Intro to New Testament professor, with whom Don had argued in class. By contrast, though, the professor teaching this overall course was a well-respected biblical scholar who was more moderate theologically. In his lectures he seemed more open to other scriptural interpretations.

Still Don had received a poor grade from Fowler on his first exegetical paper, a paper interpreting a text from Acts. He would subsequently receive poor grades on the rest of the five required exegetical papers. Fowler's comments clearly indicated that he did not respect the moderately conservative commentators on the text Don had used as his resource material, especially if they even considered a more literal interpretation of the text. Fowler's comments were generally critical of what he called speculative scholarship, meaning they were not employing the biblical criticisms in a rigorous way, or in his way. Don had sparred with Fowler in class, pointing out the biased way the criticisms were employed by liberal biblical scholars like those of the "Jesus Seminar." Don's point was that there were speculative assumptions and premises too behind such positions that were not forthright and were not irrefutably verifiable rationally or empirically.

Fowler's precepts had also caused Don to reflect more on his own that semester. Weren't there other time-tested ways of ascertaining whether something was true or not? Was not the test of how relevant and useful a truth is and whether it bettered one's life and that of others, in a way consistent with its most essential beliefs, just as valid? Had this way of discerning truth not been around much longer than the often misemployed scientific method which could never have claimed to have conclusively verified anything that wasn't reducible to a materialistic cause? If we discount this measure of truth, Don thought, would we not also have to throw out all the great values, like justice, liberty, and freedom, along with truth systems that espouse them, such as democracy, for which so many have sacrificed their lives. Still if we focus on just the truth test of how well the Christian faith has worked as its founder intended, historically and in our own time, the faith offers existential proof of its validity; a truth test rooted in lived experience rather than either abstract reason or empirical data. Don had gleaned his understanding of the "pragmatist truth test" as it regards religion from the great American pragmatist philosopher William James's landmark work *The Varieties of Religious Experience*.

Wasn't, Don had considered too, there also a logical coherency and consistency to the essential teachings, mission and ministry of Christ, as opposed to its ecclesial distortions and political corruptions. Did not this coherency itself, as opposed to seeing the teachings of Christ as all that is verifiable or worse as the ravings of a madman, also make a claim for truth? Don understood truth in this context as fallible in the sense that while our faith experiences could be inspired and empowered by a timeless and transcendent truth, human understandings of these experiences were always in need of further growth and maturation. For Don both of these truth tests argued for more than a faith's social ethics or metaphorical meaning. Taken together they argued as well for the origins and revelation, historically, of that faith. The case became even stronger when combined with contemporary written commentary on Christ and the early church by the Roman historians Tacitus and Suetonius, and Jewish historian Josephus, not to mention the New Testament Gospels and Epistles. It made no sense to Don that the Christian truth would bear out, as witnessed to in his own time, in a grace-centered lived faith, if its founder's mission and ministry were incoherently formed and historically unlikely. Christian social ethics understood from such a perspective, Don thought, was overly dependent on horizontal human agendas and bereft of any vertical mandate.

Don's challenging in class remarks had been made at the various times and junctures when Fowler had just finished, in a mini-lecture format, pushing his narrow liberal agenda. Pointing out Fowler's biases typically prompted him to flash a condescending smile, and then deflect the comment. This was irritating, but also fortunate for Don, as it did not prompt an intensifying argument between them that might have sparked an angry outburst from him. Neither was Don one-sidedly critical of what he saw as narrow liberal theological positions. He was more than open to questioning the narrow ways some conservative traditions interpreted essential Christian truths such as sin, forgiveness, salvation, and reconciliation. Don had little patience with those sectarian Christian groups where a narrow, rigid, and excluding moral judgmentalness of others eclipsed any deeper understanding of the inclusiveness of God's grace in Christ and turned sin into a top-ten list.

He still clung to the timeless transcendency of the most essential truths of the faith implicit in Christ's life and mission, culminating in the resurrection and Pentecost. Despite the in-depth reflections Fowler's precept had engendered, Don intuitively knew he was missing the spark of a faith experience that could ignite his views, as an advocate for biblical integrity into the fire of a personal, living faith. Neither did he have a clear overall theology. Typically, he seemed to not fit neatly into any, either conservative or liberal, theological camp. Don began to wonder whether, if he ever did formulate a theology, it might not be a synthesis of the most vital and relevant aspect of both camps.

Don's real issue with Fowler was the self-righteous superiority he seemed to project whenever he challenged his views on the New Testament. Despite the fact that Don had come to challenge some tenants of his own Christian tradition, he resented the overall disdain figures like Fowler seemed to have toward his religious background, or any faith tradition that differed with their views.

Don was working hard on the exegetical papers and felt Fowler's critiques biased and unfair. The downgrading of his papers tapped into the greater anger he felt toward the unfairness of life in general. Even though Don grew angrier at Fowler as the semester wore on, he knew that to survive at the seminary he could not afford to blow up at another teacher, even it happened one on one. For the time being, at least, he would have to sit on his anger.

Don also found himself wondering how a mainline Protestant seminary could not see that teachers like Fowler and Wilson were, with their narrow brand of liberalism, as closed minded, biased, and self-righteous as the fundamentalists they claimed to abhor. Over the course of the semester Don read and reflected on how aspects of these views evolved. A subset of lectures his philosophy of religion professor had given that semester on "The Enlightenment and the Reformation" offered context and fodder for these reflections. Don had learned that such liberal biblical and theological views had their roots in the enlightenment, a historical era which began to gain momentum in the seventeenth century. This philosophical and culture movement sought to elevate human reason and egalitarian principles over superstition and the ignorance fostered by oppressive authoritarian hierarchies and regimes. The danger of course was that with the dismantlement of such previous authoritarian traditions—absolute monarchies, aristocracies, and the church—human secular reason might in time become its own final authority and be enshrined to such an extent that it in turn would tolerate little dissent.

What could not be disputed was that by the later 1800s, this elevation, some would say deification, of human reason had begun to manifest itself culturally as the modern scientific worldview. Don could see that the overconfidence, at the turn of the twentieth century, in human reason's ability to solve all the world's problems had already, by his time, been undermined. Two world wars, the holocaust, the threat of nuclear annihilation, and most recently a growing environmental crisis had not just created cracks in the foundation of the modern scientific worldview, they had called the whole tradition in turn into question. The challenge this postmodern dilemma posed for many nominal Christians often boiled down to a choice between the belief that there was no unitive truth, only fragmentary relative truths, versus clinging to a traditional Christian faith. The latter choice too often being shackled to antiquated institutional and social tradition and characterized by entrenchment.

Reason as science and religion in their institutional forms had both proved themselves too easily corrupted and prone to idolatry. Science and technology within a much shorter time-span. Perhaps Don thought, then, rather than both traditions competing with one another and trying to usurp each other they might each, now recognizing the dark sides of their tradition's histories, be open to a new type of dialogue. They might then discover how they could complement and inform one another. Academic forums open to student bodies would be a good starting place. Where overly dogmatic religious and scientific views had only created polarization perhaps a humble openness to what each could offer the other, given their different understandings and approaches to truth, might ease entrenchments and lead to a more unified front against the problems of the world. A dialogue on climate change would be a great starting place. Human beings have always needed explanations of both how and why we do the things we do. This had never been more the case, Don suspected, than with the exponential increase of scientific and technological know-how and the slippery ethical slopes this can create. Don knew such a dialogue would be much more problematic and complicated than he could imagine, given the diverse schools of thought within both the greater religious and scientific communities. Nor would the materialistic scientific bias and negation of, not just religion but human spirituality, pervasive in the greater scientific community easily surrender its self-assumed stance of superiority.

Of one thing Don was sure, human reason and spirituality were both age-old defining human characteristics hardwired into us by a creator. Neither had they always been perceived as foes. The modern scientific worldview evolved out of the enlightenment. Much enlightenment thinking had its origins and impetus in the thought of great theologians like Thomas Aquinas and later John Calvin and great Jewish thinkers like Maimonides and later Moses Mendelssohn. Leading rationalist philosophers who influenced the enlightenment, who were also Christians, included Renee Descartes, Immanuel Kant in his ethics, and Gottfried Leibniz. Great scientific thinkers that presaged the enlightenment and the scientific method, like Copernicus, Kepler and Francis Bacon, were devout Christians as well. To a certain extent the prevalent view that science or reason, and religion, were or are diametrically opposed to each other has been a fallacy. With scientific advances in areas like quantum physics that question radical material reductionism, and the countless studies that have affirmed faith's health and psychological benefits, as well as the positive impact Christian social ethics can have, the barrier erected between these two great traditions is being broken down. Don could not see either human endeavor, that of religion or science, extinguishing the other.

This was as far as Don's reflections had taken him, and he knew they were incomplete and oversimplified in their analysis of the confluence of thought, historically, that led to the prejudiced liberal biblical theology and interpretations he had encountered at the seminary. Nor was he sure that they were an accurate prediction of where these currents of thought might lead, or of how they would impact the traditional Protestant churches.

Don felt the way Fowler had handled his New Testament views expressed a form of intellectual elitism. For Don, Fowler was the second narrowly liberal instructor at the seminary he had clashed with, who thought anyone who disagreed with him was not just wrong, but less intelligent than him. Don found this form of elitism, together with the class elitism he had encountered on campus, exemplified by David, a hard combination to cope with. His experience with these elitisms had touched on feelings of inferiority Don had long felt within.

Don, despite his native intelligence, had grown up in a working-class family that had often had to struggle financially. He had been the first in his family to go to college. The mannerisms and mores of his working-class Southern roots had made him stand out, or at least feel like he stood out, among the majority on campus. In Boden this had only happened in high school when he crossed paths with students from more privileged backgrounds. He recalled one incident in the cafeteria that epitomized such an instance. Don and his friends had been joking around when they suddenly overheard a group of students, sitting just up from them at the same table, imitating and mocking them. Don had challenged one boy in the group verbally, but he had waved his hand dismissively at him, and their group had then appeared to turn their backs to Don's group and change the conversation. There were of course nice, down-to-earth kids from all backgrounds in his high school who managed, despite the high school student tendency to form cliques, to make friends from a variety of groups.

The anger and at times rage, that had possessed Don since the accident, now had the unfortunate effect of amplifying every incident in his life that struck him as unfair or unjust. The academic and class elitism he perceived at the seminary had tapped directly into the deeper compounded rage that had been roiling within Don since the accident; a rage he had been trying so hard of late to keep submerged. He had barely managed in his class with Fowler to contain it. When Fowler had smirked at his challenges in class Don had felt his face tighten and turn red and a closed-mouth, tense grin form on his face. Fowler deflections to another topic had stemmed this anger tide, but his anger at Fowler had intensified as his papers continued to be downgraded.

It was from one of Fowler's classes that Don found himself walking back to his room one late morning in April. Patches of snow still spotted the ground, but this together with warmer weather hinted that winter was ebbing. For him this was a portent, he hoped, of better days to come. This turned out to be a brief false indicator. In reflecting back on what was about to happen Don was amazed how often peaceful spells in life can more cruelly set one up for the unexpected shock of a life crisis. As Don walked down the hallway and into his room nothing could have prepared him for the sight waiting for him. There sitting together on David's bed, holding hands, were Wendy and him. The look on Wendy's face said it all. For the first time her polished, classy, pleasant veneer fell away and her face turned first pale, and then bright red. Don was so taken aback that he stopped up short and stayed standing just inside the doorway, and for a few moments gazed at the couple in stunned silence. He had not been shocked when Wendy had told him that she had had a relationship with another student on campus. What so shocked him now was that it was David. How, Don asked himself, could he have been attracted to a girl who was attracted to this guy; not only attracted to him, but in a serious relationship with him? Could she not see past the ridiculousness of David's obvious façade? How could she be attracted to someone who had treated him with such subtle but still obvious conde- scending disdain? David greeted Don in his usual overly formal, slightly condescending way that was at once polite and distancing. "Well hello, Don, are you heading to lunch soon?" David asked without introducing Wendy to him. Don realized that David was entirely unaware that Wendy and he knew each other, much less had been on a date together. He also knew that David was politely asking him to leave as soon as possible. Still standing in place Don broke the awkward silence. "Yes," he said in a hesitating tone, 'I just stopped by to pick up some books. I plan to go to the library for a short time and then to lunch." The shock evident on Wendy and Don's faces, and in their body language, was too thinly veiled to fool David for long. David looked at Wendy, and then back at Don, and with a creeping look of surprise mixed with disgust he could not hide asked, "Do you two know each other?" His alarmed tone indicating that he suspected theirs might have been more than an acquaintanceship. Don looked at Wendy, not knowing what to say, Wendy immediately averted his gaze and stared down at her hands now clasped together tightly in her lap. After a few moments of uncomfortable silence, Don suddenly walked up to his desk and grabbed a couple of his textbooks and turned around to leave. "Well I guess I better get going," he said as he exited the room. Wendy and Don's silence had confirmed David's worst suspicions.

Don made no further eye contact with either Wendy or David as he left the room. Going directly to the library to study, he had trouble concen- trating and soon decided to head back to his room to drop off his books. As soon as he entered the room, he knew David had extracted a confession out of Wendy. Although David was sitting in his armchair, puffing on his pipe, with legs crossed, and feigning a scholarly poise, Don could tell there was something different about his bearing. David refused to acknowledge Don at all as he walked in, and his face had a more rigid downward-cast appearance. Don proceeded to lay his books down and then turned to exit the room. Just as he neared the door David spoke, "I know about you and Wendy." Without turning around, and feeling his anger rising, Don responded in a weary voice, "What do you know, David?" "I am well aware that you and Wendy went out on a date," David said in a pompous way that suggested that he had known this all along. Turning around, Don looked directly at David, who continued to pretend as if he was reading the book, he was holding. "We dated once, David," Don said in an irate tone. "Well nothing came of it and I am not surprised," David retorted, unable to resist shooting a barb Don's way even as he pretended to play down the date's significance. David's clear overreaction to the date together with his disdainful tone and barb had incensed Don. He felt his anger overwhelming his better judgment. Don turned around and glared at David and in an irate and indignant tone said, "And what the hell do you mean by that?" "Oh nothing," David replied with a self-righteous smirk on his face, "it's just that the two of you are so different. Wendy is a very caring person, she sometimes does things just to be kind." Don's body was sending him all the signals it did right before he lost total control of his temper. Don knew that while anger was not an invalid feeling given how David was acting, he was well aware that in his current state he was liable to overreact in an extreme way. David, sensing that he had gotten under Don's skin, smirked more noticeably, his expression hinting at the pleasure it gave him. "What you're saying is that she is too good for me," Don snapped. "I didn't say that, Don. I have to study, why don't you go do whatever you have to do to calm down," David responded in a patronizingly dismissive way.

Don knew that his anger had reached a breaking point. Paralyzed by his anger, he stood frozen, staring at David, who had gone back to reading the book he was holding. Suddenly Don took a few angry strides toward David until he was standing directly over him. "I know exactly what you meant, you smug son of a bitch, and I don't give a rat's ass. You both have poles so far up your asses . . ." David was now out of his element, he had not expected this side of Don to come out, and did not know how to handle such a direct confrontation with its crude emotional honesty and threat of physical violence. "Don, I deeply resent your tone—," David started to say; Don cut him off sharply, "I don't give a shit what you think, you can go to hell, and while you're at it take your fake Oxford English accent with you." Don knew his last remark had to sting, and still seething, he took pleasure in finally being able to state out loud what he had thought for so long. By now David was peering at Don over his glasses in stunned silence. Don, feeling his anger somewhat spent, wheeled around and headed out the door. He knew that David was more than capable of reporting his behavior to the dean's office, and that David's nastiness, which had been the catalyst for Don's outburst, could be easily denied given the polished disingenuousness of David's delivery.

Don knew he might again be in big trouble, perhaps this time be put on probation. Back home, at work, or in school, such an exchange, as long as it remained verbal, would not have been considered way out of bounds. Here, though, in the rarified atmosphere of the seminary where appearance and pretense mattered more than what was in your heart, an outburst like Don's could easily bring his stability and character into question should David file a complaint. Don stalked off to the cafeteria. He was still too angry to care much about the possible fallout. In such a pretentious elitist setting Don knew that the rules favored individuals like David, who knew how to play such games. David's finding out about the date, the incident that had prompted his jealous reaction, was something Don could overlook. What he could not was the blatant disdain David had shown him. He had felt put down not just for what he did, but for who he was.

As Don walked toward the cafeteria, he not only felt anger but the hurt that lay beneath it, as well. It felt like a giant swell of anger was lifting up the more incidental anger he had just experienced. Pushing that swell up in turn was the hurt and pain he had buried within him for too long: the pain of not feeling accepted just for who he was. Streams of anger over the bullying in middle school; over the years of emotional abuse from a father who even when sober could not say anything positive about him; over the incredible injustice of the accident—it all merged into one roiling river of rage within him. His inability to fit in at the seminary and what he saw as the rigidly liberal condescension of two of his instructors had now further undermined his self-worth. These were new contributors to the rage that was once more rising to the surface. But while Don had gained rational insight into his anger this did not equate to emotional healing.

Don walked into the cafeteria feeling like he was a time bomb about to go off. Still, as worked up as he felt, a small part of his consciousness was cautioning him to calm down, and not let his anger mount beyond a certain point. Don knew in such a state, if pushed, he might not just be capable of an outburst, but of physical violence. Don hoped the physical exertion of washing pots and pans would help calm him down. After an hour of washing pots, he did feel somewhat calmer, although he began to dread returning to his room and facing David. He grabbed his meal from behind the serving counter, and then sat down at the corner staff table to eat. Tom had already been sitting there when Don had sat down. Don was in no mood for conversation, and Tom, sensing this, gave him a knowing look and then went back to reading the newspaper he had spread out in front of him. Don resolved to finish his meal, skip his next class, and then go straight to the library before returning to his room. He had also made up his mind not to apologize to David. From Don's perspective his impulsive outburst may look worse on the surface but was not as bad as David's veiled, but intentional and probably premeditated passive aggression. For Don, the insidious prejudiced nature of David's attempted belittlement of him had made it all the worse.

Don had begun to feel his anger subsiding somewhat. He felt calmer, but was demoralized by how easily he had lost his cool with David. The guilt and shame he felt over this lack of self-control only served to kindle the lowered flame of his anger. Ironically, he was angry and frustrated with himself over his inability to curb this defense, which seemed to have a mind of its own. He was now convinced that all his strategies and attempts at self-control would not work consistently, particularly in those situations that struck the deeper chords of pain and hurt around which his anger had formed a defensive perimeter. This realization, which came to Don as he sat eating at the staff table, suddenly left him feeling demoralized and hopeless, and that he would never be able to resolve his anger issue.

Caught up in this dark mood and the emotions they aroused, Don did not see the approach of student named Jeff Warren. Jeff's voice caught Don off guard, "Are you reading that paper?" he said in a loud, abrupt, and challenging way. Looking up, Don was startled by the large figure looming over him. Jeff was over six feet tall, and while not overly heavy, had a large build. "I am sorry, but this is the chef's paper, and he'll be back in a few minutes to finish reading it," Don responded. Jeff, who seemed to accept this explanation, turned silently and glumly around and began to walk away. A few moments later, out of the corner of his eye, Don was alarmed to see Jeff walking back toward him in an angry, determined way. Jeff then proceeded to grab the paper off the table and then stalk off with it. In shock, Don turned around in his chair. Jeff had stopped abruptly about ten feet away, and holding the paper apart with his hands, was reading it. Don's emotions had calmed down some, but he still felt the undercurrent of restless edginess that he knew, under the right circumstances, could rapidly escalate into full-blown anger. Ironically, in this case, he had no real issue with Jeff other than the quickly unfolding confrontation Jeff had just initiated.

On impulse, and with his anger quickly mounting, Don rose and walked quickly up to where Jeff was standing to confront him. "The chef bought that paper, and is still reading it, please give it to me," Don said in as calm, but as forceful a voice as he could. What happened next would leave him endlessly analyzing why he had acted as he had, and why given the shaky ground he was already on at the seminary, he couldn't have just walked away, and let it go. All he could gather was that his anger at this time could, given the right provocation, go on autopilot once it kicked into high gear. Looking back Don realized that any freedom he had to exercise his will in not escalating this confrontation, would have been minimal if he did not heed, as a warning sign, the physical sensations he was experiencing as his anger mounted. This most likely would have been soon after Jeff had grabbed the paper and stormed off, and before Don had jumped up. Although it wouldn't help here, he was learning not to trust the physical and emotional signals that drove him into angry confrontations as their outcomes only created more hurt and problems, and did not provide constructive resolutions. He knew also that too often, because of the anger within, he had misread the intentions of others and disproportionately projected his anger upon them. It didn't help that Don's father had indoctrinated into him the adage that while he should never start a fight, he should be the one to finish it. This adage had made the most sense when he was in high school, but as an adult, and as his life had become more complicated, such an adage seemed overly simplistic, blind to context, and dangerous. Still even though Don had come to realize this, his body and the more primitive parts of his brain, in this quickly escalating situation, had not gotten the message. His father's authoritarian, black-and-white self-defense adage had been aimed at an adolescent who had been traumatized by bullying in junior high, and it was this adolescent part of Don that would react to the situation confronting him. His impulsive reaction here, born of shame and humiliation, and backed by his father's counsel to never let himself be bullied again had, in the heat of the moment propelled him into a negatively life-altering conflict.

So here he was caught up in a situation with his emotions primed not toward flight but fight. Don would conclude later that a perfect storm of circumstances had brought out the worst in him, in the worst possible setting. The question he would wrestle with in the months to come was why would God allow such an unlikely set of circumstances to coalesce as they did? Ironically, much later, Don would come to see the experience as a turning point in his life. At that point, no longer believing that God set up the situation, he came to accept that perhaps God had used it as part of his greater plan for Don's life.

As Don stood face to face with Jeff, he kept repeating the demand, "Jeff, give me the paper." Jeff, totally ignoring him, had continued to read the paper. Finally, Don, feeling he had no other move, reached out to grab the paper from Jeff. What happened next would remain a blur in Don's mind, but at the time caused him to react spontaneously. Jeff, in one fell swoop, proceeded to rip the paper to shreds, and then, while ripping it up, he plowed forcefully into Don using his greater height and weight to force him backward. His size gave Jeff a clear advantage in this violent shoving contest. Sensing he was about to fall backward, and unsure, if or when, Jeff would stop his attack, Don threw a hard punch to Jeff's face. He felt it connect, and saw Jeff start to stumble backward. Before the fight could escalate any more, three full-time lands and grounds workers who had stopped by the cafeteria for a coffee break stepped in and separated the two.

Don was later to learn that Jeff had come to the seminary with some mental health issues, one of which was explosive anger disorder. He had been on medication for years, and had been an excellent student throughout high school and college. Don, who was wrestling with his own mental health issues, then felt a deep empathy for Jeff. He also knew that as both Jeff and he had anger issues, perhaps for very different reasons, he should be the last one to judge Jeff too harshly. Don at times had wondered if medication might help him raise the foundation of his coping ability with his own anger. He knew such medications often came with strong side effects, and he was leery of taking anything that might affect his studies negatively. Perhaps, if he was honest with himself, he also hated the thought of conceding that resolving his anger issue might ultimately be beyond his control. More objectively, though, he recognized also that medication was often a necessity for mental disorders of a biochemical nature. Medications might be needed more generally too to raise one's coping foundation. Still, Don thought, while God could work through secondary means like medications, it was faith alone that offered the trans-formative meaning and purpose, holistically, that could heal one from the inside out.

Don recalled a story his college philosophy instructor, in relation to the topic of good and evil, had told the class. The story seemed to reassure him that the power to change his behavior still lay within his grasp. It was an American Indian tale called "The Story of the Two Wolves." In the story an Indian boy had just been in a fight with a friend. Upset, he came to his grandfather and told him of the fight. He then shared how conflicted he felt about the fight. One part of him wanted to hurt the other boy and get even with him. Another part of him felt compassion and wanted to reconcile with his friend. The grandfather then told his grandson that "everyone has two wolves within them, one that is prone to judgmentalism, vindictiveness, anger, and violence. The other is prone to patience, compassion, love, and reconciliation. They are always fighting each other within each of us." The boy then asked his grandfather, "Which wolf will win in the end?" The grandfather's response was "whichever one you feed the most." Don had always taken comfort in the story, and assumed in time he would be able to acquire a more positive mind-set through will power alone. He had read articles about the power the mind had to rewire the brain. Up until now he had thought that with enough positive thinking he might be capable of this. Now he was not so sure. Perhaps in cases like his where the roots of the pain and trauma ran so deep, positive thinking alone might just gloss over rather than facilitate healing. Medication in his case might dull the pain, and mute the anger but it too, Don thought, could not afford true healing.

The seminary had been aware of Jeff's condition and had been working closely with him ever since they had learned that he might not be taking his medication. The seminary chaplain had been seeing him regularly and had found out that the increased academic pressure, and lack of support he was now experiencing as opposed to back home in Illinois, where his family was from and where he had gone to college, had brought on a deep depression. As it turned out Jeff had not just missed some doses but had gone completely off his medication. This new information left Don feeling very guilty and wishing he had known this info, as he would have handled the encounter differently. In his heart of hearts, though, Don knew he should have been able to handle the situation better no matter what. The fact that Jeff had these challenges, and that their encounter became physical, had made Don feel even worse. But this was information, and these were reflections he would only have later.

Don retreated to the staff table where Tom was now standing. "What the hell just happened, Don?" Tom said. "The guy tried to take your paper and when I tried to get it back it turned physical," he muttered. Feeling as if his world was falling apart, Don mumbled that he needed to go, and he hurriedly walked out of the cafeteria dining room. Tom was left standing by the staff table with his mouth hanging open. Don then did something he had promised himself he would never do given his father's history. He had only broken this resolution once. In the period right after the accident he had turned to alcohol to cope. Don had forgiven himself for this given the singular nature of the shock and trauma at that time. Now once again Don would fall back on his father's coping strategy. Don had walked into town, and into one of the bars frequented by students. The bar was serving late lunches at the time, but he chose to sit at the bar's counter. The bartender, a balding middle-aged man with glasses and a kindly face, became concerned when Don ordered a fourth beer in quick succession. "Are you okay, son?" the older man asked. Don could already hear himself slightly slurring his words when he responded "never better" in a world-weary sarcastic tone. The bartender went back to wiping out glasses behind the counter while keeping a wary eye on him.

Don knew that sometime that day he would have to head back to the campus, but for now the inebriated state that was creeping over him was dulling the emotional pain overwhelming him. Late that afternoon after stumbling out of the bar, he ended up camping out at the local library in town. He felt his inebriation slowly wearing off, but still felt a little unsteady on his feet. When Don had walked into the Library, he had gone to the magazine section where there were number of armchairs and had slumped down into one of them. A librarian working behind a nearby desk, noticing that he was not reading any of the magazines, and had put his head back as if he was going to go sleep, was keeping a wary eye on him. Don, sensing he was being watched, looked up and saw her staring at him with an alarmed look on her face. With a little better balance than he had come in with, Don got up and walked out the door. As he did so he had smiled at the librarian and said, "Have a great evening," in a weary, sarcastic tone. Don then spent some time walking around the town, at one point ending up at a coffee shop, where he tried to sober up before heading back to the campus.

Later that afternoon Don started his walk back to the seminary campus. Now fully sober he began to dread the fallout that would soon confront him. Not only was he sure to be expelled from the seminary, he might even be brought up on charges. Even though he had been violently and persistently shoved back he had technically thrown the first punch. Suddenly Don realized that he had no plan B. Dropping out and returning home was not an option. He had outgrown his old friends and cut ties with them. Even with all the negative experiences he had been through at the seminary, his studies and ongoing reflections had, at least intellectually, expanded his awareness of himself, and others. This had left him feeling that he had even less in common with the old friends he had left behind. He had no desire to move back home and live with his alcoholic, emotionally abusive father, who had made his formative years such a nightmare. The harsh, stark reality hit him that he had no other place to go but back to his room on campus and hope that the worst-case, and most likely, scenario, his expulsion from the seminary, would somehow not come to pass. As he neared the campus he had no illusions. Whatever happened he would have to face it, and it was sure to be humiliating and leave him feeling utterly vulnerable and alone. He had no doubts that by the next day the news of the fight would be all over the campus. Fights on a seminary campus were not just rare events, they were unheard of. This combined with the inhibited climate of the seminary would frame the incident in a particularly aberrant glaring light. Don reached the outskirts of the campus just as it was getting dark. Rather than head straight to his room he resolved to head to the library, disappear into the stacks, and sit at one of the desks that lined the walls. Perhaps, Don thought, he would start looking for work in town in case his expulsion was imminent. Although he knew this plan, while not out of the question, was borne more of desperation than any realistic assessment of the situation. The harsh reality was that he just couldn't know for sure how the days and weeks ahead would unfold, and what kind of emotional and procedural gauntlet the seminary would make him run through. Around 11:00, as the library was about to close, Don headed back to his dorm room. As he walked through the warm, humid night Don knew one thing for sure, he had hit rock bottom, and whatever options might present themselves would be limited and bleak from here on.

The Intervention

When Don finally got back to his room, to his relief David was not there. As the days progressed he was to find out that David had requested and received an immediate room assignment in another dorm. As Don walked around campus, he knew talk about the fight had to have spread across the campus, and suspected he had now attained a lasting status of notoriety. He had seen Jeff at a distance. He did not share a class with him, and this prevented any up-close awkwardness. Don suspected the seminary chaplain and health center had stepped in, were meeting with him, and were more carefully monitoring Jeff's mental health. Still Don knew that the first couple days after the fight were the calm before the storm. He knew a letter could appear at any time in his mailbox summoning him to the dean's office. In truth he was surprised it had not already come. He did not have to wait long. By the third morning, as he stopped by to pick up his mail near the dorm entrance, there it sat, a formally addressed envelope. Every instinct told him he was in deep trouble. Reaching into the box, he could see that the letter was not from the dean. It had what looked like the imprint of an official stamp on it. As Don slid the letter out of the box his heart skipped a beat, and he suddenly felt a cold, clammy sensation come over him. It was from the president's office. His hands shook as he opened and unfolded the letter. The letter was even more official looking than the one he had received from the dean's office. It's message brief and to the point. He was to report to the seminary president's office the following afternoon at 1:00. Don was sure it was all over. The fact that the president had become involved underscored the gravity of his offense, and assured him of the course of action he knew the seminary would now take.

Don woke up Tuesday morning with an impending sense of doom, and yet somehow he also felt resigned to his fate. He knew he had crossed a line and the seminary could no longer handle him moderately and with discretion. Having the room to himself allowed a place of refuge where he could cocoon until it was time to leave for the appointment. He had made up his mind the night before to skip his morning class. He had also not gone

57

to breakfast that morning, instead eating some crackers he had brought back to the room from a vending machine at the library. He was sure that by now the news of the fight had spread across the campus. Not wanting to deal with the shocked, distancing looks students would surely give him gave him even more reason to hole up in his room until the appointment.

As he lay on his back on his bed there was no way to downplay or rationalize what he was feeling. He now felt like a total misfit, outcast, and pariah at the seminary, and was sure the administration looked at him as a dangerous liability. He looked at his wristwatch periodically to monitor the time until the appointment. He had hardly slept the last few nights and felt overtired. The fact that despite its inevitable outcome he would know his fate in a couple of hours gave him a certain peace. Finally as he turned these and other thoughts over in his head he managed to fall into a deep sleep. When he awoke with a start, he panicked momentarily wondering how long he had been asleep. Glancing at his watch he realized he had slept for nearly two hours. It was 12:45. Feeling like a condemned man about to make the final walk to his execution, Don rushed to get ready for the appointment. As he walked across the campus toward the administration building, he tried to picture the president. He had seen him once walking with a prestigious-appearing group of well-dressed men and women who Don had assumed were seminary board members. He knew all these individuals had been chosen because of their prominent status and financial ties, and included CEOs, bank presidents, and other prominent professionals. The fact that they were following him in such a respectful way, and listening intently to what he had to say, underscored his prestige, and the authority of his position.

As Don approached the administration building, he tried mentally to prepare himself for whatever dressing down he was about to receive. Anxious and totally demoralized, surprisingly the one emotion he was not feeling was the edgy, restless irritation that so often served as a prelude to his mounting anger, especially in situations where he was sure what little self-worth he still had was about to be annihilated. In his current situation, Don knew he had not only overstepped appropriate behavior on campus, but this time had way overstepped, and there was no reasonable defense he could offer. How could he defend a physical confrontation at the seminary. Given his previous behavior he could not even claim that this act was totally out of character for him and would never happen again. Don had resigned himself that he would, no matter what, remain respectful. He would speak as little as possible, and answer any questions with "yes sir"and "no sir" as his father had taught him to do when addressing figures of authority. He had not addressed the dean in this way but was determined to stick to this protocol here.

Don ascended the steps and walked into the administration building. He found himself in an oval-shaped reception area in the middle of which sat a receptionist behind a desk. "Can I help you?" she asked. "Yes," he responded, "I have an appointment with President McCall at 1:00." Pointing toward a hallway behind the reception area, the receptionist replied, "The president's office is all the way down on the right." Don found the door with McCall's name and title on it and entered. Not surprisingly he found himself in the secondary office of his executive secretary. She was seated behind a desk in an office large enough to command respect in its own right. The secretary said in a friendly, but to Don, ominous way, "Yes, Don, we have been expecting you." Without saying any more she leaned forward and pressed a button on an intercom on the corner of her desk. "Dr. McCall, your 1:00 appointment is here." She then turned to Don, and told him he could go in. As he entered McCall's office, he was startled to see McCall rise from behind his desk and walk around to meet him with a smile and then a welcoming handshake. McCall seemed taller up close, well over six feet. Balding with his remaining gray hair combed neatly to the sides of his head. He was impeccably dressed in a dark suit. The reading glasses he had on, rather than accenting an authoritarian appearance, as he peered over them looking at Don, were more than offset by the warm, caring smile on his face. Even more surprising to Don, McCall then had him take a seat in one of the two leather-bound chairs in front of his desk, while he sat down in the other chair. As he took his seat, he noticed that McCall, who was sitting back with his legs crossed, was now looking back with an intense focus that conveyed both interest and compassion.

Once Don was settled, and after a brief pause, McCall said, "So tell me, Don, what's going on with you?" The question was asked in a caring concerned way that nevertheless, he sensed, was not going to sidestep the matter at hand. Don sat further back in his chair and sighed deeply. While still aware of the gravity and possible implications of his situation, he suddenly felt more relaxed. Don was used to authority figures who were overbearing, especially in situations like this one. McCall had totally disarmed him. In addition to feeling more relaxed he also felt a strange mixture of vulnerability and openness. Don had psychologically prepared himself for the worst dressing down of his life. Nothing had prepared him for this. There was something about McCall that Don intuitively trusted.

Don leaned forward, looked down, and then back up. He started hesitantly, "Well, sir, I am sure I am here because you heard about the fight I was involved in at the cafeteria." McCall nodded his head slightly with the same mixture of interest and compassion. He then urged Don to continue. He explained the circumstances leading up to altercation, and then pausing and lowering his head, he took a step he hadn't before with anyone else, he began to share what had brought him to the seminary. As the floodgates opened, Don uninhibitedly shared about the accident, about his father, the faith his mother had instilled in him. He shared the deep faith questions he had wrestled with in the wake of the accident, and which still tormented him, and which were undermining his faith. He shared how he had hoped that his studies at the seminary would offer him deeper insights that might help him cope and renew his faith. Don talked longer and more openly with McCall that day than he thought himself capable of doing. He shared thoughts and feelings that he had even been reluctant to reflect on himself. Meanwhile McCall continued to listen with that same mixture of intense interest and compassion. Don had lost all track of time and began to wonder, with McCall's schedule, how he could afford to spend so much time with him. Whatever else Don hated about the seminary, this man transcended all that. Unless he was an incredible actor he seemed to really care. "How could a seminary like this have chosen a president like this," Don thought to himself. McCall could have easily written him off as some nutcase headache that had been dumped into the middle of his busy schedule, and quickly disposed of it. Yet here he had been listening to him for what had to be over an hour. Don was not used to talking this much about anything, much less his deepest inner feelings. As soon as he realized how much time had passed, he tried to rein himself in. "So that's what's going on with me," Don said in a slightly kidding anticlimactic way. "I know that this in no way excuses my behavior, particularly the cafeteria fight, and I am willing to accept whatever the consequences might be."

McCall smiled, leaned back in his chair, paused, and looked at Don with the same interest and compassion, but now also with a hint of preponderance registering in his facial expression as well. "We are aware of the serious issues Jeff is wrestling with. The chaplain is working closely with him. He has now fully accepted his condition, and the need for additional treatment, and is back on his medication." McCall paused and then continued, "I can tell you're working through some tremendously painful experiences, and emotions. It sounds like you are just beginning to process some of the most difficult emotions. Although I can't fathom how terrible it must have been to lose your mother and sister, or the mix of painful emotions you are struggling with, the anger you are feeling at certain injustices in your life is understandable. I think anyone having dealt with such traumatic experiences would be struggling with such intense emotions. The important thing now is to recognize, and fully accept, how much anger you are carrying around inside, and to begin to find more constructive ways to process and deal with it."

Don could not believe what he was hearing. He had never experienced a reprieve like this in his life. The one thing he had always been able to count on when he was in trouble, from anyone else other than his mother, from little on up, was a quick authoritarian judgmental dressing down, followed by a punishment. This had been the case with his father, at school, and at work. His high school principal, having called Don into his office after numerous altercations as well as actual fights, had always exhibited a world-weary attitude toward him. He had coupled this with a degree of authoritarian indifference, when meting out his punishment, that had made Don feel like he was a lost cause not worth the principal's time. There was a word that came, as if for the first time, into Don's mind that he always thought of only as an abstract theological term. It had held no experiential validity for him up to this point. Don turned the word over in head. It was the best word, the only word, to describe the feeling that someone, who didn't have to, cared about him even given the flawed, broken person that he was. That word was grace.

McCall broke Don's train of thought with another surprising revelation. "Don, I would like to meet with you again. How about next Tuesday at the same time." "Yes, sir, that would be fine," he responded. "Just promise me, Don, that if you really get worked up about something, between now and then, you will not act out on it but wait to share it with me," McCall added, rising and extending his arm for the handshake. Don shook his hand in agreement, and for the first time since the fight he smiled. In fact, his session with the president had left Don not only feeling more relaxed, but somewhat freed up from all the emotions he had not been wrestling with, and just as often suppressing. He felt the first stirrings of an inner peace that was deeper than the periods of calm between blowups that had been more happenstance. He felt cared about not for what he could be or wasn't, but just as he was. As important, Don felt freer to look at himself less defensively. Perhaps, he dared to consider, there are some good people in positions of authority at the seminary, and even among the students and faculty. Maybe, just maybe, the defensive wall he had built up around himself was not only keeping out those he did not want to get too close to, but the good-hearted people on campus who he crossed paths with every day. The anger and hurt Don still felt beneath the surface would not let him totally accept this possibility, but the seed was planted. Perhaps at least some were not keeping him at a distance, as much as he was sending them signals to stay away.

Don met McCall the following Tuesday at 1:00, and McCall yet again caught him off guard by suggesting they take a walk around the campus. Their regular meetings turned into weekly walks. Students, over a period of weeks, became accustomed to seeing McCall and Don walking together every week. McCall's head, on these walks, was always slightly bowed as he listened to Don intently. The conversation gradually shifted from Don sharing about his painful life experiences, and his sense that he was an outsider at the seminary, to questions of faith; the questions he had come to seminary seeking answers to. McCall, despite holding a doctorate in theology, never gave Don the stock doctrinal answers, within the seminary's faith tradition. What McCall did do was affirm that his emotions and his questions were reasonable and understandable, and that feelings were never wrong in and of themselves. In particular he reassured Don over and again that anger in the face of the unjust and senseless suffering he had experienced was completely understandable. McCall was as excellent and compassionate a listener on their walks as he had been at their first meeting in his office. By their third walk together an interesting phenomenon began to happen. Many students whose paths crossed theirs not only greeted McCall, but also smiled and greeted Don as well.

By the end of four weeks of walking together, as they were about to part ways on the bottom of steps of the administration building, McCall, after shaking hands with Don, paused and looked at him intently. He sensed that he was about to say something important. "Don, you mentioned that you will be taking an intensive language course at the start of the summer. I wonder if there is something you would do for me," McCall began. "If I can, sir," Don responded. "I have a close friend, he used to be the manager of the university bookstore and is now retired. He emigrated from the Netherlands to this country after the war. He had been a POW in Japan during World War II for nearly four years. He had moved, as a young man, to the island of Java in Indonesia to manage a large bookstore. Indonesia was a colony of the Netherlands at the time, and my friend moved to the city of Surabaya in Indonesia, where many Dutch citizens lived and worked." Don had listened carefully, completely baffled as to what McCall was about to ask him to do. "His name is Jop De Vries, and he has a remarkable faith story. At my request he has often shared this story with groups at the seminary, area churches, and at church conferences and retreats. Don, I would like you to do a series of interviews with him." Don was not entirely clear on what McCall hoped he, or perhaps he and Jop, would get out of this but he deeply appreciated McCall and trusted him, and so without hesitation, he answered, "Yes, sir, I can do that." "I will set up the first meeting for the first week of your summer intensive course. I already checked the class schedule for your course. It meets five days a week from 9:00 to 12:00. If Jop and you are amenable I will schedule your meetings for 1:30 on Tuesdays. I will firm up the arrangements and give you his address on our next walk. After that we will have to stop meeting, at least for a time, as I will be away at an international church conference in England for some weeks."

Don knew McCall had his best interest at heart, and believed that this experience would help him in ways he could not yet foresee. Beyond this, though, he was becoming more intrigued for other reasons. He had always loved history, and World War II history had been a topic of special interest for him. Don was not sure why McCall thought this experience could be beneficial for him. He suspected that if Jop's faith had survived the suffering of years in a POW camp that this had something to do with it. Don himself realized that for a faith to survive such an experience could not be due just to a theology that had made sense of this experience, but somehow must be wrapped up in the experiences themselves. With one foot up on the first step of the administration building, McCall turned around one last time, and once again, after pausing, gave him a prolonged look. "Don, I know you came into my office a few weeks ago expecting some severe consequence as punishment. Today I have given you that consequence, but it is one, I think, given all you have been through, that is much more in keeping with what the God we know in the love of Jesus Christ would choose. This is a love whose end goal is never judgment but transformative love through grace." Somehow McCall's words did not come off preachy, but as a natural expression of a man who truly believed what he was saying and was trying to humbly and prayerfully live and practice his faith.

As Don walked back to his dorm room, he couldn't believe the events of the recent weeks. Perhaps God was at work in his life, not causing his troubles, which after all were to some degree due to the choices and free will of the participants, but helping him to reframe these experiences in a positive, even transformative, spiritual light. There had, after all, been a series of experiences which he could not easily write off to coincidence: his friendship with Tom, whose poetry had helped him reflect on the power of grace to heal not just the mind but the heart; his philosophy professor, whose teaching style he had resonated with, and who had recommended books by Kierkegaard that also had helped him to recognize how radical faith should be, especially in contrast to the institutionalized faith of so many Christians. Then there was McCall. Don knew that as much as he appreciated the kindness and grace that McCall had shown him, he would only come to fully appreciate his influence on his life as he hopefully continued to mature and grow in his faith. Don also suspected that these interventions, by key individuals, were part of a long series of ones God's hand was weaving into his life at critical times. While he might not always have been able to see such interventions in the past, Don was determined, despite his ongoing faith doubts and struggles, to remain more open to recognizing such interventions in the future.

Interlude

D on went to meet McCall for their last walk and talk together. Don knew he was going to raise the first interview he was to do with Jop De Vries. Toward the end of their walk, as anticipated, McCall remarked, "Don, I set up the first meeting between you and Jop. It will be two weeks from today at 1:30. Jop is fully on board, and he looks forward to meeting with you. You can plan on at least five consecutive weekly meetings. Here is the address, and the first interview question." As they approached the administration building, McCall stopped walking, turned, and handed Don an envelope with the question inside. "As I had mentioned before this will be our last meeting for awhile. I will be back in a few weeks from the conference. The remaining questions will be sent to your mailbox. My prayers go with you, and I hope you will find Jop's story as enlightening as I did."

Arriving at the front of the steps to the administration building, Mc-Call paused and seemed about ready to shake Don's hand and say good-bye, but then said, "One more thing, Don, you should know I was a pastor for many years after receiving my doctorate. I was chosen as the president for the seminary because I brought a pastoral style to the position. It was hoped that my leadership and example would help balance out what some thought was too much of a formal and academic atmosphere on campus. There are many students and faculty who I have gotten to know who are not of that frame of mind. The academic pressures of a school like ours can cause these students and faculty, in very different ways, to seem overly serious, reserved. Give yourself some time, and give them a chance, and in time you may yet make some of the closest friends here that you will make in your entire life."

Don nodded and smiled at McCall, feeling a deep gratitude that he could not articulate verbally. He then shook hands with McCall, and said thank you, with an expression and in a manner that conveyed these feelings as best he could. As Don walked slowly back to his dorm room it dawned on him that McCall had indeed pastored him through one of the most difficult times in his life. Sitting back on his bed in his dorm room Don opened the envelope McCall had given him and read it. The address was 472 Hawarden. Don did not know in what part of town Jop lived, but the town was not large, and he could get directions in town. The question simply asked, "Can you tell me something about your family background, and what led you to make the move to Indonesia."

Don was becoming more excited about the prospect of meeting Jop, and hearing the story of his experiences in the camps. He intuitively sensed that McCall felt he needed this experience to grow in his faith understandings, and to further process his emotional pain and grief. Jop's story, from what McCall had told him, was primarily about how his faith had been shaped and even transformed by his camp experiences. Perhaps this was key, in some way, to what McCall thought he needed. Don had made the arrangements to stay in his room over the two-week break, between the end of the spring semester and the beginning of the summer intensive course. He had obtained his Hebrew textbook and started to study ahead. The remaining weeks of the spring semester had unfolded in an uneventful, calm way. Don had done well academically, receiving two A's and two B's in his courses. He had even managed to pull his grade, in his class with Fowler, up to a B based on the grades he received on his midterm and final exams. His academic success that semester was partly due to the fact that he had plunged into his studies as a way to distract himself from his troubles, and partly due to the special interest he had had in two of his courses. Still, despite McCall's intervention and help, Don needed some time to debrief emotionally from the traumatic events earlier in the semester. During the break, the campus, and particularly the cafeteria, were blissfully devoid of students, at least in Don's mind. This helped Don's emotions settle even more.

Don continued to work a few shifts a week washing pots through the summer. As usual he ate with Tom at the corner table in the cafeteria. Tom and his girlfriend had continued to invite Don over for dinner. Don had also bought a biography on Andrew Jackson and had read it every chance he had. Jackson, due to formative issues, had struggled with a volatile temper most of his life. Don resonated with Jackson's anger problem, even if he didn't agree with many of his political views, or his treatment of the Indians.

Breakfast during the summer was between 7:00 and 9:00. As Don walked down the hallway, he would pass the first-floor lounge, a large multi-purpose room with numerous overstuffed chairs, arranged informally, and a TV sitting in one corner of the room. The room also served as an alternative place to study. Walking by each morning around 7:30, Don had noticed what he assumed to be the same Asian international student sitting in one of the large armchairs. He had first noticed her in the library vending room. Glancing sideways as he walked by, Don observed that she was sitting by herself with her legs crossed on one of the chairs. What Don found strange was that she was sitting there staring straight ahead without a book in her hands. Neither was she watching TV. Don found this behavior curious. He assumed she, like him, must be taking one of the summer intensive language courses. He imagined that, as an international student, she might be quite lonely, even homesick. She appeared to be in her early twenties like him. Don hadn't stopped to talk to her, figuring that her accent and any language difficulties might make such an introduction awkward. Still he felt for her, as he knew all too well what it was like to feel lonely, and like an outsider.

Each morning on his way to breakfast, during the two-week break, Don continued to notice that this girl was sitting in the same strange way in the first-floor lounge. He was equal parts confused by her behavior and very curious about it. He also felt drawn to a girl who like him seemed to be off by herself, and who for totally different reasons, was unlike many of the other students on campus. If he was honest with himself, Don, from the first time he saw her in the vending room, also found her attractive. Petite, with jet-black hair, fine features, and a ready, if shy smile, he had thought her pretty, but with all that was going on in his life during the spring semester, together with what he thought were their cultural differences, he had not thought it realistic to try and get to know her.

The break, though, found Don in a very different emotional place, and campus atmosphere. These factors along with finding himself now in a situation where every day provided a prime opportunity to introduce himself to her had caused Don to have a change of heart. Toward the end of the second week Don had made the decision to stop by the lounge and introduce himself to the girl. That Thursday he set out for the cafeteria shortly before 7:30. Instead of passing the lounge Don stopped and stepped just inside the door to the lounge. Wanting to be sure she understood him, he spoke a little louder than usual and introduced himself in a simple straightforward way. "Hi, my name is Don, I have noticed you sitting here every morning on my way to the cafeteria." The girl had looked up as Don walked in and smiled at him in an open way, which had made him feel less awkward. Then she spoke. "My name is Cindy Chang," she said in perfect English, with a slight Midwestern drawl. Don suddenly felt foolish and guilty that he had projected a stereotype onto Cindy. "It's good to meet you, Cindy. I hope you don't mind, but I have noticed you sitting here every morning, and wondered what you were doing?" As soon as Don asked the question, he worried that his question might be perceived as nosy, critical, or both. Cindy immediately put him at ease with her response. "I am meditating," she answered, looking up at him with an open, friendly smile on her face. "Meditating?" Don asked. "Yes, I practice a form of Buddhist mindfulness meditation. Meditating helps me cope better with stress, and when I meditate in the morning, I feel more centered the rest of the day." "Are you a Buddhist?" As soon as Don asked this he realized that this was a silly question given that she was studying at a Christian seminary. "My mother is a Buddhist, my father is Christian. I was raised Christian. My mother taught me this meditation, and since Buddhism is a non-theistic religion it is easy to adapt a meditation like this one to other faiths like Christianity." Don had learned enough about Buddhism in the comparative religion course he had taken in college that he was able to nod, and indicate that he understood what she meant. The Buddha had made it clear to those that followed him after his enlightenment that what he was offering them was a spiritual method to end human suffering. The Buddha thought this alone was the deepest and truest human form of liberation. The Buddha's four noble truths and eightfold path were a direct product of his enlightenment experience meditating under a Bodhi tree. They also formed the content of his first great sermon. Don could recollect all this from his comparative religion class but was not sure how Cindy was adapting it as a Christian meditation, and so he asked Cindy about this. "As I focus on my breath, inevitably my thoughts wander. Without judging them I just observe them and as they fade away, I refocus on my breath. Just before I refocus on my breath, I surrender these thoughts and emotions, things I might be denying or am overinvested in, to Jesus Christ." Cindy had said this in an instructive but friendly way. Revealing what little he knew about Buddhism, Don said, "But what about the Buddhist belief that being liberated from suffering means extinguishing all desire. Isn't that what Nirvana means?" "I see a parallel between the Buddha's teaching of the middle way and Christ's teaching that while it is okay to enjoy life one should not get too attached to worldly things," Cindy responded. "I understand meditating," Cindy added, "as a way to detach from those things we crave or have an aversion to. This helps me re-center myself in God's grace and love in Jesus Christ."

Surprisingly this made perfect sense to Don, and he began to wonder if meditation might not be beneficial to him. Wanting to find out more about this intriguing young woman, he asked, "So where are you from, Cindy?" "My father is a biology professor, and had studied at an Ivy League school in this country before going back to Taiwan, where he met and married my mother. Shortly after they got married my father felt there would be more teaching opportunities in America, so he applied and was hired as an assistant professor at the University of Chicago. My parents moved to Chicago, and that's where my older sister and I were born. We grew up in the suburbs." Don could not believe how open Cindy was, and how easy it was to talk to her. He had never thought, when he first saw her in the vending room, that Cindy was the kind of person he could relate to so easily. Cindy then paused, and asked, "So tell me a little about yourself, Don, where are you from?" Even a few months back if anyone had asked this question he would have become instantly uncomfortable and would have quickly deflected the conversation in a different direction.

This time Don felt no such reaction coming on. Something had shifted in him since the cafeteria fight and McCall's intervention. He had hit an incredible low, followed by the liberating spiritual high he had experienced in the grace God had extended to him through McCall. In fact, high might be the wrong word as it usually implies something fleeting, or that passes as some intoxicant wears off, be it chemical or psychological. Don's experience had given him relationally an experience of God's grace, and something in him had begun to change. This experience had somehow loosened his previous rigid defense against sharing anything about himself. His faith had been revived by this divine balm, and he now longed to be liberated from the anger that held him prisoner, even as it protected him from feelings that threatened to overwhelm him. Don knew he had much healing that still had to happen, but he now trusted that God would break into his life with his abundant grace in ways yet to be experienced. With his faith rekindled, Don, for reasons that he did not fully understand, at this time and place, had felt open to sharing with Cindy.

"I am from a small town in Kentucky called Boden. My roots are pretty working class. My father works for a car manufacturer on the out-skirts of town, and I almost followed him into this line of work. I inherited a degree of intelligence or academic ability, combined with an analytical bent of mind from my mother, and in the end just couldn't settle for my father's life path." Don had already shared more easily with Cindy than he had with anyone other than his mother and McCall. While he still felt comfortable sharing with Cindy, he decided not to overshare. He was just getting to know her and was hoping there would be other opportunities to get to know her better and share more of his life with her. Intrigued by the potential benefits that meditation might have for him, and sensing an opportunity to spend more time with Cindy, Don, after pausing, asked Cindy if she would be okay if he joined her occasionally to meditate. "You can join me every morning if you like," Cindy responded happily. "You might have to give me some instruction to start out. I understand generally what you said about how it can be used in a Christian context but am not clear on technique," Don replied in a slightly diffident way. "Be glad to. Can you come a little earlier, say around 7:00, that would give us more time." "No problem," he responded. Not wanting to delay Cindy any more from returning to her meditating, Don remarked, "Well I will leave you in peace, but I will see you tomorrow around 7:00." Cindy smiled and said that she would be here as he turned to leave. As Don walked across the quadrangle to the cafeteria he began to realize that he was getting two educations at the seminary, the academic one and the extracurricular one that God seemed to be offering him. God's chosen instructors were not seminary faculty, but were even more critically needed and effective: Tom, McCall, Cindy, and soon Jop were all part of God's faculty.

A Growing Bond

The Monday of the first week of the intensive Hebrew class had finally arrived. Don was glad to have more of a schedule, even though the class would require a minimum of six hours of study a day. Other than the interview itself, McCall had asked Jop if it was okay for Don to tape the interviews. After his Tuesday morning class Don readied himself for his walk to Jop's house. He had asked for directions, over the break, from the owner of a small bookstore in town. Don headed out, address and directions in hand.

Don had to walk to other end of town from the seminary, a walk of a couple miles. Since his arrival at the seminary his Pontiac Catalina had largely remained parked in the seminary parking lot due to mechanical problems and a lack of money to get the car fixed. Walking, for Don, had proved not only to be his primary form of exercise, but when necessary, a way to calm his nerves and sort out his thoughts. As it turned out, Jop lived on a side street off of Palmer's Main Street at the other end of town. It took about twenty minutes for him to walk the distance. His directions indicated that he should make a left off Main Street, and then a quick right. Don soon found himself in front of a quaint-looking Cape Cod. Double-checking the house number on the mailbox, it was indeed Jop's house. It was unpretentious and yet inviting. Don walked up the sidewalk to the front door and rang the doorbell. He heard footsteps approach from the other side of the door. A dignified white-haired woman who appeared to be in her seventies opened the door. "Don?" she inquired. "Yes, ma'am," he replied. "Come on in, Don, Jop is expecting you," she responded. "I am Jop's wife, Marie, Jop is waiting for you in his study. He would have come to the door himself, but he has been struggling with some hip problems of late." Marie then instructed Don to follow her through a cozy living room with a fireplace at one end. When Don had first entered the home he had also seen, through an arched entrance way, a small kitchen at the front of the house. Marie led Don into a fair-sized backroom whose walls were lined with bookshelves. As he followed Marie into the room, he noticed a white-haired man sitting with his back to him in a large leather armchair. A rolltop desk sat against the back wall with a wooden swivel desk chair in front of it. A window between the nearly floor-to-ceiling bookshelves on the outer side wall of the room let in the muted light of the sunny day through the partly opened slatted window shades. Don could see that Jop had been reading. A green shaded lamp with a tall stand offering the necessary light for Jop to read by. "Jop, Don Campbell is here to meet with you," Marie announced, alerting him to their presence. Jop, leaning on one arm of the chair for balance, immediately stood up and turned around to greet Don. He was a tall man, even taller than McCall, with broad shoulders. He had taken off his reading glasses and laid them on a small coffee table next to his chair as he had risen to greet Don. This allowed Don to get a fuller impression of Jop's face. Like McCall's, Jop had an open, friendly, and inviting expression. Also like McCall, the remaining white hair on his head had been combed neatly to the sides of his head. But his voice was quite different. "Welcome, Don," Jop said as he directed Don to the other leather-bound chair in the room, located on the other side of Jop's chair. "Thank you, sir," Don replied as he walked over and sat down in the chair. Jop had a thick Dutch accent that his time in America had apparently not modified. The way he had said welcome, in a down-to-earth way, totally devoid of pretention, gave Don an impression of the man as a straightforward and pragmatic individual. Still, as he looked around the room, he could tell not only that Jop loved books, but that he was a very well-read, educated man. On a shelf just above the chair Don was about to sit in he had noticed a number of books by Kierkegaard. "Have a seat, Don," Jop said in the same gracious and yet matter-of-fact tone. "Marie, would you mind getting us some coffee and cookjes," Jop said, using a Dutch/English hybridized word for little cookies. Marie nodded and left the room. "I was usually the one to get the coffee and cookies, but since I developed this problem with my hip my wife has taken this on. Having coffee breaks with cookies is a Dutch custom much like the English with their tea breaks. It helps slow us down and is a way of offering hospitality to guests. Also, Dutch coffee made the old-fashioned way tastes very different from American coffee. Half a cup or mug is filled with rich espresso-like coffee, the rest of the cup is then filled with hot milk or cream. Chickory and anise are also added for flavoring. Marie soon returned carrying a tray with two mugs of this coffee and a plate of Dutch windmill cookies. Jop handed Don his mug and then took his. "The cookies are not really Dutch, they are compromise I had to make living in the States," Jop said. "I became an American citizen many years ago, so I feel I should incorporate something American into these old Dutch rituals. Besides, real Dutch cookies are hard to get," Jop then added. "I think these days many in this country need to learn to slow down and could benefit from such a custom." "My mother always insisted that we share at least one meal a day together as a family, and a more formal dinner on Sundays. I think this was her way of slowing us down," Don said as he took a cookie off the plate, ate it, and then took a sip of the coffee. The coffee was full-bodied and delicious. Creamier, sweeter, and smoother than any brewed American coffee he had ever drunk before.

The coffee break, really more of a hospitality gesture, had given Don time to look up at bookshelves on either side of the window and against the wall in front of him behind Jop's chair. He tried to do this subtly as he looked over the mug he was sipping from. Numerous small freestanding framed photos had been placed in front of the books in various places on the bookshelves. Some of them were of Marie and Jop as a younger couple. Three children appeared in a few of these photos, with Jop and Marie, which appeared to be from the late sixties. As the youngest looked like he was at least five or six, at the time, Don guessed they were now all grown with families of their own.

At the near end to Don on the bookcase behind Jop was a framed black-and-white photo of Jop with a dark-haired, olive-complexioned young woman. They were sitting close to each other on the steps of a building, in what looked like Indonesia, holding hands with happy smiles on both their faces. In a smaller framed picture next to this one was the photo of the same young woman holding what looked like a newborn baby. Don knew that Marie was American, and that Jop had met her when he had come to this country. It followed that the children with them, in the more recent pictures, were from this marriage. But who was this other woman and child? Could this have been from a previous marriage of Jop's in Indonesia? If so, what had happened to her? They seemed so young, full of life and happiness. Don glanced around the office and noticed numerous framed prints of Dutch paintings hanging on the walls. Turning slightly in his chair, Don had also noticed a framed photo of what appeared to be Jop with his three brothers, sister, and parents on the corner of his desk.

Don had nearly finished his coffee, and taking one last sip he looked back toward Jop, who had settled back in his chair, crossed his long legs, and was now looking back expectantly at Don. "So, Don, we should get to the business at hand. John [McCall's first name] did not tell me much about you, but did ask, as you know, that I allow myself to be interviewed by you. I am also guessing that he did not tell you much about me except probably that I was a Japanese POW during the Second World War," Jop surmised in his same friendly but forthright and practical tone. "It is my understanding that you will be interviewing me five times and taping it," Jop added. "Yes, sir, if that's okay," Don said, pulling a small cassette player out of the backpack he had set down next to his chair. "Please, Don, I am not one of your professors, just call me Jop from now on." Then pausing, Jop, leaning forward before sitting back again, said almost apologetically, "I will try to fit my whole story into these sessions. As you may also know I have given many talks about my experiences in the camps to church groups, and conferences, but I generally give a summary of these experiences. This will be the first time I will be telling my whole story in such detail. I may need an hour or more for each session to do this. We may also, depending on how things go, need an extra session. Are you okay with that?" Jop inquired. "Yes, sir, I mean Jop," Don answered, feeling somewhat uncomfortable addressing such a dignified, erudite older man so informally. The fact that Jop wore his learning so lightly made this more informal relationship easier. "So, go ahead, Don, ask me the question John gave you for this interview." Don unfolded the paper he had put in his pocket and looked at the question. He then looked up at Jop, who was sitting back with his hands folded in his lap, silently awaiting Don's question. Don suddenly felt awkward. The question seemed an awfully personal one to ask this distinguished older man he had just met. Still, as Don looked at Jop he seemed totally on board and comfortable with sharing the personal information he was about to during these interviews. Even though McCall had given it to him, Don tried to read the question as if it were his own: "Can you tell me something about your family background, and what led you to make the move to Indonesia?" Don said as he looked searchingly at Jop. The question was simple and straightforward, but he intuitively knew it would open the door to another time and place and a wealth of experiences that set Jop on a path that led too much suffering.

As Don looked at Jop and waited for his answer, Jop smiled, and sensing that he was ill at ease, said, "Don't worry, Don, I have shared this part of my life story with many groups. I had to smile because these memories now seem so long ago, and I was such a different person then. When I talk about myself as I was back then, it's almost like I am talking about a different person, a young man whose struggles I no longer strongly identify with, except that they were at a critical stage in my development, and without them I would not be who I am today.

"Well, as John probably told you, as a young man I moved from the Netherlands to Surabaya, Indonesia. Indonesia at that time was a colony of the Netherlands." Don had turned the cassette player on just before asking the question, and other than when he had to turn the cassette over, his job now was to listen, and not interrupt. He wanted Jop's story to flow uninterrupted so as not to break Jop's train of thought. McCall had given Don just enough questions to frame Jop's story, and he was determined to stick to this format. "I grew up in the city of Rotterdam, which is in the province of the southern Netherlands often called Holland. My father was a successful art dealer there. He had come from a humble line of longshoreman working in the harbor of Rotterdam. He was the next-to-the-youngest of six brothers and had shown a spark of personality and intelligence. At six feet seven he looked older than his seventeen years. My longshoreman grandfather, wanting to give him a leg up in the world, had approached a distant relative, who was a successful art dealer, and asked him if my father could work as an apprentice art dealer for him. At the time, in the later 1800s, this was still a primary way one could learn a trade. The distant cousin, a kindly, married but childless man, having met my father and been impressed by his sociability and intelligence, agreed to give it a try.

"While such apprenticeships did not always work out, as the trade was not always one for which the often coerced young man or woman had an aptitude, my father fortunately turned out to have a natural aptitude for this business and established his career with this art gallery. Over time he also grew close to the owner of the gallery. Eventually the old art dealer died, and my father took over the business. As smart and capable as my father was, he never left his working-class roots behind. His language often slipped into more working-class Dutch expressions and under the right circumstances he could swear as well as his longshoreman father and brothers. At six feet seven he was a very large man with a domineering manner. He combined his forceful personality with an extensive knowledge of the art world of the time. In his work he used this in skillful ways to sell paintings, while continually developing the extensive network of customers who bought paintings from him.

"At home his authoritarian nature was expressed with less subtlety. He so dominated my three brothers and one sister that he controlled almost every part of their lives. My mother, a gentle, loving woman who had a simple but deep faith, was his opposite. My father had no tolerance for anyone who questioned his opinions or decisions. He had a simple saying, 'I am the easiest person to get along with, all you have to do is agree with me.' If any of his children disagreed with or questioned his authority his temper could erupt. He would curse with a booming voice while waving his hands wildly. My father used our fear of his anger to get his way. His size alone was enough to cow my brothers and sisters even as young adults. My mother was the only one who could calm him down at times like these. She had a way of deflecting his attention to other matters; his work, or some matter related to the staff. My father's success afforded us servants. We had a couple of maids and a gardener. One maid and the gardener were part time, the other maid was a full-time live-in staff member and helped out around the house in a variety of ways, including helping to make meals in the kitchen.

"Even my mother knew it was fruitless to argue with my father, and that it would only escalate his anger. While he never physically abused any of us, his domineering nature, backed up by his intimidating size and temper, kept the family under a kind of dictatorship. His children, even though it was never pleasant to live like this, having grown up with this behavior thought of it as normal. On a good day my father remained relatively calm, but on a bad day almost anything could set him off: a newspaper story, a difficult day at work, or even an undercooked meal. My mother dreaded going out to eat with him, as he inevitably would find fault with the waiter or waitress, or the food, which he often sent back for one or another reason.

"His outbursts were almost a daily event, as even on good days while the outbursts were less common, something during the day would set him off at least once. When angered he could stay sullen and disagreeable for hours. My father was born in the 1870s. It didn't help that at that time and in the early part of the next century the culture was still very patriarchal, particularly in wealthier families. Many who have asked me why my mother put up with this behavior do not understand this. A wife could be divorced and left penniless, children could be cut off. Many fathers of course did not abuse their station at this time and oversaw their family life benevolently. My father was somewhat unique in his ability to intimidate and cow my siblings. Neither did the culture, at the time, condone any disrespect on the part of children, even as young adults, toward their parents. My oldest brother, Piet, handled my father by towing the line. He was quiet and religious like my mother, and as an adult became a Dutch Reformed minister. My next-oldest brother, Wim, was a good-natured fellow whose favorite saying was 'the greatest worry is no worry of mine.' He had a way of letting everything roll off his back. He was the son who later took over my father's art gallery, although, having little business sense, over time, ran it into the ground. My next-oldest brother, Hendrick, who we called Henny, was an epileptic, and was the one family member my father toned down his anger around so as not to set off a seizure. My mother was also more protective of him. Without modern medicine his seizures could not be controlled, and he died of a prolonged seizure when he was a teenager. My father, despite his hardened outer core, was devastated and never fully recovered from this loss. My mother, equally devastated, leaned on her faith, and was better able to cope with Henny's death. My sister, Dorothea, who we called Zus, was strong-willed like my father but lacked his anger issue. My father, perhaps because she was his only daughter, went a little easier on her. Still living at home, well into her twenties, our father insisted that she be home by eight in the evening, particularly if she was out with a young man. When my sister, at the age of twenty-eight, had been proposed to, my father still required that they seek his permission.

"I was born in 1917, when my parents were in their mid-forties. I was what was called in Dutch a slipperje, or mistake. I was also fourteen years younger than my next-oldest brother, and barely came to know Henny before he died. It may have been partly because of Henny's death that my father was so overly protective and controlling of me. He controlled every part of my life growing up; the school I went to, the friends I was allowed to have, the recreational activities I could become involved in. He wanted to know where I was at every time of the day, and if I questioned his authority I would receive the full brunt of his bombastic, verbally abusive temper.

"The problem was, of all his children, I in my youth was the most like him, and I had been born late enough that the times were slowly beginning to change. By the time I was sixteen I was nearly as tall and as strong, given his age, as him. Until this time I had been in awe of him, and had not rebelled in any significant way. When I was six or seven, I remember holding his hand as we walked through a neighborhood near the art gallery. Suddenly our way was blocked by two men in a heated argument who were shoving each other. My father, who towered over them, grabbed both men by the backs of their shirts with his huge hands and pulled them apart. I still remember the cowed, subdued looks on their faces after he let them go. As we went on our way my father acted as if nothing had happened.

"As a teenager of seventeen I was full of rebelliousness. I also had a quick temper that my siblings did not possess or had never exhibited. It was the early 1930s and, starting already in the '20s, old-fashioned customs and mores in Holland and elsewhere in the West were becoming more relaxed. Economically, too, Holland was recovering from an economic depression, although because of my father's business success our family had not suffered any financial deprivations. I was running with a circle of friends, both boys and girls, whose parents seemed more forward looking. I soon began talking back to my father as I increasingly resented the degree of control he exerted over my life. He wanted me to forego university and become an apprentice to him in the art gallery. I had by this time made up my mind that I wanted to go on to the university and earn a business degree. I had been dating a Roman Catholic girl a year earlier and my father had been successful in breaking off my relationship with her. I was determined not to let him derail my hopes of enrolling in the university. We had been arguing over the fact that I had been consistently coming home later than the 7:00 curfew he had set for me. These arguments had, on a couple of occasions, almost led to a physical confrontation between my father and me. My mother, fortunately, had always been there to separate us and defuse the conflict. What I don't find easy to share, as it still haunts me so many years later, is that when my mother would intervene in our fights my father would often turn his anger on her. He would yell at her, and criticize the way she ran the house, cooked the meals, as well as for other imagined offenses. It was more the anger with which he said these things that hurt her than the criticisms themselves, but I thought it was abusive nonetheless. The reality was that my father loved my mother dearly, and could not have lived without her. They had met and married in their later teens, and by now knew each other so well they could anticipate, as such couples often can, what the other was about to say and do.

"My father was also very hard on my mother's father, who lived with us. We called him Opa, and I was very close to him. He was a kind, gentle, soft-spoken man, and an easy target for my father. He had worked hard his whole life as a shopkeeper in a store that sold bedding wares. After he retired, and my grandmother had died, in the days before there were any social benefits, he had no choice but to live with my parents. The anger my father had often directed at my grandfather had seemed particularly cruel given his age and dependent status.

"In the spring of my eighteenth year I had applied and been accepted to a business college in Rotterdam. I was due to start that fall and planned to continue living at home. My mother and I, colluding in arguments against my father to let me enroll at the college, had worn him down, and he finally agreed to let me start at the college in the fall. He was adamant that he would only pay the tuition if I agreed that upon graduation I would join him and work at the art gallery. I had never really promised to do this but had not said I wouldn't do it either. By this time, though, I knew that the last thing I wanted to do was become an art dealer, I was feeling increasingly restless and wanted more than anything to see something of the greater world, as well as get as far away from my father as I could.

"The one thing that aroused my anger at my father more than anything else were his attacks on my mother. One night when I came home and walked into the house I could hear him yelling at my mother in the dining room. I had arrived home late, just as dinner was finishing up, which had probably helped set my father off. He was yelling something about the meal not being worth eating. While our live-in maid typically cooked the meals, my mother oversaw the process. As usual I could hear my mother pleading with my father to calm down. But this evening there was no calming him down, and his tantrum seemed to go on and on. As I watched this scene unfold from the entrance to the dining room I felt my own anger rising. Finally losing control, I took a few steps further into the room and screamed at my father, 'What the hell is wrong with you? You are nothing but a bully who takes out all your anxieties and frustrations on the family.' His attention and anger immediately shifted in my direction. 'What did you say, boy?' he said as he quickly came around from the other side of the table, and walked into me, backing me into a corner of the dining room. 'I said you are a bully. I am now nearly your size and no longer afraid of you, and if you don't stop, I will stop you.' 'I would like to see you try,' he then said to me, using his immense size to push me back against the wall. By now my anger had turned into rage. I pushed him hard and he was forced to take a step back. My shoving him had momentarily stunned him into inaction. I took advantage of this to slip out of the corner he had backed me into. Fearing that when his momentary shock had worn off, he would be even more enraged and might physically attack me, I went to the head of the dining room table and grabbed a knife we used to slice the cheese with. I held the knife in front of me just as he came near me. My mother was now in tears. My father, still angry and cursing, threw a dining room chair across the room, and then looked at me in silent rage, but did not approach me. I stormed out of the house and went to a friend's house and stayed there until late in the evening.

"When I finally came home that night, I was relieved to find that my father had not waited up for me. In fact in the days and weeks that followed he totally ignored me. It was as if, even though he allowed me to stay at the house, he would otherwise not acknowledge my existence. I purposely arrived home each night after dinner and ate the meal my mother had set aside for me. My mother quietly assured me that he would come around, and I just had to give him time. While she encouraged me to pray for a reconciliation, she did not ask me to apologize. I understood why. I knew that while she loved my father dearly, she also knew how difficult he could be.

"Two years later, still living at home, I graduated from the college with a bussiness degree. What neither of my parents knew was that I had made plans for my future more radical than any my father could have imagined. Indonesia in the 1930s was still a Dutch colony and remained so until after World War II. There were over a hundred thousand Dutch expatriates on the island of Java alone, most in the cities. Many young Dutch men and women at this time would move there for a year or two, sometimes longer, to experience something of the world, and perhaps as well, like me, to make a break from an overbearing parent. I had applied and been accepted as the manager of a large bookstore in the city of Surabaya on the island of Java. I was to leave on a ship for this destination at the end of the summer.

"When I finally broke the news to my mother, after some tears, she seemed to understand but told me that this would break my father's heart. My father, meanwhile, had begun talking to me again, and I could tell he wanted to reconcile with me but did not know how. I had made my mother promise not to say anything about my plans. A few days before I was to leave, I wrote a letter to my father explaining my decision and sealed it in an envelope. I told my mother where the letter was, and instructed her to give it to him after I had left. She cried and we hugged the day I left for the harbor of Rotterdam and for the ship that would take me to Indonesia. I still remember her parting words so typical of her: 'My dearling, I hope to see you again, but in case for some reason I do not, know how much your father and I love you. My prayers go with you, and I will leave you God's hands now.' I later regretted putting my mother in the position of having to tell my father of my leaving, but at the time I could not figure out another way to make the break.

"I arrived a week later in Indonesia. Owners of the bookstore had helped arrange an apartment for me in the city of Surabaya, where the bookstore was located. I started my new job within three days of my arrival. The bookstore, all on one floor, was large. Ceiling fans cooled the hot, humid Indonesian air. My office was off to one side of the store in a cubicle formed by dividers made of bamboo. I should tell you, for reasons already shared, that I had arrived in Indonesia as an arrogant, and underneath the surface a somewhat angry, young man, at least with individuals who abused authority or ironically questioned mine. Despite my mother's best efforts, I had at best a casual, naïve, and superficial faith. Also like my father, I had a quick temper, and while not as verbally abusive, I could be cutting and honest to the point of cruel with anyone who questioned my status as the new bookstore manager. This included the bookstore staff and occasionally a difficult patron. My staff consisted of a couple Dutchmen, a few Indonesians, and one Chinese employee."

Jop had shifted positions in his chair a number of times as he had shared the formative part of his life story. Don had been listening intently, and had noted some parallels between Jop's father's abuse of his mother and his own father's treatment of his mother. He had also become aware, as he was sure McCall had intended him to be, of the parallels between how Jop and he had struggled with anger issues, partly as a result of their father's behaviors. After Jop had shared about how he had begun his work at the bookstore, he had suddenly paused and taken a drink of the remaining coffee in his mug. Putting the mug down, he turned back toward Don and resumed talking. "Usually with groups I offer a less personal summary of this part of my life. I hope I didn't go on too long. John thought it important that I go into more detail in these interviews." Then with a bit of a sparkle in his eye, Jop added, "Knowing John, he probably had more than one intention in setting up these interviews. It wouldn't surprise me if he hopes to put together some kind of book based on my experiences.

"John came to the university bookstore, where I worked as the general manager, when he first started at the seminary. He came to my office and introduced himself to me, and we struck up a prolonged conversation where I shared something of my background, including my POW experiences. By the end of the conversation he had asked me if I would be willing to give a talk at the seminary on my experiences in the camps. Through the planning of this and subsequent talks John set up for me we became close friends. John is a bit of a spiritual opportunist. He is always looking for opportunities to minister to others, as well as for individuals who have the potential to minister to those in need. He is God's free agent, not motivated by a professional ministry role, as much as his deep faith that the Holy Spirit can be found, among other places, at work at the crossroads of people's lives. If only we would pray for the eyes and ears to see those in need at such times, John believes, then the Holy Spirit could work through us, to help such individuals."

"I believe Dr. McCall came into my life at such a critical time," Don replied, and then continued, "and I am glad you shared all this, Jop. My father too could be verbally abusive, although he is an alcoholic as well. It gives me hope that you were able to rise above all you went through, much of which I still have to learn about, and were still able to become the man you are." Jop smiled and leaned forward. "Don, I was not able to overcome my issues on my own, had I tried to do so on will power alone, I would have most likely have become like my father, or perhaps worse. What happened to me during the war years could have easily caused me to become more angry and bitter towards others and life in general. I will start sharing some of these experiences in our next session together.

"Come," Jop said, "you must be on your way. I understand your taking an intensive language class which involves much study. Before you go, though, why don't we have a prayer." Jop then leaned all the way forward toward Don, clasped his hands together, lowered his head, and began to pray: "Lord, thank you for bringing Don and I together for your purposes. May he come to see my difficult life experiences, and his, as wounds and scars that we will have to bear through life. May he come to understand that he will continually need the healing balm of your loving grace made available to us in countless ways, to heal both new wounds, as well as old ones that may be reopened. May he wear these wounds and scars as a proud spiritual warrior for your kingdom. May he, as he grows old as I have, bent over and wearied from the blows life has dealt him, take pride and solace in the faith and knowledge that God has used him not in spite of, but through life's troubles as his knight of faith to further his greater plan for humankind. Amen."

As Jop walked him to the door, Don thanked him for his time and for sharing such personal memories with him. "No thank you needed," Jop replied, "old men love to share their life stories. I just hope it in some way will be of help to you." As Don walked home he felt as if he had just put down a good book. He knew whatever happened to Jop during the war years had had a huge impact on Jop's life. The year Jop had arrived in Indonesia was 1938.

War and Internment

Don could not wait until the following Tuesday. He already felt a bond developing between him and Jop. Meanwhile he tried hard to buckle down and study for the intensive Hebrew course. The study of languages had never been Don's strong suit. He had taken German for two consecutive years in high school and had received a C and B minus, respectively. Two of the lowest grades he had ever received. He was determined to earn at least a B in this course. It helped that it was more for reading ability than speaking. The classes met from nine to twelve five mornings a week. Don was trying to put in at least six hours of study a day. To have extra spending money Don had signed up to wash pots through the summer. He was washing pots three nights a week, after which he studied for an additional two or three hours late into the evening. One part of his daily routine he looked forward to was meeting up with Cindy in the first-floor lounge. At first, he struggled with the meditation sessions they had together. It irritated him how easily his mind wandered away from his focus on his breath. The thoughts that distracted him varied widely. It could be bodily sensations like a rumbling stomach reminding him of breakfast and how hungry he was, it could be anxiety over how he was doing at his Hebrew course, or curiosity over what Jop would be sharing with him next, or all of the above and more, in a runaway stream of consciousness. When he finally caught himself in such a state of distraction he immediately got irritated and forced himself to focus once more on his breath.

Don had a tendency to shift his body around in an impatient way when he was trying to snap himself out of his distracted state, and Cindy took notice. When she inquired if he was okay, he said, "It just irritates me that I can't stay focused on my breath." "One critical key to mindfulness meditation is not to judge yourself. The thoughts and feelings that arise during meditation are fodder for becoming more self-aware. Just observe them, including any emotions, in a detached way until they begin to subside, and then without judging yourself, surrender whatever it was you were thinking about to God as you exhale and refocus on your breathing," Cindy instructed. She then added, "You could also try a more focused variation of this meditation to help tame the mind. This meditation involves a mantra which can help you become more open to surrendering your whole self to God or mindful of what might be blocking this. The mantra goes, 'All that I was, all that I am, all that I will be.' Breathing normally with every exhale, you say each part in turn. Early in my meditation practice, in my teens, my mind wandered a lot too. This meditation helped me develop more focus and kept me in the present moment. I still use it occasionally on days where my mind is particularly restless." Cindy, changing the subject, then inquired, knowing nothing as far as Don knew about his anger issue and the incidents he had been involved with on campus, "Do you get irritated easily?"

Her inquiry startled Don, and even though he liked and trusted Cindy, her question hit awfully close to home. Without perhaps intending to, Cindy's question hinted at his anger issue. Don hesitated a moment, and then looked over at Cindy with a surprised look. He felt his face redden as he debated with himself how best to answer her question. Cindy looked back at him and recognized that she had struck a chord of some kind. "I am sorry, Don, you don't have to answer that question, that was too personal." Sighing, Don's head and shoulders slumped forward. He wanted to move forward in learning to deal with his emotions, particularly his anger. One way to do this was to share something of his past, perhaps in degrees, with select individuals he liked and trusted; to be cautiously vulnerable. "Funny you should ask," he said, looking back up her, "I not only get irritated easily, I have an anger problem." He could see Cindy sit up straighter and tense up a little. Don suddenly wondered if this had been such a good idea. The last thing he wanted was for Cindy, who did not know him that well, to be afraid of him. Trying to reassure her, he quickly added, "I never get angry at those I am close to, it's always with strangers or people I don't know well. I was bullied for a time as a kid and I tend to overreact when I feel bullied. If I am close to someone and they give me a hard time I know underneath it all they still care about me, and we'll get past it. After being bullied in junior high, I thought there must be something wrong with me for them to pick on me like that."

Don paused, realizing he had shared much more than he intended to. "Sorry, Cindy, I didn't mean to run on like that, I just didn't want you to think I was dangerous or something." Cindy, who had been listening intently, looked over at Don and took his hand. Smiling in a caring way, she said, "I don't think you went on too long, I am glad you trust me enough to share what you did, it couldn't have been easy. By the way, it hasn't always been easy being Asian American. I got stereotyped a lot in school growing up and even since then." Don's face flushed red again, realizing that he been guilty of this, and he hoped Cindy hadn't picked up on that.

Don sensed that Cindy and he had just bonded on a deeper level. Not wanting to hold anything back, he made the impulsive decision to share about the accident as well. Don promised himself he would tell her about it, but not go on too long about all the emotional issues it left him with. "Cindy, there is another layer to my anger which I am just beginning to accept and process. It stems from a car accident that happened when I was in my last year of high school." Don paused momentarily, he couldn't believe he had started down this road, and began to worry that he was going to come off needy if he continued. "Were you hurt in the accident, what happened?" Cindy asked in concerned way. "My mother and younger sister were killed in the accident." "O, Don, I am so sorry," Cindy responded immediately. "I am handling it better now than I have in a long time." Don had decided not to share any more details about his family and the accident at this time. Still he wanted Cindy to understand his anger problem better, so he decided to try to explain how the accident had contributed to this problem. Perhaps she could even help him to understand how meditation might help him learn to handle his anger better, which would turn the conversation toward a more pragmatic end and alleviate some of the drama.

Cindy had grown silent after making her empathetic remark, and was still looking at him in a calm, patient way, waiting to see if he had any more he wanted to share. Don found himself admiring the way she had listened to him so calmly and patiently. He hoped one day he would be able to do this. Listening to the problems of others had been difficult for him. It reminded him of the pain he had denied inside of himself for so long. "The thing is," Don continued ,"I have also been very angry at the injustice, the unfairness of the loss of my mother and sister. I have been angry at the world and at God too. It's taken me a long time to begin to accept just how angry I have felt inside. Occasionally all this anger would spill over, and has caused me to overreact, but again only with people I didn't know well who I thought were giving me a hard time. Most of the time, though, my anger turned into depression. I somehow was internalizing the anger. I was angry at myself. I felt so helpless, and vulnerable that there was nothing I could to do to save them." Don suddenly felt himself overwhelmed with emotion and he began to choke up. This was the first time this had happened to him, no doubt because he had talked with only a couple people about these feelings, just McCall and now Cindy. As he looked at Cindy, tears, despite his best effort to control his emotions, welled up in his eyes. Cindy again reached out and held his hand and continued to look at him with an unaverted compassionate gaze. At once Don realized why Cindy had elicited his emotional response, there was something about her look of compassion that reminded him of his mother. Don sighed deeply and looked up at the ceiling. Regaining his composure, he looked back at Cindy, and in a teasing tone he asked, "So now that you know some of my deepest, darkest secrets, do you think meditating could help me with all this?"

Cindy smiled and let go of Don's hand. "Yes, I think it could help. Of course as a Christian I believe that it would be beneficial if you understood this meditation as a vehicle, a kind of devotion, to help you become more aware of God's grace, and how much God loves you in Christ." "Now you sound like a good Southern Baptist, Don said teasingly." "I do?" Cindy said. "That's a first." Then Cindy added, "You know, Don, there are two things I have learned from years of meditation that might be helpful to you. They are lessons I learned from the Buddhist tradition, but I think you can find direct parallels in the Christian tradition. I went through a difficult period in my junior year of high school. I had been very studious all through school, partly because my parents placed a very high value on education, and always had high expectations of us academically. If my sister or I came home with a B we were lectured and told that we were not trying hard enough. By my junior year I began to resent this pressure. My friends, who were under less pressure academically from their parents, seemed more carefree, and while they earned good grades, for the most part, a B was not an occasion for a tirade. I began to feel angry about having to measure up to such a high standard, and I started to rebel. I stayed out later than I was supposed to, drank alcohol with friends, and dated boys who my parents didn't approve of.

"The end result was that my grades started to suffer. Finally, my parents, realizing that I was in a real crisis mode, became more patient and understanding. One night I sat down at the kitchen table with my mother and shared how angry I was at having to live up to such a high standard, one that most kids in America didn't have too. To her credit my mother didn't lecture me. She said, 'I can see how angry you are and I know it's left you feeling very confused. Your father and I are willing to back off a little on pressuring you to do so well academically, but hope you will rein in some of your rebellious behavior too.' I told her I would try, but still felt angry, and was confused. Getting good grades is important to me, but I just don't want it to be the most important thing anymore. My mother then shared some Buddhist wisdom with me. It is sometimes better not to stir muddy waters but to wait for them to clear. As a teenager it took me awhile to fully understand what she meant, but the older I got the more I appreciated the wisdom in this saying. From a Buddhist and meditative perspective this saying reminds me to observe my emotions, especially anger, without having to act out on them. This isn't always easy, especially when you are really worked up. Those are the times where a regular meditation practice helps. I also discovered on my own that it helps to observe the self, among our many selves, that is feeling the anger. There is a danger of both seeing that injured part of you as a fixed part of yourself, and all that you are. What I have learned is that while you still feel the emotions, you can, like a surfer, ride the crest of these stormy waves by observing them in a mindfully detached way habituated through meditative practice."

"I think I understand," Don said, "and I could see how that might help someone like me cope better with my anger. The only thing, Cindy," he said with a questioning tone, "is that as God's grace is becoming very important to me, I don't think detachment by itself is enough for me. I recently had an experience that affirmed my faith that God loves me and forgives me. I am not sure how to reconcile the Buddhist teaching of detachment with this aspect of my Christian faith." "I know," Cindy replied, "I had to wrestle with that as well. I read a book in a pastoral care class recently I found helpful. I think the author's name was Henri Nouwen. In this book, and I can't remember the title, he talks about something called 'living the question.' What he seems to say is that sometimes when we are wrestling with some issue, or question, and no ready or easy answer seems to come to us, we must wait patiently until the answer comes from within with the help of the Holy Spirit. It might be good, then, sometimes to get out of our head, and to practice prayerfully trusting that the Holy Spirit can work through mindfulness meditation." "I think you just gave me a parallel to the Buddhist saying to not stir muddy waters," Don replied. "I suspect, though, that putting this spiritual wisdom into practice is a lot harder than it sounds." Don added. "I think you're right," Cindy said, laughing, "that's why mindfulness meditation is called a practice." Becoming serious again, Cindy added, "Once more, remember that detachment does not mean denying the value of an experience. It just means that we may need some distance at times to gain perspective."

Don looked at Cindy with a smile and expressed his gratitude. "Thank you, Cindy, that was really helpful. I really appreciate your taking the time to let me share, and that you have shared with me as well. I totally ruined your meditation session though." Glancing at his wristwatch, Don realized that it was after eight, and he would have to rush to eat breakfast in the cafeteria to make it to class on time. "I better get going or I will miss breakfast, but I will be here tomorrow, and promise not to derail us," he said, rising to leave. "Wait, Don, I told you there was a second piece of Buddhist wisdom that might help you, let me share that with you before you go. I will try to be brief. It is more of a teaching than a saying. What it basically says is that suffering can happen to us in two ways, or by two arrows. The first arrow is the suffering that happens to us that we cannot help or control. The second arrow, or kind of suffering, can be caused by how we react to the first arrow. I think what this means is that while some suffering is inevitable, we often make that suffering worse by how we react to it, especially if we do so in impulsive, destructive ways. I am not sure if that is helpful to you or not, but at least you got your money's worth." Without missing a beat, Don replied teasingly, "I didn't pay you anything." "Well maybe you will think of something. But you better go now or you will miss breakfast," Cindy said teasingly. "Aren't you going to breakfast?" he asked her. "I have some leftover food in a small freezer in my room. I will eat that shortly. Right now I want to meditate for a bit." "Understood," Don said, backing toward the door. "See you tomorrow morning," he said as he turned to leave.

As Don walked quickly toward the cafeteria, he went over the two pieces of Buddhist wisdom Cindy had shared with him. The first one, the saying, he understood at least intellectually, particularly within the Christian context within which Cindy had shared it. He knew he overanalyzed things and needed to just let things be more often, prayerfully trusting that answers would come; answers that, at times, might be experiential and not just rational. The second one, about the two arrows, he had to think about more. But if Don understood it correctly, this one might, if he could somehow put it into practice, motivate him to allow time to calm down, and consider the impact his anger might have on him and others if he acted out on it impulsively. It also occurred to him that there was more than likely a parallel in Christ's teachings that stressed constructive assertiveness as a way to channel anger. Christ had warned against vindictive, abusive behavior that was hurtful both to ourselves and others. Christ had also set the example of a disciplined prayer life during which difficult situations and feelings could be surrendered to God and processed.

Don treasured the insights Cindy has shared with him, and was determined to remember them so that he could put them into practice. He also knew that if he continued to rely on will power alone, given the intensity of anger he had experienced, he could fall into a trap. During low stress times he could delude himself into thinking that if something happened that sparked his anger, he could control it. This had not worked in the past, and he had to fully accept this fact. Don was just beginning to trust in the power of God's grace, and considering where he had come from emotionally and spiritually, he wanted that grace to remain a critical part of his healing process.

Don had been attending Sunday services at the seminary chapel regularly, but had found most of the sermons by the chaplain, and the guest preachers he lined up, had focused overly on theological and biblical arguments that appealed more to the head than the heart. On the Sunday before Don's second interview with Jop, though, a guest preacher had delivered a sermon from Paul's Letter to the Philippians that exhorted them to rejoice always in all kinds of circumstances. Don got the main point of the sermon, that if you lived out of a relationship centered in Christ, as Paul had, then this relationship could cause one to live out of a deep inner peace, contentment, even joy, no matter the circumstance. This, however, had the effect of making Don realize how far he still had to grow in his faith. He then recalled Jop's prayer, which offered him much reassurance. In his prayer Jop had prayed for him to remain faithful not in spite of all his wounds and scars in life but because of them; to wear them with a humility that allows them to become badges of honor as we let God's grace transform them for his plan and purposes. Romans 8 popped into Don's head at that moment, which he could not recite word for word, but where he knew Paul had written about how all things can work for good when we align our will with God's.

On Tuesday morning, the day of the next afternoon interview with Jop, Don swung by his mailbox, and as expected found the envelope Mc-Call's secretary had sent to him. He had wondered why McCall had his secretary give him these remaining questions piecemeal. The only thing that made sense to him was that McCall wanted Don to focus on only one question at a time, perhaps so that he would listen in a more focused way to each question in turn. As before, he opened the envelope and read the question silently. He then whispered the question to himself, "What events occurred in your life that led up to the war and your internment as a POW?" "Here we go," Don thought to himself. While this question, and interview, may not yet reveal the intense, dramatic, and Don guessed tragic experiences Jop had in the camps, he knew this interview would set the stage for the sharing of those experiences.

Anticipating his time with Jop, Don felt unusually distracted in his Hebrew class that morning. By this point, Don, while still invested in his studies, was beginning to see that there were other ways to cope with his anger issue, as well as the fallout from his anger, other than plunging himself into his studies with blinders on. He also was beginning to realize, from the individuals he was crossing paths with, Tom, McCall, Cindy, and Jop, that God had him learning on two tracks. He was not sure, as of yet, how to reconcile or balance these two tracks. He was finding that what he was learning from these unexpected spiritual guides were more beneficial to him than what he was learning in class, which did not offer ready or relevant support and resolutions to the anger and hurt he felt inside, and with which he struggled. As he wrestled with feelings of anxiety before and in class that Tuesday morning, Cindy's first lesson suddenly seemed to offer a helpful insight. He would not stir these muddy waters right now. Coupling this Buddhist saying, of not stirring muddy waters, with the Christian understanding she had offered, referencing Nouwen, he would wait patiently and prayerfully for the answer to come from within with the help of the Holy Spirit.

Don couldn't wait to get out of class. He grabbed a quick lunch and headed out to Jop's house. Arriving at the front door, he knocked. Once again, he heard footsteps approaching and Marie's welcoming smiling face appeared as she opened the door. Marie once more led Don into the office, where Jop rose and greeted him with his same down-to-earth hospitality. Shortly after, Marie had brought in the tray with the Dutch coffee and cookies. However traditional it might be, Don was really beginning to appreciate this hospitality ritual. There was something about sharing food and drink that not only helped slow him down, it offered a way to break the ice, and transition to the weighty matter at hand. Perhaps most importantly it had helped to create more of a bond between Jop and him. It had made him feel more welcome, and relaxed, and given him a sense that he was no longer a stranger. The thought fleeted through Don's head, it is no wonder Christ chose to dine with others so often in his ministry.

Jop put his mug down, leaned back, and folded his hands in his lap, indicating that he was ready to begin the interview. Don asked the question without hesitation this time. "Can you tell me about the events in your life that led up to the outset of the war, and then to your being taken prisoner?" Jop began his talk, "I adjusted quickly to life in Indonesia. Despite the fact that the Dutch were their colonial masters, the Indonesians I got to know at the bookstore and in my daily life proved to be a warm and open people. As manager of the bookstore much of my time was taken up with office duties such as book orders and other paperwork. What I quickly found that I loved most, though, was answering questions of the customers. I was often asked to recommend excellent authors from every genre of literature, including history, theology, and philosophy. I soon found myself reading reviews and a synopsis of many of the bestselling books, in many cases this led me to read the works themselves. This is not something that is required of bookstore employees today, at least in America. Neither did I have to do this during my many years as the manager of the university bookstore. I was fortunate that I had a generalist's curiosity, and liked reading books from a variety of genres while working at the bookstore in Surabaya.

"When I first arrived in Indonesia, I was unsure how long my stay would last. I originally decided to stay at least a year but was open to staying longer. I knew, almost right away that I had found the right career as a bookseller. While working as an art dealer would have involved working with customers, my love of books made it the ideal product for me to sell.

I reluctantly had to admit to myself that my love, and any ability I had, of working with the public, in a more general way, had probably been inherited from my father. One morning, only weeks after beginning at the bookstore, I was doing paperwork in my office and chanced to look through my open office door. I saw a young woman with dark hair and an olive complexion. She was looking at books laid out on a display table near the front of the store that was adjacent to my office cubicle. She looked both exotic and beautiful to me, and I stared at her a moment too long. Sensing my look, she glanced back at me. Not wanting to in any way appear like a voyeur, I saved the moment from awkwardness by immediately asking her if she needed any help. I had asked her the question in Dutch, as the great majority of customers were Dutch expatriates. The question wasn't totally disingenuous, I was always looking for an excuse to break away from my paperwork, which I viewed more as a chore. I could not deny my primary motive. As a single young man who found this woman particularly attractive, I was taking advantage of my role to make a connection with her. While I was tall with blond hair and blue eyes, I had always been drawn to petite, dark-haired women.

"She had responded, 'Oh that's okay, I am just looking.' I could not let it go at that, and had to find some way to keep the conversation going. I could tell from her response that she was Dutch, but her appearance was not typically Dutch. I rose and walked over to her and introduced myself. 'My name is Jop, I am the bookstore manager, is this your first time in store?' 'Yes, I am Irene Cohen, I have only been in Surabaya for a couple of months.' My heart leaped at this bit of good fortune as it gave an opportunity for further conversation. 'That's interesting,' I told her, 'I have only been here a few months as well. I am from Rotterdam. Where are you from in the Netherlands?' She replied that she was from Amsterdam. I knew there was a large Jewish community in Amsterdam and was sure given Irene's last name that she was at least of partial Jewish extraction. I then asked her if she had come by herself. 'I did,' she responded, 'I was trained as a school teacher and wanted to travel. I learned about a job offer here in Surabaya teaching at a school for Dutch children, and I decided to take it, at least for one year.' 'I have a business degree, and wanted to work as a manager in a bookstore. I also wanted to travel. I too learned of a job here, and decided to take it for at least a year,' I responded. There was a brief pause in our conversation as for a moment neither of us knew what to say next. Not wanting to let this opportunity pass, I took a huge chance given that we had just met and the mores of the time were such that romantic relationships moved slower than today.

"I asked her if she if she was free that night. Irene looked searchingly into my eyes. It was as if she was trying to discern intuitively whether I was a person of character she could trust, and someone she was interested in.

From the moment I saw her large brown eyes look shyly up at me, I felt a chemistry with her that I could not explain, that I had not felt with any other girl I had known. After a few seconds she broke the silence, smiled, and said, 'Yes, I am, what did you have in mind?' I couldn't believe my good fortune. I told her I didn't have a car, but that I could meet her here in front of the bookstore around six. I mentioned that there was an excellent Indonesian restaurant only a few blocks away, and if it was okay with her we could eat dinner there. She replied, 'That would be fine.' I smiled at her and said once more, but this time in a teasing way, 'And again, ma'am, if you need any help, please do not hesitate to ask.' Irene in an equally teasing manner replied, 'Well thank you, sir, I will keep that in mind.' We looked at each other for a few more moments, smiling, and then I thought it best to end the conversation before things got awkward. I told her I better get back to work but was looking forward to seeing her tonight."

Don had noticed that as Jop shared this memory he looked like he had been transported back in time. As this special memory seemed to fade, a whimsical smile was slowly replaced by a sadder look that lasted only momentarily and seemed mixed with timeworn acceptance. Jop then resumed with his recollections. "I rushed home immediately after work and changed my clothes. Indonesia in August was very hot and humid, and even wearing khaki shorts and a loose-fitting cotton shirt, one sweated so much it was not uncommon to change shirts at least two or three times a day. As I raced back to the store front, I could see that Irene was already standing there waiting, holding her purse in front of her with both of her hands. As I neared the storefront I smiled and waved, and Irene waved back enthusiastically, rising a bit on the tips of her shoes. Irene had a girlishness about her with just the right mix of refinement and down to earthiness that seemed in perfect balance.

"As we walked the few blocks to the restaurant and shared light conversation, I learned that Irene was in her early twenties like I was, and that she was one of three sisters. Her religious background mattered little to me at this point so I did not ask her about this, and did not plan to bring it up that night unless it came up naturally in conversation. My rebelliousness and anger at my father had caused me to detach somewhat from my Dutch Reformed heritage, and the institutional church. I still believed in God, in a very superficial, naïve, and as yet unchallenged way. I had also been drawn more to works of philosophy in the bookstore than theology. The one exception was the philosopher/theologian Kierkegaard. There was something about the way he challenged traditional institutionalized and nationalized Christianity that I resonated with, as I did with his description of faith as something that required a radical subjective leap. All of this seemed to challenge the rigid doctrinal Calvinist Reformed tradition I had grown up with, and this especially appealed to me. Still, if anybody had asked me what my faith background was I would simply have told them Dutch Reformed."

What reading Don had done of Kierkegaard had appealed intellectually to him, but had not been informed or affirmed by a lived-out faith, much less any faith experience, as it hadn't for Jop either as a young bookstore manager. Kierkegaard's allusion to the leap of faith every individual Christian should make had resonated with Don. This was a leap over religious belief, that one ascribed to but did not live out, to a passionately lived-out faith. What additionally necessitated this leap was the rationally unfathomable central paradox of the Christian faith, Christ's incarnation. Could an infinite God, beyond time and space, form a transcendent union with humanity within time and space? That this God could take human form, the incarnation, in Christ was a contradiction that lay at the very heart of Christianity. To Don, Kierkegaard had suggested that this paradox could only be resolved with God's help from beyond, mediated by Christ's Spirit through a lived-out faith. Neither could there be any scientific or rational proof for such an infinite and transcendent God given that our experience of that God would be qualitatively different from any limited to our materialistic sensorial reality. For Kierkegaard, Don had read, even the historical revelation of Jesus Christ did not provide objective proof of God, but could only point beyond itself to the subjective experience of its truth.

The catalyst for this subjective experience, once again, was a leap from a mere assenting to, or interest in, religious belief systems, to a subjective experience of the Christian faith as one that is lived. Don had also been informed by Kierkegaard that while religious belief systems could provide a pattern for faith, if too systematized and/or institutionalized they could supercede a faith-centered life. Kierkegaard's works had often been written pseudonymously so that the reader, without knowing his position, might overhear arguments that would cause them to critically self-reflect. Clearly Kierkegaard, Don had discerned, did not want to enlist and indoctrinate followers, but to prod his readers, of their own free will, to the precipice of a subjective leap to a passionately lived-out faith.

Don had resonated with Kierkegaard's qualitative leap of faith. This gave him reassurance that such a leap might finally help him surrender—his compulsive strivings, intellectually and academically, to resolve the anger he felt over the injustices in his life—to God. Don had intuitively felt as well that an experience of God's grace had to be an integral part of any faith experience resulting from such a leap. He had also understood from his readings of Kierkegaard that this was not generally speaking a leap to blind obedience but to a lived faith; a faith life that does not preclude spiritual struggle or uncertainty of belief but can offer holistic transformation and quench the soul's deepest thirst. Moreover, Don had thought, was it not most often when we wrestle with the angel, as Jacob did, that we are blessed with a new identity and future?

Kierkegaard, Don had read, had been highly critical of the state-run Danish Lutheran church of his day. Don could see parallels between the religious conventionalism of Kierkegaard's time and the faith-stifling conventionalism and institutionalism within many church traditions in his own time. In the latter case, however, this conventionalism and institutionalism could be driven as much, if not more, by social mores and traditions than dogmatic or doctrinal beliefs. Don had read two of Kierkegaard's works, *Either/Or* and *Fear and Trembling*. He had also read a lengthy introduction to the former translation which had given Don a summary of Kierkegaard's life and thought.

Even though Don had questions about Kierkegaard's existentialist theology/philosophy he knew aspects of it would influence his own developing faith understandings. Foremost among these were Kierkegaard's leap of faith, and his critiques of conventional Christian belief and the institutional church. Here, Don had thought, was a thinker with such brilliant nuance and analysis in his writings, particularly regarding the psychological and moral aspects of faith, that he did not feel competent to critique them. All Don could do, given his formative understanding of Kierkegaard, was to note where he did or did not resonate with him.

"But I digress," Jop then continued, "where was I, oh yes, we were walking to the Indonesian restaurant. What became apparent, whatever our religious differences, was that Irene and I shared much in common. We were both well educated, but were not interested in impressing anyone with how much we knew, rather it just made our relaxed conversation that much more interesting and rich. We covered a wide variety of topics at the restaurant that night, from our philosophies of education, to literature, to politics, particularly relating to the Dutch colonialism; although we had this discussion in more hushed tones, lest the topic become apparent and offend anyone. Both Irene and I agreed that European colonialism was in decline, and this was probably a good thing, not realizing how hypocritical we were being as we enjoyed the status and fruits of Dutch colonialism. The evening seemed to race by even as we dallied over coffee after dinner.

"After we left the restaurant, I walked Irene slowly back to the boarding house where she had rented a room, and which had a common eating area and living room. When we reached the front of the building I made no attempt to kiss Irene good night. Observing the mores of a well-bred young man of the time, I thanked her for a wonderful evening. She in turn thanked me. Irene hesitated just long enough, before turning to go inside, for me to pop the question I knew I wanted to somehow ask. 'Irene,' I said, 'may I see you again?' She then gave me that same searching look she had in the bookstore. Her brown eyes had a wonderful mix of innocence and trust that would have won my heart there and then, if she hadn't already. 'I would like that very much,' she finally said. I had trouble sleeping that night. I had had numerous girlfriends since the age of sixteen, although I had usually gotten to know them as part of a group of friends that traveled around together. This was different. There was something about my relationship with this girl that seemed fated. Not only did we share much in common, including many interests and views, she had intangible qualities about her that I found very attractive.

"As I lay in bed that night with the mosquito netting surrounding my bed and the ceiling fan gently humming I couldn't help but wonder, since I had fallen so hard and so fast for Irene, if I was indeed falling in love, or merely infatuated with her. After a few more dates both Irene and I knew that ours was destined to be a long-term relationship. A few dates turned into many, and the weeks turned into months. The mores of the time precluded cohabitation, but even so we were spending all our free time together. We spent nearly every evening and weekend at my apartment, which though small, a bedroom, tiny kitchen, and living room, offered more privacy than the boarding house where Irene was staying. Over time we began to introduce each other to our respective colleagues and the friends we each had made, many of which soon became mutual friends. There are pictures of Irene and me, taken by some of these friends at this time. I selected one to show you." Jop then picked up a black-and-white photo from the coffee table next to his chair and handed it to Don. The picture showed Irene and Jop together on a small couch. Irene was reclining back against one side of the couch and her legs were across Jop's lap. Jop looking handsome, in a 1930s way, with his blond, slicked-back hair, neatly pressed khakis, and nearly knee-high white socks. Irene fit Jop's description perfectly, petite, her dark-brown eyes glowing with a combination of youthful optimism and love. Don smiled appreciatively and handed the photo back to him. Jop then resumed talking.

"By the end of the first year Irene and I were engaged. We both sent letters back home that broke the news to our parents. Letters came back from my parents congratulating us, while gently inquiring about Irene's background. I guessed that this was my father's input, even though the handwriting was my mother's. Irene's parents also wrote back with congratulations, and were less concerned about background, religious or otherwise, than practicalities such as when the wedding was, where we would live, and were we thinking of staying long term in Indonesia now that we were planning to get married. We both enjoyed the letters, which made us homesick, but at the same time were glad we were far away from what we knew, if we were in Holland, could be the interfering influence of certain family members. In one of the letters Irene received from her parents there had been cryptic references to Germany, and the threat of war.

"Irene had shared with me that she was of partial Jewish heritage, but that her Jewish paternal grandfather had converted to Christianity for reasons that were unclear to her. The fact that both Irene and I shared a superficial faith investment had already made this a moot issue. Irene and I were married in October of 1939. We had agreed to ask the pastor of a local Dutch Reformed church we had occasionally attended together to officiate at our wedding. Irene and I then moved into my apartment, which we soon outgrew. We then found another bigger apartment nearby. It had the same number of rooms but the rooms were larger.

"We had both been aware, through letters, that tensions were escalating in Europe. With the German invasion of Czechoslovakia and Poland in 1939 and their subsequent annexation, the threat of a war that could engulf Europe seemed increasingly likely. Still when word came, through newspaper and family letters, informing us of Germany's invasion of the Netherlands in May of 1940 it came as shock to us. After all, Holland had proclaimed its neutrality, and we naively underestimated both the imperialism and evil of the Nazi party which now ruled Germany. While there had been clear indications of Nazi anti-Semitism we were totally unaware, at the time, of the horrific evil that would be perpetrated by the Germans against the Jewry of Europe. As it turned out Irene's family would be relatively safe given the conversion of Irene's grandfather, who was now deceased, and the partial Jewish ethnicity of the rest of the family. Still both of us worried for the safety of our families, and aging parents. We knew no matter what happened they would be in for the hardships a German occupation would surely impose. Bombings had already reduced much of Rotterdam to rubble. Harassment and executions of anyone who displeased an occupying German army and food shortages were givens.

"I had also become aware, again through newspapers and well-connected friends to the local Dutch colonial government, of the growing threat of Japan. While not imminent in the first year of our marriage, it cast a growing shadow of anxiety over the joy we knew during that period. By the early spring of 1941 we found out that Irene was pregnant, and we were full of joy and expectation over this future little addition to our family. Our little girl, who we named Renee, would be born in December of 1941. We created a nursery in a corner of our now larger bedroom. Even this joyous news had a shadow cast over it by the increasing reports of Japanese aggression.

"Then came the news that I was to be called up to serve in the Royal Dutch Army in the artillery. I had had, like most young Dutch men of eighteen, to train and serve in the Dutch army part time back home. I had done this at the same time I was studying for my business degree. My service at the time was more like serving in the National Guard in the US. After an initial summer training period, I had, for about eighteen months, to spend one weekend a month training at an army installation near Rotterdam. There are pictures of me with friends in uniform at this time. The Dutch army then and now was more relaxed than the American military, and the training in no way prepared us for action in an actual war. The Netherlands had grown too confident of its neutral status.

"Even though, in the event of war, I knew I could be called up, it was not until the growing threat of war with Japan that this became a pressing reality to me. Early in March of 1942 the news we had been dreading came. The Japanese had begun their invasion of Indonesia. I quickly found myself in uniform and reporting for duty to an artillery unit. My rank was that of Corporal, and because I spoke English well I was to serve as a liaison between my Dutch artillery division and that of the English and Americans on the island of Java. The battle of Java did not last long, with the Japanese version of blitzkrieg encircling and overwhelming our combined forces.

"On March 8, 1942, the governor general of the Dutch East Indies spoke over the radio and said that the Dutch East Indies Army had capitulated, and that as officers and soldiers we had to follow the orders of the Japanese army. For some ten days there was a vacuum. Our army just faded away. We were ordered to take our weapons to the nearest police station and go home for the time being. But hundreds were not anywhere near home. There were Australians and Americans; there were Dutch people from everywhere in East Java with no place to go. We gathered people to our home in Surabaya. We lived together in our home on Billiton Street. I was the only staff member apart from our Indonesian workers. I called a staff meeting and we opened the store. We knew life would go on one way or another, as it had in the Netherlands after the Germans occupied the country. I remember meeting my first Japanese soldier, and officer, who wanted to buy some English novels. He was courteous and we spoke English. Later, though, my Indonesian employee, who spoke some Japanese, told me that the Japanese officer had inquired whether I was Dutch or American. He bought some novels and paid in Japanese currency.

"Life seemed to go on, but no phone connection was available. My wife and child were in Malang Java with friends. Though I had hoped to make contact I was unable too. I hoped they would return. The house was full with people who had no place to go. In our bedroom, where in the corner we had so caringly set up the nursery, now slept three Dutch people I had found roaming the streets. One night when I returned from the book store I saw a truck full of Japanese soldiers driving slowly through our district. I ducked into a side street and let them pass.

"On March 19, this strange period of being civilians ended. The radio announced that that day we all had to report to the town hall of Surabaya. Those who did not report were threatened with death penalties. There were hundreds of men, all in civilian clothing, with little suitcases, backpacks, bundles, etc. We just waited for hours before we were marched off to the Jaarmarkt, a large exhibition complex we had visited each year. Japanese soldiers walked around us, but there was a kind of incomprehensible relationship that first day of being prisoners.

"Once inside I looked back at the gates. They were shut, guards had been posted, and suddenly I knew that this was what thousands had experienced in many previous wars. We were no longer free men. We had no idea what would be awaiting us. We were driven into the main hall where we could not sit down, and for twenty-four hours were standing, leaning against walls, and one another. There was a rumor that the building would be blown up or burned down, but nothing happened. We were aware that life would never be the same. We wondered about our wives and children. We tried to see in the darkness of that first night some hope, but it all was very uneventful. The next morning we were fed some weak porridge, and assigned to buildings made of bamboo.

"So we began with the resilience most of us had because we were young. We had to adjust to sleeping on hard clay floors. We learned fast to eat out of helmets we had found, and eat with our hands because we had no eating utensils. Most of us looked at it as a kind of camping experience, maybe a few weeks, and then the Americans would free us. After a few days women began to bring food to the Jaarmarkt. They took dirty clothes and returned them the next day. It was a strange kind of internment, people moving in and out of the gate with the Japanese guards hardly interfering. They were just not organized enough to take care of some seven thousand Dutch, English, and Americans within a very limited area of space.

"Soon this early period was over. Women could no longer bring food and work details were organized to work on the partly destroyed airfields. Apart from having us work on the airfields, the Japanese had a definite plan to humiliate us in the eyes of the Javanese. We were transported on trucks like cattle, and often stopped in heavily populated Indonesian sections of Surabaya. The people looked at us with blank stares, which neither expressed hatred, nor caring. We assumed that the very fast defeat of their colonial masters, who had been a colonial power there for 350 years, had not yet been grasped by them.

"As the weeks passed a pattern was set. Outside, slowly, a net was woven around the European community of women, children, and men who had been civilians. On being transported to the airfields we often saw women and children; some found their husbands and shouted messages to them. We were not mistreated, but when the food from the outside ceased to come in, we began to experience the limited food rations. This still did not create a hunger problem; it just did not satisfy our European stomachs. This was one way the Japanese had been able to move through Asia at such a rapid pace; almost no extra backpacks, just rice and some dried fish for meals. Our armies had field kitchens, and heavy backpacks. Most importantly we had no training in jungle fighting. We were in no way prepared to face the Japanese on a war footing.

"All contacts with the outside world were cut off except through medics, who each day were still permitted to travel to the hospital in the city. The real change came when the first man was beaten by the Japanese guards. I vividly remember the incident. We had to greet each soldier, bow, and remain in that attitude until the guard had passed. That man had not bowed, and it seemed perfectly justified during the beating that the man had defended himself. Three other Japanese soldiers rushed in. In witnessing the brutal beating, we suddenly understood that we were not prisoners of war, but inmates of a concentration camp. It took us a long time to understand this mass frenzy of the Japanese beating us. Often when the beating was over, the almost embarrassed Japanese soldiers would walk away. It was a strange syndrome originating in a society that was so different from ours They did not see beating us as a cruelty; it was part of a culture which would find its beginnings in centuries-old ways of life, of religious experiences, of making offerings to the gods, especially the emperor, the divine descendant of the early goddess of Japan, and we were the sacrificial lambs. All of that was totally obscured in those early months. We only perceived it as being slaves of the conquerors. We realized that even more clearly on Good Friday when the survivors of the battle in the Java Sea were brought to our camp. Their condition was indescribable."

Jop suddenly seemed to have become aware that he had reached a natural place to stop. He reached over and took a sip of coffee from his mug. "This may be a good place to end the interview. I have answered your first question as fully as I can." Don thanked Jop, and rising to leave was once again escorted by him to the door. At the door, Jop remarked, "Don, I know this is a lot to take in. I know very little about you, and do not need to. I know hearing my life story in such detail may be too much to absorb." Don quickly reassured Jop, "You have no idea how much I look forward to these interviews. I wait with anticipation through the whole week for the next one." Jop, with a mix of the humble down-to-earthiness Don had become accustomed to from him, said, "John obviously thought my story might be of some help to you. Hopefully some parts of it will."

As Don walked back to the campus, he knew Jop's story from here on would only get more dramatic and tragic. He had begun to gain some perspective on the tragedies in his own life, and suspected this perspective would only grow. He already knew Jop had been a POW for over three years. He also had known from his own historical readings that Japanese POWs had been treated with increasing brutality as the war dragged on. Don had seen pictures, in a book, of liberated Japanese POWs that looked like walking skeletons. He could not help wondering, given Jop's obviously second marriage to Marie, an American women, what tragedy had befallen Irene and Renee, but he would have to wait to hear in the upcoming interviews about this and just how much suffering and loss Jop had to endure.

The thing that troubled Don most now was how hearing from someone who had endured most likely greater suffering and injustice than he had was going to help him process his anger. Would it not just make him feel guilty over what could be seen as wallowing in his pain and loss, while using anger as a defense against dealing with the pain he felt inside. A less emotionally charged, more reflective part of Don realized that just because Jop had to endure so much suffering did not mean that his own suffering was not legitimate and that he had a right to a healing process that might take awhile. In a more constructive light, it occurred to him that Jop's faith and personal relationship with God in Christ might have survived and thrived precisely because his suffering had been so great. This gave Don hope that his faith could be revitalized as well. As the old adage goes "there are no atheists in foxholes." Still, Don wondered, not everyone's faith grew in such horrific circumstances, so what had happened to Jop and those like him that nurtured their faith rather than extinguished it? Certainly it was not the suffering and injustices themselves that fostered faith, but the faith experiences of the men that had resulted in a changed attitude, perhaps radically so, toward their circumstances in the camps.

The week went by quickly. Other than when meditating together, Cindy and Don took time, both before and after, to share more details about themselves with each other. Don's Hebrew intensive class seemed tedious and boring compared to time spent with Jop, but Don had come to appreciate the future benefit the study might offer him in being able to read some of his favorite Old Testament texts in the original language in which they were written. Don was still leaning toward a teaching career, and could also

see the future applications that being able to read Hebrew, even at a rudi-
mentary level, might have in teaching. This would be particularly the case
with lectures he might give, in a religious studies area, that would touch on
key Old Testament texts. Don held himself to his minimum of six hours of
study a day. Still, anticipating his time with Jop gave him something to look
forward to and helped motivate Don in his studies.

Painful Farewells

The following Tuesday morning, as usual, Don went to his mailbox and found the envelope the secretary had put there. He opened the envelope and read the question: "Jop, can you share about your suffering and loss in the camps and how your faith was shaped by these experiences?" Arriving at Jop's, and having enjoyed the refreshments Marie had brought, both Jop and Don prepared to settle down and begin the interview. Jop eased back in his chair, his world-weary smile conveying to Don something of the sadness the memories that he would be sharing were already calling forth. Don reassured himself that Jop must be okay with the question he was about to ask, and he was sure Jop had shared these memories with the many groups he had given talks too. Don opened the folded paper in his hands that he had just retrieved from his shirt pocket. After reading it he looked up at Jop and waited for him to begin. "Well we're getting to the crux of it, aren't we, Don?" Don wasn't quite sure how to take this statement or respond to it. "Suffering and faith," Jop continued, "in all its forms, are often two of the most difficult things for Christians to reconcile. The inability to reconcile these two is what prevents so many people of faith from healing, or even from holding onto their faith." Don now knew where Jop was going. He also was beginning to understand better why McCall had enlisted Jop to help him.

"Don," Jop continued, "my answer to this question will take longer than planned if that is okay with you." Don assured Jop that it was. "I am not sure of this, as I have not gone into such detail before with anyone about these experiences. The times in the camps where the suffering was not yet so great are what I will share first. In the following interview I will share some of the more profound experiences of suffering and loss I experienced in the camps as time went on. My faith journey, in the camps, was intertwined with these experiences and was an organic part of them.

"I think I left off telling you about the time where we first fully realized we were being treated more as if we were in a concentration camp than as POWs. I think I also shared that we had just received the casualties from

the battle of the Java Sea. When I had fought with the Dutch artillery regiment against the Japanese, we did not see the casualties we inflicted. It was
war from a distance. I did not experience the true brutality and barbarity
of war until we were POWs in the first camp. As I alluded to at the end of
the last interview, we realized this more clearly on Good Friday 1942, when
the survivors of the battle of the Java Sea were brought to our camp. Their
condition was indescribable. They were covered with oil from the sunken
ships. Reaching the Java beaches, their wounds were covered with tropical
ulcers. They lost more than half their weight; their eyes were just staring.
We still had supplies and were able to clean their wounds. I volunteered as
a medic because we were short of army medics in the camp. After several
weeks most of them were recovering well.

"In 1942 we began the camps without chaplains, and we ended in 1945
without them. In 1942 we were still utterly clergy dependent. But by 1945
our Christian community in the camps had grown strong under the total
direction of lay people. At Easter 1942 we were humans crying out in the
darkness, and nobody answered. There is a Dutch Christmas hymn which
says: 'Bound in the darkness, deserted by people and God.' We had no notion that clergy were not our anchors, but only our co-Christians who had
chosen to serve the church, or faith community, full time. As Easter 1942
came and there was no service for seven thousand men hoping that there
would be one, we felt deserted by our pastors and God.

"That Easter time was not a desperate time yet, even though the first
beatings had occurred. The secret radio in the camps was listened to eagerly.
The Japanese had still not landed in Australia and rumors kept everyone
thinking that the invincible Yankees were about to land on East Java, and
we would be the first ones liberated. The wounded of the Java Sea Battle
were doing fine. The Easter service was dropped without much further ado.
Easter 1942 would have passed by unnoticed if something had not happened that Easter morning while I was on duty in the English wing of our
very primitive sick bay. I was recording temperatures when suddenly it was
quite still. Then there was a clipped English accent. When I turned around,
I saw an English naval officer standing between the wounded sailors and
reading the Easter Gospel. He was not a chaplain. It was an English military
procedure that when no chaplains were present, an officer would read from
the Bible, and say the prayers from the Anglican Book of Prayer.

"After listening, I went on with my work not realizing that this was
the first of a long road of uninvited experiences. Only later did I become
aware that the idea of a lay person ministering had been lodged in my innermost being. I had no idea at the time that anyone but clergy would lead
worship, visit the sick, pray, listen, console, share loneliness. In 1942 the

work on the airfields demanded more and more of our men. The men began to suffer under the tropical sun, with not enough rest, food, and drink
during the day. Women often stood outside the camp. Some were caught,
they were brought inside the camp, tied to a tree, and had their hair cut
off. We were helpless and could not interfere; both men and women had
been beaten by the guards.

"After a few months, the men were used to working on the Japanese
airfields. In the beginning I was part of the work detail until I volunteered
to work in the sick bay, where there was a great shortage of medics. Being
without alcohol, cigarettes, and with limited though still sufficient food,
there was a toughening up of our bodies.

"There was a notice on the camp bulletin board. A Salvation Army
worship service would be held. It was signed Captain Helmhout. The Japanese didn't seem to care. That Sunday morning, I found a dozen men sitting
around. Captain Helmhout was also a Salvation Army officer. He was as-
sisted by a former youth pastor. Leijder Hovenstroop was a dynamic man,
but short tempered. His talk was hard to follow, and contained contradictory ideas. In spite of his strange exegesis, he was the only one among seven
thousand prisoners who refused a Japanese order. Each morning the entire
concentration camp had to stand at attention in the center of the camp
in order to bow toward the sun. Our guards told us that the emperor descended from the sun goddess. In bowing we both prayed for the emperor
and thanked him for taking care of us. The Japanese told us that we were
cowards because we had surrendered instead of seeking death. We actually
considered suicide cowardice, and living on as we did in the camps required
more courage than to seek death in battle.

"Anyhow we bowed each morning accompanied by the unmelodious
screams of the guards ordering us to bow deeper. Quietly we mumbled rather
uncomplimentary things about the emperor and his soldiers. Hovenstroop
saw it as a challenge not to bow before any strange gods. To our great surprise
he was not beaten. In his half Dutch, half Japanese he explained why he took
the stand and the Japanese commander excused him. Another courageous
clergyman was the Dutch Reformed pastor Rev. Samuel Van Hoogstraten.
He had been a missionary to the East Javanese, later our pastor, and then
had become a personal friend. He had been the one that had married us.
He smuggled all kinds of short letters from the women outside. If caught he
would have been shot. He visited our sick, and the wives of prisoners who
lived in Surabaya. This had been allowed by the Japanese commander at the
time who was a more humane person. Later in the war Hoogstraten was taken
prisoner by the Japanese secret police. He was tortured beyond belief, kept
three years in dungeons, and finally in 1945 he died of total exhaustion. In

his last hours a Bible and the company of others were denied. He did not die alone. Man's plan could not thwart the God he served.

"In June another transport of Dutch people came to our camp. Another element of Christian experience came with them. They were Christians who had found a new challenging way of life. They practiced an ecumenical worldwide movement. They were part of the Oxford Group. It did not have members, one could not join. One was part of it by living a lifestyle which was unique, a reminder of the early church. Its central thought was that in the New Testament both Jesus and the early church spent much time in prayer and listening to God, through the guidance of the Holy Spirit, who would come to comfort and guide his followers. Their theology was fairly liberal, though conservatives felt very much at home in the Oxford Group, because the real emphasis was on the Christian life and ethics rather than on dogma. Crucial was how the Christian related at home, at work, and the world at large. I had heard about the Oxford Group before the war. Their beginnings were at Oxford University in England. At that time the movement seemed to me to be a bit over the top. At this time in the camps I felt my schedule was too busy to take time to listen to God daily. Soon, however, I found friends among them. They came to the sick bay and often stayed overnight with the dying.

"Earlier in April my wife had brought our baby, Renee, then four months old. It would be the last time I would see her in the camps. The following day a friend of mine, a medic, who regularly drove to the hospital for supplies, told me that each day he could take one sick bay person to the city hospital and invited me to join him, and spend a day, outside the camp, with my wife and child. He said he would pick me up by 4:30 p.m. This gave some uneasy moments, as anyone missing Japanese roll call was presumed missing, and the punishment for being found outside the camp was execution on the center field of the camp. But Freddy, a most easygoing chap, although late, finally, happily drove in and we made it with five minutes to spare.

"In early July 1942 a new Japanese commander arrived. All mistreatment stopped. He had a small pedal organ brought up for the Protestant and Roman Catholic services. He arranged for family visits. Things in the camp were still bearable. We had thought the war would not last long anyhow, the Americans will soon free us. By the end of July this belief had evaporated although things seemed to have improved in the camp with the new commander. In July 1942 the women came in by droves, some with children and many with prams full of food and clothing. The women knew about the English and Americans and brought supplies for them too.

"One of my new English friends, Dennis Moppet, joined us. My wife happily included him in her gifts. It is strange what one remembers. Irene had brought me some sewing supplies and part of it was a little pair of scissors in the form of a stork. I used it until nearly the end of the war. A guard found it and considered that it could be used at a weapon. He hit me with his cane over the head and took the scissors. It had been her last gift to me. She had not brought the baby. When the bell rang indicating the visiting time was over we just stood there. It was another farewell. There was the first one when she left for Malang to stay with friends. There was the visit with the baby, and now this one. Still the goodbyes were getting easier. I do not remember what either of us said. We had been married two years, and even before the war I had been away for weeks either on business or military exercises. We longed for better days when we would have more time together as a couple and family.

"Until 1942 we had been permitted to have religious services. On the Queen's birthday on August 31 when we sang our national anthem, we were suddenly ordered that no groups larger than ten could gather. All musical instruments had to be turned in, but the organ was forgotten. We had learned from experience never to do everything the Japanese told us to do. We continued with services anyway. In June when I was leaving the English services, I walked with the young Englishman Dennis Moppet. He came from a small town south of London, called Lewes. It was one those guided encounters in life. It became a friendship for life between two young men. He told me in detail about his family. He had already met my wife on the visitation day. He came from a deeply religious family, and had two younger sisters. At times he read to me from their letters, which he had received just before the war in Singapore.

"Slowly we began to talk about God, about faith, and then he invited me to me a small group. This was partially a study group, they were talking about the Lord's Prayer, and welcomed outsiders. The Dutch had nothing of this kind. Apart from Captain Helmhout's service we were in a total vacuum. It was only when the Oxford Group came that a small assembly of the Dutch was created. I invited Dennis to that group, where the discussion centered on suffering. Most spoke some English and tried to include Dennis. He was able to follow our talk more or less. I think it was at this time that I became aware of another dimension of faith, that of a co-suffering God.

"Until this time I had enjoyed the group of coworkers in the sick bay. Because we had been assigned to day and night duty, the four of us had a small room of our own. I was not really eager to go out at night. The days with the sick were long. We had a monopoly game and played it night after night. The only visitors were rats, but we even got used to their presence, and made big traps to catch them. We also had a dog. Nobody knew where that terrier came from. At that time, we were not suffering from hunger, and the dog was quite safe. Later dogs and cats became welcome additions to our meals.

"I began to absent myself from the monopoly games. The others wondered why religion seemed to become of greater interest to me than monopoly. But the figure of Jesus of Nazareth began to fascinate me. I had accepted that he was half God, half man; a kind of gentle figure telling parables, healing people. In our studies I found a dynamic in that man of Nazareth that had never come through in all the sermons I had heard in my life. It had never occurred to me to take the Bible with me when I left for the war. I had attempted to lead a fairly honest life as a businessman. We went to church most Sundays and enjoyed the sermons Hovenstroop gave. But my interest was nominal at best. At home we read the Bible after dinner, and a book by Stanley Jones: *Triumphant Living*, which friends, the Van Beekkerks had given us as a wedding present.

"My English friends and my Oxford Group friends challenged me to dig deeper. They did not challenge me by singling me out; they were far too caring to pressure anyone. Their interest was contagious. Dennis and I continued to have long conversations. I kept him informed about the Oxford Group and how, at times, I tried, as one of the ways to live out your faith, to have a quiet time. We promised to begin an experiment in prayer for each other and for our families. It was the first time that I consciously began to talk to that rather unknown Being. I began to think about my brother-in-law, Bram Corstanje, whose faith had provided an unusual experience for me. I lived with them for close to a year when my mother was rather ill. My teen years were pretty lively and she needed rest. I was sixteen and Bram was twenty-eight. His pastorate in the small town of Franeker was very busy. He was a pacifist and Christian socialist. As a result his life was difficult. Suddenly at twenty-nine he died. He had contracted tuberculosis from a man, a parishioner, who he had visited regularly. I was alone in the room with him when he died. Shortly before his death he told me, "If my suffering is ever of any service to you, then I don't mind it." I did not quite understand that, but now in the concentration camp, and through these study groups and conversations, Bram became most real, and I began to get a glimpse of what suffering was, and what it could mean for others. But only a glimpse, as life that first year, in retrospect, was still tolerable.

"I found Dennis a job in the sick bay kitchen, which saved him from having to go out and work for the Japanese in the airfields. We often met and worked together. In the evening we talked and thought through the implications of being Christians. In many ways it did not appeal to me, because it implied unconditional norms; e.g., unconditional love. It meant that to be a Christian was that Christ would be an overwhelming first priority, and that, at the time, still seemed an impossibility. I had no Bible at this time. One of the English chaplains lent me his copy from time to time. On the inside page his mother had dedicated her son to God, as Hannah did with Samuel. Dedicated him so that he could make a difference in the world, and this Tom Goss had, particularly in the concentration camp, been busy beyond belief. He had started small groups everywhere; spent hours with the sick, had friends in all the bamboo barracks.

"In September all the English left. Saying farewell to Dennis and Tom was a hard thing to do. Dennis gave me his Royal Airforce Badge, and I gave him my Dutch Artillery Insignia. He opened his Bible and read Psalm 121, which ever since became a central part of the Psalms for me. We promised to return them to each other after the war. Shortly thereafter we got our first Dutch chaplain, Carel Hamel. As official services were now forbidden, Carel Hamel held short services with small groups all over the Jaarmarkt camp. He held dozens on Sunday. Outside in turn we would be watching the Japanese guards and if they approached, they would warn all inside, who would then get busy washing clothes, etc. Once they had passed, we resumed the worship, which consisted of some Bible readings, a short exhortation, prayers, and very softly, the singing of some Dutch hymns we knew by heart. At times when we were caught, we received a bashing with the butt of the guard's gun. Chaplain Hamel was indefatigable. Each day he conducted study groups on the Bible, and related subjects. His services generally lasted about fifteen minutes. In one week he held about sixty services and reached some eight hundred different people in our camp.

"In the fall of 1942, the food rations were diminished. It was at this time that the sick bay was filled from corner to corner. Those who had not been sick before received less food and became sick. As more people died, many more men began to ask about study groups and services. Carel Hamel did what he could, but suddenly he was put on a transport, and October 19 he was deported to Thailand to work on the railroad to Burma. He became a legend. The book *The Soldiers' Chaplain* portrays the man as he was, even though he hardly talked about himself. The next Dutch chaplain to us was Emil Schaeffer, who was more institutional in his ministry. He started confirmation classes, and when the Japanese once again allowed services, he had a chapel build out of bamboo. He then had benches built for the chapel. He later organized a church council for this church and formed a choir. He had a gift for leading worship that involved lay participation.

"A group of Mendonese, or Indonesian soldiers that fought for the Dutch, had formed their own church group. They too formed a choir. They had beautiful deep voices which reminded some English of the choirs in Wales. For them God was in the midst of the camp. One of them made a cover for my New Testament which Emil Schaeffer had given me. He embroidered the letters *NT* and a cross on the front cover. Forty years later I still use this Bible, and it reminds me of that Mendonese friend. The Mendonese had their own church services, and lay leaders who spoke in their own language. I wondered why, until Chaplain Hamel came, no Dutch lay leader had ever led a service The Oxford Group had their own meetings, but not worship services. Here were lay leaders just like in the early church; fisherman, and businesswomen like Lydia, with a single theologian Paul. This became a seed in my mind.

"Chaplain Hamel encouraged lay involvement in worship, and in new ways, which had nurtured this seed within me. Carel Hamel had worked more on a one-to-one basis, and did not care for anything institutional. This was a contrast to Emil Schaeffer's pastoral style which was more institutionally oriented. Yet both chaplains had their merits in the way they nurtured the spiritual lives of the men. Schaeffer organized a church council that represented men from fundamentalist, Calvinist, Unitarian, and Salvation Army backgrounds, among others. The men of this ecumenical group were ones who founded 'The Church Under the Cross,' as the main church in camp was called from there on. The name came from Martin Luther, who wrote: 'A Christian's heart still rises above, even if the church finds itself under the cross.'

"With Christmas upon us, the question arose how and why does one celebrate Christmas in a concentration camp? We had been prisoners for some ten months. We had not seen our families in half a year. Some of our people had died, and the sick bay was now always crowded. I think it was partly because of Western culture, and because it would be a tie to our families, that we still wanted to have a Christmas celebration. Then there was a spiritual need that many had as well. A need for rebirth, new beginnings, new hope, and an awareness that the God we worshiped was not distant.

"A year back, the night of December 24, was when our baby was born. We went in the blackout to the clinic, where a midwife and Javanese nurses were around us. All windows were covered with black shades, and that night, when our girl was born, we still could rejoice, for maybe the Japanese would never come back. This Christmas of 1942 I thought of Joseph and Mary, far away from their home, uncomfortable surroundings, smelly shepherds, foreigners called wise men. It was not all that much joy for this young family those two thousand years ago. I tried to picture my little daughter now a year old, but I could not. Compared to the coming years, this first Christmas in a camp was still festive. The Japanese had allowed us to have a Christmas tree, women were permitted to bring in some extra food and clothing.

"A concentration camp is a microcosm of the world outside. Among us were different kinds of artists; painters who earned extra cigarettes drawing people. The artists made an altar background of three panels. It was about four feet high. It portrayed the Holy Family and was very appreciated because they worked with very limited means. For this larger Christmas Eve service the different church groups came together. The Mendonese joined us with their choir, and also provided a wonderful group of flute players.

"Emil Schaeffer called our attention to the artist's work, which showed a cradle, and over it hovered a cross made of big wood branches. He called us to the reality of this Christmas and said something like: 'We are not at home but in a concentration camp. Our wives are not here, our children will not see us, nor we them. There are no presents under the tree. We have three thousand men here, some very sick, a few near death, little food, hard work, bad treatment, and yet one thing remains the same. Christ is in our midst, whatever Christmas means to you, and that is why we are not alone. That Christ can be in all of us, in our homes, in the city, and elsewhere. It simply means we are bound together this Christmas. It may be worse next Christmas, if the war is not over. We will always be bound together even with our loved ones, because that is what Christmas is all about.'

"He then asked us to look at the cross, and then at the cradle, and told us that the cradle without the cross is pure sentimentality. The cross without the cradle is hopelessness. He concluded, 'As long as you live, never separate the two. These years are our learning school. Use them well. We are not alone in it. God, you, and I are in it together.'

"It was a sobering experience and thank God the chaplain did not give us tinsel. We could cope far better with that reality, and our feelings of having been away almost a year now. We sang some carols; one was 'It Dawns Already in the East, the Light Shines Everywhere.' One stanza of which was 'Those who are bound in the shadow of death deserted by God and people, begin to see the light of the early dawn.' A year later, in Japan, somebody reminded us of this Christmas sermon of 1942 and the terrible Christmas in Osaka. We had absolutely no problem seeing the cross beyond the cradle.

"In March 1943 the Japanese again suddenly withdrew permission for worship services. The church council ignored the order and, as in September 1942, we stood guard outside, while the worship proceeded inside. One time, when a lay leader, David Kuyken, was leading the service, a Japanese guard came in. David could have pretended to read from a book other than the Bible, but his marvelous way of speaking made it clear to the guard that he was not reading something from just any book. He was taken to the guard's house. Through the interpreter he told them without hesitation that, of course, he had been preaching the Good News, what else? He added that he would never stop doing it. It was one of those rare moments where the Japanese were stymied. If David had broken one of their common rules, e.g., smoking in the barracks, not meeting the guards on time, taking it easy at work when the soldiers passed, they simply would have beaten him. But, one who wanted to express their religion? They finally called on the English chaplain and he came running in his Anglican gown as hundreds of men stared. The guard could hardly keep up with him. He repeated what David had said, that he would never cease to preach the gospel either. Finally, they locked them up for twenty-four hours, but never touched them. Next Sunday they were given permission to resume the normal worship service.

"The year had gone by fast. Transports had come and taken people out. In January the English RAF people came back, including Dennis. I was able again to find him a place in the sick bay kitchen. It was great to see him again. Work in the sick bay had cemented some precious friend-ships with the people I worked, including Dennis. I did a lot of visiting with the Oxford Group. One Siestse Van Dyke became a friend for life, long after the war we were in contact. I was also good friends with his wife, Truus. Siestse suddenly passed away in 1960, to a degree as a result of the prison camps. His passing from this reality left an empty place which has never been replaced by another.

"The Oxford Group under Siestse had a weekly discussion and sharing group. Everyone was welcome. Each week someone gave a talk on a subject related to life in the camps. The discussions were so animated that they often continued after the "lights out" signals were given. Many people who had been estranged from the church throughout the years took a new look at Christendom, and began to attend the Sunday Services.

"It was interesting that none of the chaplains ever showed any interest in the Oxford Group meetings. It was purely a layman's movement where pastor's and laity intermingled with no one more important than the other. I wondered if this was threatening to clergy and chaplains within the camps. Chaplain Tom Goss, who had been transported back, among others, with Dennis, said it was a splendid group, and that it did its own work well, but that he had other commitments to keep. Dennis told me that in his bar-racks a group of soldiers had begun to meet every morning for five minutes just before the Japanese roll call. They formed a circle, had a short prayer. Around them, as if by common consent, all conversations ceased.

"All these events added up to the fact that, when people were jerked from their normal existence, there was room to search for new values to sustain them. So what about that God; did that God know anything about us here? We searched and dug deeper than we ever had done before in life.

Though life was not easy that first year, this search was not yet based on utter wretchedness, but on loneliness, on being separated from those we loved. All this touched by a sometimes long-forgotten reality, God! What role did this deity really play in human lives, in countries at war? I was fully part of it because my childhood beliefs, which I had accepted in naïve ways growing up, would no longer sustain me. I had felt utterly broken up leaving my young family a year earlier. Any vestiges of those childhood beliefs had left me, and I had not yet found a reality to replace it. The Bible Emil Schaeffer had given me was full of quotation marks, and it was good that I finally began to doubt much of what, at one time, I had accepted with rock-hard certainty.

"Now forty years later these question marks have become exclamation marks, although some questions remain, and I would not want to do without them. English chaplain Tom Goss once said, 'If you know all about God that you want to know, then you don't have a God but an idol.' Even Christ in Gethsemane had his questions; on the cross his last one dealt with having felt utterly deserted by that God he had served. Why? So we too struggled on. In truth, that first year opened doors to many of us. At first we were hesitant to step over any threshold. That only began to become urgent in the second year of concentration camp life."

Jop suddenly paused, and stopped talking. "Don, I have again been talking for a long time, and hope I have not lost you along the way." Don, who had had trouble staying awake through sermons his pastor had given back home, had not only had stayed awake through Jop's recollections, his interest in Jop's experiences in the camps had only grown. "Actually, Jop," Don responded, "I am finding your story not only interesting, but personally relevant." "I am glad to hear that," Jop replied, "that is what John and I both hoped would be the case. In the next interview I will be sharing some of the most difficult times in the camps." As Jop led Don to the door, Don thanked him again, and began his walk back to the seminary.

On the walk back Don found himself more lost in thought than usual. He intuitively sensed the personal relevance of Jop's story to his own faith journey. Yes, they were very different in time, place, and context, but the broader themes of Jop's faith journey and struggles resonated deeply with him. Like Don, Jop had entered his major life crisis with a naïve, still-formative faith; like Jop the accident had left Don asking deeper faith questions, and struggling to find answers that might help him make sense of the suffering and injustices he had experienced; like Jop he was encountering individuals at critical times who became spiritual guides for him. He had not yet experienced any great insights or epiphanies. Perhaps this too would happen, but for now it was enough that he felt himself on a spiritual journey again, and not trapped in a spiritual wilderness created in part by his anger. The choice to go to the seminary might have been his, but he was beginning to believe that it was part of God's plan for him as well, or God was making it part of that plan. The interplay between human free will and God's will for us was one of those questions Don had wrestled with, and one he suspected he would continue to wrestle with. He certainly did not agree with Calvin's doctrine of predestination that taught that God had already willed ahead of time which individuals would be his elect or saved. This contradicted Don's Baptist belief that accepting God's grace involves not only soul searching, but a decision to surrender one's life to Christ as one's personal Lord and Savior. He had wrestled with this theology as well, but at least it allowed some room for free will. If it had been part of God's plan for Don to attend the seminary, he had been completely unaware of God's, or the Holy Spirit's, initiative here. For Don the choice had seemed to be made more out of desperation than anything else. Perhaps Don thought the only true faith choice we can make, recalling what he could of his readings of Kierkegaard's, was the radical sub-jective one that leaves reason behind and leaps the chasm of doubt and/or superficial religious belief to a passionately lived-out faith. But did this not require God's assistance in the form of the Holy Spirit? Perhaps, Don thought further, we are freest not before but after we have made a leap of faith. Maybe it is only then that we are freed up from the things that truly enslave us, unfulfilling relative truths, and transient worldly obsessions. As he neared the seminary Don resolved once more not to fall into the trap of overintel-lectualizing his faith, for while theologizing and philosophizing had its place, in the end, Kierkegaard had cautioned, it won't lead you to a living faith. True faith, especially as it regards God's grace, Don had already begun to realize, involved an openness to an experience of that grace; one that offered the deepest possible validation of its truth. A validation that in turn led not just to a belief in that truth, but a passionate desire to live it out.

The next week went by uneventfully. After all the drama of his first year in seminary Don found the routine of the weeks of the intensive course a pleasant change, even though the fall semester might bring new challeng-es with it. One key exception to the routine, other than Don's interviews with Jop, were his morning rendezvous with Cindy. He looked forward as much to seeing her, perhaps more so, than to meditating with her. Don had become well aware of how much meditation could benefit him. He still struggled with the Buddhist ideal of detaching from what the Buddhist's called rising conditions; that combination of desires and aversions that one could become too attached to either by clinging to them or denying them. Don's Western sensibilities had ingrained in him the belief that at least some of these experiences became an integral part of who he was. He had

had trouble accepting the Buddhist belief that this Western understanding of self was illusory; that the self was continually changing, like the flickering of a flame, and as such had no fixed or permanent reality. He could accept that many of his rising conditions and aversions had arisen due to traumas in his life, and that if healing could occur here, he would have to let the destructive aspects of himself dissipate. Don found reassurance in Scripture that we could be freed from these parts of ourself. He knew that the transformative love of Christ, like the refiner's fire (Malachi 2:17—3:6) might free him from parts of himself that were inconsistent with what God created him to be and wanted him to become. But Don also clung to his belief that such Christian attributes as faith, hope, and love might find permanent expression through his sense of self.

Cindy's advice to adapt the Buddhist understanding of "no self" by surrendering all the thoughts and feelings that arose during meditation to Christ, as he refocused on his centering breath and exhaled, had been helpful. But Don had even wrestled with this adaptation to his Christian faith. He couldn't help but wonder if this adaptation, minus adherence to the no fixed self-belief in Buddhism, would make it impossible to experience the most liberating effects of this meditation. In Buddhist belief, if there is no fixed self then it becomes much easier to let go of all the baggage one attaches to the self, such as all Don's anger and self-recrimination. The question that troubled Don, given this Buddhist doctrine of "no self," was that to experience the full benefits of a meditation fundamentally designed to liberate one from any fixed sense of self, didn't one then have to let go of any sense of self?

Don had shared this concern with Cindy, and her initial thought was that he was confusing losing all sense of self with detaching from a fixed sense of self. She had teasingly said, "You think too much." Then in a more serious tone she advised him to trust that God could use meditation to help him, even if Don didn't fully understand how. She had also reminded Don that there were, depending on interpretation, parallels between Christ's teaching in Matthew 10:39 that "he who finds his life will lose it, and he who loses his life for my sake will find it" and the Buddhist teachings of detachment from self.

She suggested as well that there were parallels between Buddhism and, in a metaphorical reading, the biblical story of Abraham's near sacrifice of Isaac. In this interpretation Isaac meant everything to Abraham. The parallel here having to do with the transformative spiritual experience availed one when they surrendered all they are and have been to God through a meditative practice. Wasn't the point here that we must be willing to sacrifice everything, which often takes the form of the fixed, ego-centered views we have of ourselves, before we regain all that we are in a more detached, open-ended, and liberated spiritual way. Cindy then added, "Many great Christians had found that in letting go of or surrendering false pride or a broken sense of self to God's grace, that God then gave them back a liberated sense of self, free from guilt, shame, and any other negative emotions that had imprisoned them. Wasn't John Newton's heartfelt confession of shame and guilt, one stormy night aboard the slave ship he captained, a prime example; a radical conversion and transformation that led him to ministry and to penning 'Amazing Grace'?"

"You may still wrestle with anger," Cindy then cautioned, "but you will no longer see that part of you as permanent and unchangeable. You will no longer feel imprisoned behind the rigid confining bars of a fixed negative view of self. What I have taken from Buddhism is that we and the world around us are constantly changing, and what traps us is the dangerous illusion that this is not the case, particularly as it relates to fixed negative views of ourself. We end up denying or clinging to things in unrealistic ways. How is this inconsistent with a radical life-changing Christian faith experience that affords a humble openness to God's ongoing transformative will for us? A process of transformation which is able to liberate one from the bondage of many ingrained negative behavior patterns while facilitating continual growth." Then pausing, Cindy looked thoughtfully at Don and said, "And if we were created to be continually growing in God's loving transformative grace, then might not hanging onto too fixed a sense of self be illusory from a Christian perspective?" Cindy had shared this knowing that Don needed this parallel understanding between Buddhism and Christianity in order to more fully embrace mindfulness meditation, something she knew could be of help to him. Don treasured Cindy's input, and knew it would take time for him to process it and perhaps adapt it to the meditation practice he was developing. But he was amazed at the wisdom she had gained from prayerfully adapting her meditative practice to her Christian faith.

Still Don was experiencing benefits from the meditation. He was able to gain objectivity on some his most troubling thoughts and feelings. Don had found the image of riding them out like a surfer on the crest of stormy waves helpful, and could see how this benefit from his meditative practice could kick into gear when his anger got aroused in everyday life. Cindy and Don had also gotten to know each other even better. They chatted, now, both before and after their meditation times together. Don had learned more about Cindy's difficult teenage years How she had to walk such a tight line between living a normal American teenage girl's life, while respecting her parent's values, which were so steeped in their Chinese culture. The fact that her parents socialized almost exclusively within her father's Chinese Christian church had made them less open to many American cultural mores and customs. After her rebellious period Cindy had found balance by rededicating herself to her studies but not to such a degree that it left little time to socialize with her friends. She also continued to go to church every Sunday with her parents, and while dressing tastefully, did so wearing clothes of her choosing and more in keeping with American trends. When things still got tense between her parents and her, she consoled herself that college was around the corner, and even if she lived at home, her parents would by then certainly loosen their strictures on her. Cindy and her sister, Linda, both had typical American names, a concession on her parent's part to ensure the girls would have an easier time adapting to American culture. Linda had a much more pragmatic temperament. She had pretty much kept her nose to the grindstone in high school, and in college had chosen premed as her major. While Cindy knew her parents loved both of them equally, at times, she felt that the chemistry between her sister and her parents was stronger. Cindy had shared with Don that her independent free spiritedness had often cut against the grain of her parents' Chinese cultural values.

What may have caused problems with her parents, though, was one of the things that Don found most attractive about Cindy. It was a personality trait that he strongly resonated with, and was helping them to bond; this, and that they both were very reflective about the deeper questions in their lives. Don had shared how close he had been to his mother, and how much he despised his father for the way he had treated her. This was more information than he had shared with anyone about them, including McCall.

Don did have a problem with Cindy that he kept turning over in his head. They had become friends, and were on the way to becoming close friends; closer than any male friend he had ever had. As attracted to her as he was, he so valued this budding friendship that he did not want to jeopardize it by asking her out. If, for some reason he could not foresee, she would turn him down it could ruin this friendship, and he was not ready to risk this.

Don also continued to feel conflicted about his sense of self and the meditating he was doing. He had found Cindy's instruction intellectually satisfying, but emotionally a part of him still wanted to believe that there was something unchangeable about the human soul. Deep down he knew this, in part, had to do with a deep longing he had to be reunited with his mother and sister in the next life, just as he had known them in this life. Still he felt hopeful that this conflict would resolve itself, trusting that God could use this meditative technique in ways that he might yet not understand. Don had found Cindy's advice to trust God and her earlier reference to Nouwen's pastoral insight to "live the question" helpful.

One insight that Don had gained from Cindy, in one of their after-meditation chats, offered a particularly strong parallel between the teachings of Christ and Buddha. What Buddha had termed the middle way between the extremes of the ascetic life and one of indulgent pleasure, was a mindfulness state where one could enjoy worldly pleasure in the moment without clinging to them. Christ, in passages such as Matthew 6, in his Sermon on the Mount, had affirmed our need for the basic necessities, or comforts, of life as long as we kept his kingdom as a priority. But more than this Christ had by his life and mission exemplified how one could enjoy life, as he often did when eating and drinking with his disciples and others, without losing sight of that which does not whither. Both Buddha and Christ then advocated a middle path through life. This insight gave Don confidence, as he tried to tried to find common ground between the two traditions, that at least in some ways they shared the same source of divine wisdom.

The Hawaii Maru
(a POW Transport Ship)

When Don found himself at Jop's house that next Tuesday afternoon he knew he was about to hear about Jop's darkest days in the camps. He wanted to hear about these experiences of suffering and loss in the camps and knew they might help him in ways not yet fully grasped. Don's depression had lifted for some time now, and he wanted to continue to focus on the positive in his life. He was afraid that hearing about the suffering and loss Jop experienced in the camps might trigger some depression in him; that he might resonate with some aspects of Jop's experiences, that they might tap into the deeper emotions of grief he had only partly worked through. The insights he had gained from both Jop and Cindy had made him realize that he still had much work to do in confronting and accepting the darker parts of himself. He knew too that in dealing with these parts of himself, and the experiences that had contributed to them, he must do the additional work of finding constructive ways of expressing and channeling the behavior that resulted from them. He knew the greater part of this work was not just in learning some techniques, as he had meditating with Cindy, but in the disciplined way he, tenaciously and prayerfully, employed such techniques in his everyday life.

The coffee and cookies that Marie, once again, brought Don and Jop helped them transition into the interview. As they settled back into their chairs and had put their nearly empty coffee mugs down Jop began to speak. "The first part of what I am about to share, Don, will not sound too bad. Starting on April 18, 1943, I was to be transported to three different camps. The short stays in these three camps were a relatively pleasant prelude to the longer darker days that followed, and which then persisted until the end of the war and our liberation.

"In April 1943 our first concentration camp, which had been a kind of home, despite some horrors, was closed and slowly emptied. A group of dysentery patients were ordered to be ready to leave. Generally, the Japanese asked the Dutch or English commanders to put the lists of transports together, the sick, the strong, the old, and the young. It was a painful task, our physicians were consulted, choices were made. But who was really strong could be hard to discern. Also, the area they were sent to mattered. Areas like Amboina would see few survivors return nearly two years later. They had to be helped off the trucks by fellow prisoners. They were, by this time, in states of utter exhaustion, emaciated, and many near death. Many never returned, including Dennis Moppet. Two ships on their way to Amboina were sunk by American or Australian submarines; none the ships were marked as carrying POW's. Two close friends drowned. One of them a Jewish friend and fellow bookseller in Surabaya, Sammy Lezer. The other was a cousin of mine.

"I had worked in the sick bay for nearly a year; had never been sick, but had been troubled lately with a stubborn case of diarrhea. Dr. Wulf, our oldest physician, gave me a checkup and put me with the sick transport because it had medics. Wherever our transport was going it would be the first time I had left the city, the city I came to, Surabaya, as a young book seller in 1938. Though the sick transport I was put on was the first to form, it was the last to leave.

"It was a nightlong journey. First, we were taken by truck to the station. I had lived in that greater neighborhood. The streets looked dirty, the houses neglected. No women anywhere except near the station. We all craned our necks looking around, but none on our truck found anyone they knew. Gradually we noticed that it had gotten cooler. We finally arrived in one of the healthiest places on Java, Bandoeng, on West Java.

"The new camp was really a POW camp. It was housed in the barracks of the Dutch East Indies Army. The camp was in excellent shape. After living for over a year in a camp with Bamboo huts, muddy paths surrounded by rats, where we had eaten poor food, it was welcome change. We had no idea that there were some real POW camps around, and of all things we had landed in one. Even the camp church met in a real chapel. We were treated like POWs. The mystery of this was soon solved. There had been a lot of money in the hands of the officers and Japanese camp commander. He was nice, but also very corrupt. So, to mutual benefit, life was quite agreeable in Bandoeng.

"A Dutch Reformed chaplain by the name of Piron was the next spiritual guide God placed in my path. He was loved by all; still a young man barely in his thirties and untiring. He spent hours with the unchurched. Rev. Piron had progressive ideas and wanted independence for the colonies. He led a study on the book of Romans. This unlocked the door to a theological letter which I had never understood. As a matter of fact, it was the first time I had begun to read the Bible myself this year. The concept this book began to unlock for me, under Piron's tutelage, was that of God's grace in Jesus Christ.

"Chaplain Piron, later in the year, was sent away on another transport to Sumatra. The ship was sunk and most of the prisoners drowned. He landed on a raft with others. A man swam toward the raft. There was no place for him on the overcrowded float. Chaplain Piron went into the ocean, helped the man onto the raft, and quietly remained behind in the ocean. He gave his life the way he had lived. He was truly a man for others.

"The few weeks in Bandoeng were a vacation compared to the Jaarmarkt. We celebrated our second Easter there with the celebration of Holy Communion. On May 5 all of us who had come from Surabaya were sent on a transport again. If we liked Bandoeng we found the new camp was even better. Again the camp commander, fortunately, was corrupt to the depth of his soul. He followed the rules of the Geneva Convention on POWs. There were two camp stores, even a few little restaurants where we could buy Indonesian food. From the moment we arrived we were paid in Japanese currency, ten cents a day, and could buy food. It seemed like reopened paradise. We worked in wool mills, sitting on benches behind looms. It was a welcome change from working in the sick bay for a year.

"The Tjimani Camp also had a large number of Oxford Group people, and this prompts me to introduce one of the most remarkable Christians I have ever met. One who had experienced the Christ as a contemporary reality in the Oxford Group. Pieter Volten was a lawyer; short, dynamic, always on the go. I had first met him in Bandoeng when I was standing in line for food. A man behind me in line said: 'Isn't this a great experience, this standing in line for food?' Since I had just arrived, I assumed that he was one of those nuts who had lived in that splendid camp from the beginning: I reacted rather silently, but he smiled and said, 'In a waiting line the man in front of you, and behind you, may need you.' May need me, what for, I was thinking. What did he have in mind? He gave me the key: 'What an opportunity to share your hope and faith, to encourage the other if necessary.'

"It proved that he had seen me in the chapel. Pieter had a deep belief that if one went to church, one was either alive or not. He seemed to assume I was alive, why I never knew. He confronted and challenged me with the fact that Christians do not have a private faith. He never spoke in pietistic language. He was intoxicated by a love of Christ. He simply talked, listened, and encouraged. Also, he never cornered another but gave them plenty of room to get out and remain friends. Neither did he decide if others were Christians or not, had to be converted, or needed to have the Bible read to them or prayed for. He was simply a brother! He cared, he was contagious. The manner in which he lived from day to day was such that his words were lived. Each moment was a unique encounter with another human being.

"I can recall Pieter and me attending one of the Oxford Groups at Tjimani, whose only purpose was to do Bible study. I was most embarrassed when Pieter interrupted the pleasant discussion and said, 'You know the purpose of Christendom is not to study the Bible without end, but to relate to others. I don't hear anything about that.' Pieter offered the group and me some key insights. 'You know if I listen God speaks, and if I listen and begin to obey what I hear, God is at work in and with me.' What he taught us was that the organized church taught much about how to listen to God, but little on how to obey God in the midst of our lives in the world. He also taught them and me that human beings are not just meant to be logical creatures but are full of little selves all trying to get our attention. He taught, and himself demonstrated, the value of setting aside quiet time and writing down our thoughts not to let them dictate to us, but to sort them out in a prayerful mind-set with the help of the Holy Spirit.

"The one other thing I learned from Pieter was to take risks not recklessly or in a way that was thoughtless of the other. Rather to strike up conversations with others where the need and opportunity arose. Sometime after learning this I began striking up conversations with those I worked with at the mill, such as with a medic, and was baffled that they were not interested in what I brought up. Sharing my frustration with Pieter, he said, 'You talk too much beyond the experience and interest of the other. A Christian should begin where the other is, not where the Christian is.' So I toned it down and found that letting them lead the conversation presented the best opportunity to ask questions of a deeper kind.

"Pieter also reminded me of two works I had read in the bookstore by Soren Kierkegaard, *Fear and Trembling* and *Sickness Unto Death*, which is despair. Kierkegaard's emphasis, in these books, which I now recollected, on the radical nature of faith, helped to stretch my mind subsequently as a POW. In the Oxford Group one man laughed when I raised the idea that God was in the camp. A former banker said, 'That's what I did years back when someone shared that possibility. The idea did not let go and in the end I found God was quietly observing me as I dealt with clients.' Later this same man confided in me, 'You just have to give others time, you're not the only one who has been laughed at.'

"The Tjimani POW camp was a necessary interlude for my psychic and spiritual development. We stayed only a short time in the camp and before we could regain our strength, we were informed we were to go on a transport again. We had been there from September 1 to September 26 of 1943. The next camp the transport brought us to was Batavia. We stayed only four weeks here. It was another transit camp. Daily people's names were put on lists for Singapore, and transit camps, in Burma, China, or Japan.

"On September 26 we were taken aboard the Makassar Maru. It may have had accommodations for nine hundred people, but three thousand POWs were put in the ship's holds. Our destination was Singapore. It left from the same dock where I had arrived in 1938. Food in this camp was low grade and barely enough, but we compensated, when working on an airbase, by eating plenty of coconuts. The climate in October was bearable. The barracks, formerly English barracks, were in good shape. We often talked about death in the Singapore camp. Maybe it was because we thought we might go to the horror of the railroad camps in Burma. Each time a man died it brought the awareness this was someone who could have lived a full life and had been robbed of that destiny.

"The chaplain, David Kuyken, led our final Sunday service in the Singapore camp. The liturgy made us mindful of all the young Dutchmen whose lives were ebbing away. For a time we sat in silent prayer. Soon after this we were put on the next transport. The chaplain had reminded us that in the future absence of clergy we could rely on lay leadership, and that this had been all there was in the early church.

"This really opened the door to a new understanding, for me and others, of the Church Under the Cross each time it re-formed. We came to understand that we were all ministers, each responsible to God in Christ to grow and mature in our faith, each responsible to God in living out our faith wherever we might be—in work details, outside the camps, in the sick bays, etc.—churchgoing being only one part of our spiritual life in the camps.

"On November 6, 1943, we were put in the holds of the ship *Hawaii Maru*, which in itself would be our sailing concentration camp for thirty days, from November 6, 1943, to December 5, 1943. We thought that this journey was the worst that would ever happen to us. We had to climb down two ladders in the holds of a rusty old ship. Three thousand men climbed down. It took three hours and screaming guards all around us. It had been a passenger ship once. We discovered portholes which we opened in spite of orders not to touch them. A slight breeze came through.

"Each person was allowed an area about six feet in length and the width of one's shoulders. Water was distributed once a day, and food twice a day, a strange-looking rice with dead bugs. As we were driven down, I was separated from all my friends. We stayed for two days in the tropical heat of Singapore harbor, but were not allowed to move around, except for bodily needs. They were taken care of in an ingenious, but hardly sanitary way. A long board was attached with ropes to the railing, but the board was outside the ship. With so many men having to climb the two ladders it meant that many who already had poorly functioning intestinal systems, never made it to the deck. There was no place to wash clothing, and the smell in the holds became incredible. Soon dysentery broke out. The only way to get fresh air was through the portholes.

"Human beings are rational animals, they have the ability to choose. Circumstances may be either good or bad, but people decided in the ship how to live. We were so much on top of each other that certain rules were drawn up; not by discussing them, but by common agreement. It was the only way to live through this experience. We stuck to the little space we had, there was hardly any bickering or grumbling, except when we stood in line for food, which took hours. Then minor fights occurred. In general the men made the choice to come through this ghastly experience in the best way possible. A deck of cards appeared. My neighbor had a miniature chess game which we played many times a day. We began to know each other; listened to endless stories about wives and children, pictures circulated. We talked about books and shared the few books we had in our corner of the ship's hold. We speculated about Japan, and meeting Japanese who were not in the armed forces.

"It was semi-dark as the portholes allowed the only light available. Sleeping on the hard boards was no problem. We had slept for weeks at the Jaarmarkt camp on the bare clay ground, our shoes being our pillows. The ship was a testing laboratory. We underestimated potentiality in ourselves, which at least I was not aware of. The point was the choices we made and not the conditions in the filthy ship. It did not make us supermen; it simply made us accommodate each other better than we had done before.

"Near Saigon we landed in the tail of a typhoon. According to a first mate of the merchant marine, the ship was in some danger of capsizing because the wind factor was dangerous. Probably on account of limited food rations, nobody I knew became seasick in our corner. We were tossed from left to right and just hung onto to each other. In the pitch dark of the night it was like an unreal movie. One optimist said that at least no American submarine could torpedo us in that storm.

"When the storm left, we began to move around. It took hours to crawl on hands and knees, around people, lowering ourselves to the center of the holds and moving through narrow hallways. We heard that the storm had tossed down gallons of sea water, and most people around the ladders had been drenched to the skin. Pieter Volten was always somewhere seeing a fellow, either planned or not, in need. I still see myself standing in that corner of the ship wondering where he was. Obviously caring for someone. Finally,

I saw him squatting near a very sick man. He waved at me from a distance, and asked how and what I was doing.

"I knew what he meant, how was I relating to others. Being a Christian means to relate on all human levels: physical, emotional, and spiritual. I tried to relate to my neighbors. I played chess, told stories, listened to others about their families. Most hesitantly I tried to get to know my immediate neighbors on a deeper level. I really was not eager yet to share my basic Christian concepts, except in a nice discussion that remained on a certain plateau. I was amazed after talking about God how some others opened up. They shared how fearful they had been in the storm, after trying long-forgotten prayers.

"Finally, we reached Taipei, then known as Formosa, a Japanese colony. Fresh water was stocked, and we were allowed to come on deck in groups of fifty. The blue winter sky was warm enough. I had been on deck daily to use the bathroom board outside the ship. At first, it took some conviction to do this, for climbing over the railing dozens of feet above the waves of the ocean was a new adventure in satisfying one's physical needs.

"But now I could walk around. We looked differently after two weeks in the holds of the ship. Our tropical tan had worn off, and it was strange to look at the pale, sunken cheeks of many men; all of us covered with half-grown beards. But the fresh air and the sun were a bonus. The next day we left Taipei and back to dark holds we went. One of the recreational aspects was to look through our porthole at the other ships in our convey. This view suddenly took on a fearful dimension. We heard the barking of the anti-aircraft guns in front of the ship. We first thought it was another drill until our ship shook as if it had been lifted out of the water. We realized that we were being bombed. We heard planes overhead, and saw bombs falling into the water uncomfortably close. There was utter silence in the holds. Faces were taut. We knew of ships having been torpedoed by America submarines, unaware that there had been POWs on board, for no ship was marked that way by the Japanese.

"There was a big explosion and through the porthole we saw the ship next to us had been hit. It soon was listing badly, and lifeboats were put overboard. I saw tense faces. Some lips were mumbling prayers. I thought about my family. It was my wife's birthday, November 27. They were never far from my thoughts. That morning, as always, I had prayed for my family that we might be back tougher on her next birthday in 1944.

"I knew that it was not raw courage in me, but that it was what we call grace, just another name for God's strange love; not coming in from far away, but already there to be discovered in oneself. I began talking with others; softly talking. I do not remember what I said but it had something to do with trust in God. We prayed that God would see us through: 'Your will, not ours Lord' ended most of these prayers. Suddenly Christ's prayer in Gethsemane became crystal clear, except that he could choose, and how atrocious a choice for a young man. If we died, it was not by choice, but as victims of war.

"The bombing seemed to taper off. At one point some voices began to sing a Dutch hymn while the bombing went on, more off than on. In the corner where Pieter Volten sat, smoke, like a lazy billow, began to roll through the holds. Hesitating voices joined in singing a Dutch hymn, of which one of the verses went, 'Fierce storms may rage, everything around me may be night, God, my God will protect me. God will watch over my being.' Soon, as the voices grew louder it permeated the holds of the ship with peace, calm, and courage.

"The lifeboats of the ship next to us were headed for the *Hawaii Maru*, and suddenly we heard the familiar Japanese screams, driving people into the aft and holds of our ship. We had been separated from our fellow prisoners since we left Singapore. They came down the two ladders, but there was no grumbling, we just made space for them.

"We never understood why the planes left and had not finished us off. Maybe they were Chinese bombers not as accurate as the Americans. Much later we realized another escape might have occurred. We could easily have been finished off, pilots radioing their bases and pinpointing our convoy. We noticed suddenly that we were alone on the ocean. The rest of the convoy had left us. Were we a sacrificial lamb, a decoy? We stayed all day at the spot where there had been bombing, and left by night. We were never bombed again, nor did we ever catch up with the convoy. We also speculated that other bombers had found the rest of the convoy and finished the job, by sinking all the ships. We zigzagged for days and finally reached Shanghai, where we stayed for several days. It was early December now and the cold winter days in Shanghai did nothing to comfort us, except we were safe in its harbor. A few days later we reached Japan.

"That same night, two years back, on St. Nicholas Day, we had celebrated with friends from Malang. The baby room in our house was proudly shown; ready to receive our first child. Two days later Pearl Harbor was bombed. The baby room was never used. Now two years later I knew nothing of my wife and baby. Were they alive? Where could they be? No contact for all this time. The weather was frigid. Five years of life in the tropics had thinned our blood and though we were happy to leave the rattrap *Hawaii Maru*, the intense cold seemed little improvement.

"On reaching the dock soldiers sprayed us to delouse us. Fortunately we were immediately taken through a long tunnel under the sea arm to the city of Modji and put in a big hall. It was cold there, but there was light, some food, and colored water which was called tea. I looked for Pieter and other friends. Then the transport was split, one going south, one going north. Pieter and others went south. As the line began to form a line, I stood near them. I was biting my lips, for now there were none left of my Oxford Group friends, or other church friends. Pieter smiled, and I will never forget his final words: 'Till we meet again, Jop. If not on earth, then the communion with God will have been completed.'

"When we were liberated and in Manila, I heard Pieter's completed communion with God had happened eight days earlier. In the mining camp Fukuoka, where he had been, Pieter had developed a severe fever and cold and was unable to go to work. When he half collapsed, the Japanese guards had ordered him to stand at attention. When he was unable to do so, they beat him to death with the butts of their guns. So ended a remarkable life in this world, to find the greater reality in the next experience of living. I lost a man who had been instrumental in the changing of both many others' lives and my own.

"The next morning, we reached Osaka in a drizzling rain and camped in the middle of an industrial complex. There were four hundred American marines, caught in northern China. They greeted us and told us that the place was not bad, after getting used to it. It was the Tsumori concentration camp, our destiny until May 1945. Of the three thousand men who left the Tjimahi camp, only 339 were sent to Osaka, Japan. Others stayed in Singapore, went to the Burma railroad, on to Fukuoka in southern Japan. The night we arrived, St. Nicholas evening, December 5, we sat surrounded by utter misery. It was near 20 degrees below zero. One Eurasian chap was near death; few spoke up and there was an eerie atmosphere in our barracks, and probably in the others too. I looked around and thought of Pieter Volten, Siestse Van Dyke, and Dennis Moppet thousands of miles south in the Amboina region of Indonesia. They probably were involved with others around them. On board I had opened up to others, but here I did not know a soul. Who would want to hear comfort in words, if their greatest need was food, warm clothing, a fire?

"It was a strange Saint Nicholas evening. I remembered the great Christmas Eves in the past with the family, the presents, love of family. But that Saint Nicholas Eve I got a present too. I am not sure what to call it, maybe courage. Maybe, for by nature I tended to take the most cautious ways. I got up and saw misery everywhere. People had their hands under their armpits to keep warm. I walked to the nearest corner without any clear perception of what I was going to say or do. Suddenly I found myself beside a Dutch man by the name of Goosens. I had been in Christian groups with him before. He was a rigid Calvinistic thinker for whom the trappings of faith, at times, seemed more important than the faith they served. Still he had a tremendous faith that all things were in God's hands, and that we should trust in God's will.

"On the *Hawaii Maru* he had expressed this dominant aspect of his faith, and it had provided comfort to some. His generally stony face, now ash grey with cold, though, did not invite conversation. He was probably the last one I wanted to talk with about the camp church comforting others, but there was no one else. Had God made me trip over Goosens? God has strange ways for us. It dawned on me that I should at least talk with Goosens. The topic was an obvious one. Each time when we entered a new camp, whether there were chaplains or not, the community came to life in various ways. Courses were offered, in many fields of study, choirs, and even acting groups emerged, regardless of how feeble the health of the people.

"There is in us, at least in most of us, an indomitable drive to stay alive, mentally, physically, and spiritually. All the above mainly dealt with staying mentally alert. All of us by this time knew that we had been at least turned a quarter off our normal psychological axis, and it was the human element in human beings to fight this. Then when the camp community began to function, generally weeks later, a camp church began to emerge, a service would be announced; but tonight, we could not wait, one man was already dying, despair was all around us.

"That a camp church did not have to begin with a group of people, a council, doing some planning, that was in my grasping like the book of Acts, the early church that had just swung into action because of Pentecost through the work of the Holy Spirit. That night Goosens and I were called to be the church of Christ in this barracks! The stony-faced Goosens nodded at me as I told him that I was on my way to the nearby corner of our barracks. Without saying a word he got up and followed me. I knew he had been an elder and hoped he would help lead the formation of this new camp church. He had, I thought, shared in my thinking.

"The nearby corner happened to be filled with a group of professional colonial Dutch soldiers, great experts in profane language the least promising crowd to initiate a camp church, even with the Holy Spirit working around us. They looked up. Goosens remained silent, so finally I began to talk. I only remember saying that we had each other for support, and that I believed, in my understanding of faith, God was never absent. God knew all about human suffering through Jesus, in whom God was present in a very different way than anyone else. God was still present in each of us, whether we ever had thought about it or not. That God would be able to make a difference here, this hour and any hour. I then stopped, feeling totally inadequate, thinking they would probably tell us to cut it out, and get lost.

"I recognized one older soldier, a trumpeter, always boasting about his latest experience in a brothel. He stared at me, and a faint feeling in me wondered about what I had just said; God in him too. He nodded slowly, as if he was trying to recall something far back in his life. It was just a morsel of hope in this fool's paradise. Some distant memory of a Bible verse, where Jesus was said to be a friend of whores and traitors.

"I asked, 'Would you be willing to talk to the God in us? Talking sometimes helps, I think.' Several nodded and began to close their eyes, I did the same and again I waited for Goosens. It was painfully silent; he did not pray aloud, he who must have uttered hundreds of prayers as an elder and churchgoer. So I talked aloud to that creator of ours, without ever remembering what I said. When I finished, the old trumpeter took my hand and simply said, 'Thank you, mate.' As I lay in my bed in the barracks that first night I wondered about how God works in such seemingly small interventions. Perhaps by Goosens remaining silent God had been able to take this new faith initiative through me. Whatever happened that night in the corner of our barracks, it was the beginning of the Church Under the Cross, and from that night on, each evening we met to close the day together with the Creator Spirit.

"I was soon to meet Captain Warren Minton. He was one of the few officers, American or Dutch, with a deep commitment to his men. He interceded repeatedly, and more than once was beaten for insisting that the Japanese provide more medicine and food. He and I studied American literature together during most of the time in Tsumori camp. He was also the one who got me interested in this country, and after the war helped me to come to this country. His main valor was his humanity. He was also a leader in the American camp church.

"It was only a year back, but it seemed a decade. The Jaarmarkt was a bad camp, but it was fairly heaven compared to the winter, the darkness, the polluted air in the harbor district of Osaka, Japan. It was probably the saddest Christmas ever. There was too much death, hunger, hopelessness among us. Yet there had been something very meaningful that evening. We had worked, as usual, in the factory that day, but the night was not dark, it was light in our experience. At times the most encouraging experience does not come in the moment of victory, but in the deepest point of a gloomy valley. At our moment of despair there was a moment of singing, praying for our loved ones, of hope, though there was little to hope for. The hope was our co-suffering God, regardless of how we perceived the eternal.

"The year 1944 began with a somber mood. Dozens of people were dying or already dead. For each one there was a Protestant or Roman Catholic service and Captain Warren Minton attended each service. We got up at 5:30 a.m.; a bleak morning hour. The wind was always penetratingly cold, almost blowing through us. Our camp had eight barracks. When we returned by 5:30 p.m. there was a small coal fire in the center of the rectangular barracks. We had received Japanese uniforms, which at first caused some hilarity. They were too small. We looked like huge caricatures of the Japanese; little caps, on our shaven heads, sleeves far too short, the same with our trousers, but we were still warmer than we had been before.

"The entire camp had been divided into work details at various factories around the camp. I was part of a detail marching off each morning to the harbor area. We were handed over to Japanese civilians who took us in small groups to our assignments. At noon we returned to an area with tables. The invariable fish soup was served, with sick-looking pieces of bread. If one was lucky, one might find a fish head in his dish.

"It was another reality to work with the Japanese civilians. It seemed like we were entering another world. The fact was that they were shy, and remained a bit distant throughout the time we worked together; mainly because they feared the guards too. They sprang from the same roots as the guards. Since they had not been exposed to the mystical atmosphere of the Samurai military culture, they seemed to relate to us, as people. Still their devotion to their emperor, a descendant of the sun goddess, was unmistakable.

"Going back to the barracks Saturday night we never knew if all our friends would still be alive. Quite a few people wanted to join the camp church. The church council simply suggested they would be received by statement of faith. There was no time to prepare the men for any confirmation classes, as held in previous camps. It was out of the question. At this camp it was like walking a thin line between life and death. Even the ability to study together was an uncertainty. Seemingly quite healthy people might start coughing, have a temperature a few hours later, yet sent to work by the guards, come back with pneumonia, and die a day later.

"One of the men, who had been in the corner Goosens and I had visited that first night in Osaka had come to the camp church from the beginning. His name was Pierik. He was a colonial soldier of little education. Often in our discussions during the church services he apologized for cursing so easily, but nobody gave it a thought. Then he too fell sick. One of the elders visited him and told me that Pierik had asked if God would really accept him. Literally he said, "I know so g.d. little about the Bible, and I am a child in the faith." Questions like these were important to these men because they had probably never been in church, or church school

Or they had threatened them with a dour god to whom they had to give an account of all their sins and then they might, or might not, be forgiven. It was a primitive faith, but it was a faith.

"Teaching was immaterial at this time in the camps. A relationship with others, and God, was the crucial point. Christ had made this possible through his presence in his earthly life, and now we call that presence the Holy Spirit. Pierik nodded as we spoke. He had trouble speaking in his dreadful effort to get air in and out of his dying lungs. We still remember his smile, his face changing into the outward portrayal of a man who felt at rest. The medic told us that his breathing during the night became much easier, and he passed over effortlessly.

"I witnessed other men dying during this period with a simple faith that helped them through this passage. I recall one who in his last hours quietly sang the words to a Dutch Hymn, 'I have had faith and therefore I sing.' Walking back that freezing night I happened to look up at the star-studded sky. I stopped a moment between two barracks and thought of the star-covered nights at Java. Heaven was not anymore for me a special experience, but a relational experience, so heaven was not necessarily up and down.

"God was in our life both as Abba, a loving parent, and the creator of the universe. Pierik had passed over to the Abba who also had created those stars, and yet that Abba's concern, all through the Bible, was with the suffering and deserted. Pierik's body had been killed by a lack of medicine, but he was beyond reach of those who had killed him by withholding needed remedies. As the Japanese could not touch the stars of Abba, they could not even touch the real self, our undying self.

"So many had in one way or another been a beacon for me to grow spiritually, and to liberate myself. If I close my eyes, even now, I can see them again. Through all these years I have deeply hoped that they know how their example comforted and educated me.

"One Japanese coworker told me that it had been one of the coldest winters he had ever been through. In February 1944 I got a cold, the next day I had some breathing problems, and Dr. Ort put me in the small sick bay. Telling me that it was much quieter there. I was not really aware of the implications to be placed there. Not everyone died who entered that small barracks next to the kitchen. It was always filled from corner to corner and pleasantly warm because of its limited space. The medics there served with great care. One of them who attended the camp church, a former schoolteacher, Wim Verhoff, was always alert and seemed to know when someone needed a word of encouragement.

"When my fever got higher and higher, he spent a great deal of time with me, putting cool rags on my forehead and softly talking to me. One morning the places left and right of me were empty. Both men had died during the past night. It never occurred to me that I might die, too, and it was only later that I learned how close to death I had been. Wim had fed me personally to make sure that nobody would steal my food.

"The next morning Dr. Ort came to make his rounds and stopped at my place. I was half asleep. He took my pulse and told Wim Verhoff, 'Take his time.' He thought I was in a coma and I could not hear him. Maybe I was, but later I became aware how people even in a very deep coma could understand what people in the sickroom were talking about, and I was most careful after that not to discuss my patients' cases in their presence.

"Later Wim Verhoff told me that the Japanese required the exact hour of death of each patient: a bureaucratic measure which didn't inspire them to send medicine. However, that week they did. The death rate had become so alarmingly high, and the number of workers in the factories decreased daily, that they finally brought in a new home remedy for pneumonia, sulphonamide. It was then the first effective treatment for pneumonia. The small sick bay held some twenty-five men and most of them had pneumonia. We all got our shots that same morning. In the end only one man and I survived that week. For all the others it had been too late. I still see the other chap standing up, and dancing around, because he had suddenly felt so well. Nevertheless, without any warning, he collapsed and died. His body had rejected the new medicine.

"A few days later I was transferred to the larger sick bay. Dr. Ort welcomed me and said, 'Welcome, De Vries, it is good to see you. I had not expected you to pull through.' What is it to return from death? Why? The camp church always prayed for all in the death sick bay. What kind of God was it who pulled me through and not the others? It felt like a double dose of responsibility which God had descended upon me. I had survived and so many others had died. Maybe life or death depends on miniscule matters: some physical, some spiritual, and I wanted to live for my wife and child. But I am sure that the others had wanted the same. Pierik, the man who had quietly sung the Dutch hymn as he did, the fellow who had danced around in excitement that he would live, only to collapse and die.

"I have wrestled with this question for many years. The final answer I found was that someone, outside myself, wanted to care for me, and did. He loved me unconditionally whether I had gone to that next reality or stayed on in this world. In the end I knew that I was not to solve the problem of 'why.' God who never gave an exact answer to Job or to Jesus of Nazareth went beyond giving answers. The Spirit was giving of itself, if only we would leap in faith into the arms of Abba, the New Testament Father Being. And those who never leaped in this life? The reasons were countless why people did not find God before dying.

"We saw in the loneliness of camp life that many had never been given any resources, and had no notion of the caring Creator. Could the patience of the One Who created them carry on long after this earthly life would be over? Out of the life and death experiences came, like a path in the jungle, an insight of the Christian as a coinherent lover of humankind. I could not solve the matter of 'why,' the only other survivor in that bay died.

"It was at that time, when I was thrown back into this world, that I began to understand the healing work of Christ, not just physically, but also in the healing of the whole person: those oppressed by fascist, communist, or capitalist governments, the physically troubled, the suffering, and in so many other forms. We talked about it, and my friends not only understood, but I perceived how innocently I had just steered my life in the direction of my own success. It did not break me into pieces, but I was glad now to have learned about living again to a much fuller degree.

"I remember when it was my turn to lead the service, I told the story of Jesus healing Lazarus, but Lazarus in the end died again. I tried to say that this was what we all had to face. Jesus knew this, and so did Lazarus. Jesus loved his friend so much that he called him back to live on in his life; and this life, as long as we lived it, it was crucial what we make of it."

Jop suddenly paused. "Don, this might be a good place for me to stop. The next set of experiences start with a clash between those who insisted on a more institutional type of Christianity, in the camps, and those with more open-ended ecumenical and lived-out experiences of faith. I will also share with you a pivotal miraculous experience I had in the camps. As you recall, I had mentioned earlier that we might need an extra session for me to share my POW experiences in greater detail. Next week's session, our fifth, will be the extra one. We will then end the following week with our final session, and with my sharing about our liberation from the camps."

Miracle in the Camp

The week in between Don's fourth and fifth interviews of Jop turned out to be even more routine than usual. Nothing eventful happened that Don could recall, except that he waited with excited anticipation for his next interview with Jop. McCall's question for him to ask Jop had remained the same, but Don knew the experiences Jop would share next might well offer some of the faith understandings he so desperately sought. The week seemed to pass quickly, and Don once more found himself sitting across from Jop, waiting for him to start sharing the next installment of his camp experiences. Jop did not keep him waiting. He took a couple sips from his mug of coffee before he put it down and looked to Don to re-ask his question. Pausing for a few moments, Jop then began to share his recollections of some of his most difficult, and transformative, experiences in the camps.

"The hard winter finally killed itself in the face of spring. I do not know why we had waited so long to celebrate Holy Communion. We decided to celebrate it on Good Friday in 1944. The camp kitchen gave us some left-over strips of rice which otherwise, because it was burned, would have been thrown out. We used an army mug as a chalice, with water instead of wine. For several people, who had joined the camp church, it would be the first time to celebrate communion.

"There was an uneasiness about this, because it was such a sacred matter. Later that month it was decided that Goosens, the strict Dutch Calvinist, would design the articles of the institution of the camp church. They were doctrinal statements, and I wondered how important they were to this time and place. The three articles of unity drawn up by the Dutch Synod of Dordrecht, so crucial for Calvinists, were part of it. It also stated the church council would make sure that only those who really belonged to the believers would have access to communion. In the reality of everyday camp life, those articles never made any difference, and nobody was ever denied communion. The most important article was that each member was a fellow minister to the others, at the camp, and at work. The way a member carried out his daily relationship, from Christ to others, would determine if one was a Christian. It was to see in everyone the image of God, as Christ did.

"The articles did not survive long, as they were lost during one of the many Japanese inspections. Joost Wentwick, a leader in the church camp, was a wide-open Christian, and so lovable, that excluding anyone from Holy Communion seemed an unnecessary action. Other church camp leaders did not want to be exclusive but adhered to the holiness of the sacrament and reminded all who partook of this. Goosens, however, was the inflexible Calvinist who, from criticizing my marking up my New Testament to refusing to be part of a camp church community that would not stick to these articles of unity of the Reformed faith, could not give ground even when the trappings of religion threatened to extinguish the true Spirit of faith in the most dire human circumstances. People were still dying in the small sick bay while we were discussing the need, or not, of those articles of faith. One night the medics carried the corpses of three men into our barracks. We had lost so many men in that barracks that the camp commander had made it a morgue as well. As a few of us looked at the three dead men we were strangely silent. It was then that we uttered the word 'obscene.' We had talked as a council about the articles of faith to be accepted in order to join the camp church, and these three men had died at the same time.

"I told the others I was quitting the camp church council. One of my fellow members, a man named Kortweg, who was silent at first, put his hand on my arm and said, 'I feel the same way, but it will tear the camp church apart, and that will be just as obscene.' We talked some more, and decided to accept the articles of faith and then just ignore them. The reality was that most of the men in the camp church could have cared less about accepting or rejecting the articles of faith. I came to begrudgingly respect Goosens strong theological sense, and the importance, at times, not to be vague about what one believed. Yet it was a more important step for me to differentiate between human understandings of God, and sharing the love of God in Christ in relationships with others, particularly in the camps." Jop paused to take a sip of coffee.

Don found himself wondering about all the contemporary Goosens in so many traditional churches. For while an epidemic number of traditional Christians may not be dying physically, it could be argued they were spiritually. With secular culture increasingly challenging, mocking, and marginalizing the faith, was not the church in a radically different way in a precarious state? Were the preoccupations with and entrenchments behind institutional church forms, on the part of contemporary Goosens, in their own way not also obscene? Was not the force of faith, as had happened so often in Christendom, being replaced by the forms of religion? These thoughts passed quickly through Don's mind, after which he once again directed his attention to what Jop would share next. Having put his coffee mug back down Jop resumed.

"The spring and summer of 1944 were mild and sunny. The death rate quickly dropped. I was now working inside the factory. Dr. Ort had said that he would like to keep me longer at the camp for recuperation, but that I was now one of many who were less weak than others, and given the criterion of the Japanese he had to send me back to work. With working inside the factory, and the mild spring weather, I regained strength.

"Working in the factory offered the chance to get to know the Japanese factory workers. We talked through broken English, and the most fragmented Japanese, from my side. The difference with the guards, many of whom were Korean, and the factory workers did not seem obvious, but slowly we trusted each other. One time I showed them pictures of my wife and child, and a shy smile appeared on their faces. One woman nodded several times, and then said something that I only understood later, after a friend who knew more Japanese than me had translated 'senso yeroshikenai' as 'war is not good.'

"As the war progressed that term was used more and more by the Japanese. The brutal training of the army soldiers had changed the conscripts and made them different from the blue-collar workers. They all felt in them that imperceptible murmuring of Japan's archaic and in reality racial soul. They obeyed its prompting and the legends of the past were so deeply believed by each Japanese that they reminded me of extremely fundamentalist Christians who forbade any question of what the Bible teaches. For generations it had been taught, and lived, that they were (through the emperor) all descendants of the sun goddess. It was the consolation to the lower classes, and fertile soil to the Samurai upper military groups.

"Every day we had to face the guards. They would search us, and if the slightest contraband was found, they would hit us with their gun butts. It was in the fall of 1944, a chilly day, that I was assigned to clear iron scrap from the rotary drums. We were always amazed about the lack of industry. The Japanese often used oxen and human traction. Neither could we understand the Japanese cruelty and abuse of POWs, given that they had to be aware of the rules of 1929 Geneva Convention governing the treatment of prisoners. One time a worker was electrocuted because bare electric wires hung over our heads. The iron scraps were put in the rotating drum together with iron cast ship implements which the factory produced. Then I had to pull a handle, and the drum started rolling. The iron scraps' function was to clean the new implements of rust.

"It was a gray day, and after I had shoveled the iron scrap out of the last drum, I rested on my shovel. Of course I checked if any guard was doing the rounds. I had crossed paths with remarkable Christians in the camps. Their insights often offered me just the message I needed at a particular time, and had nurtured not only my faith, but my understanding of how to live it. Still an anger was welling up in me. The winter was coming; we had now been away some two and half years from our families. We never heard anything after their last visit to the Jaarmarkt. There was an anger about the lostness of years, of being twenty-seven and having already spent three birthdays in concentration camps. Suddenly in a mood of utter anger I kicked the heap of iron pieces, which flew back and landed on the tip of my boot. I did not curse God, but vented all my anger, and grief in a torrent of emotion to God. My kick, at least, had released the tension, and I was ready to start work again, when I noticed the piece of iron on my boot. It startled me. All the pieces had different forms, leftovers, and cutoffs, waste material, less useful than anything else except to get the dirt and rust off the iron cast tools. I slowly bent over and let the iron scrap rest in my hand. It was in the form of a cross four inches long. I kept staring at it, forgetting all about the guard who might come along at any time. I never speculated how it got in the heap, how just this piece hit the door, when I kicked the heap apart, how it landed on my boot. There are a million accidental events that happen on any given day. Somehow, this seemed like a message and an answer to my self-questioning a short time back; what in God's name am I doing in this God-forsaken place? It had been in the same mass of scrap iron for days. I had shoveled the scrap in the rotating drum over and over, to glance off the big implements and remove the rust.

"The cross in my mind had always been a big question mark. How could a man on a cross, two thousand years back, have any usefulness in our time? Slowly I began to perceive that the event might have a purpose now. Jesus of Nazareth was put on a cross by people who absolutely rejected the unconditional love of God expressed in that cross, and then shared by Christians with others. People came and lived and died by that cross, and the strange power of that cross went on in human beings generation after generation unexplainably. People died for it in fierce confession of their faith, in giving their lives for others. The cross was never totally gone from this world, whatever happened outside Jerusalem in AD 33. Now it had jumped onto my boot. I let it roll back and forth in my hand. This little insignificant piece of iron scrap had cleaned far more important pieces of iron, it was only an implement. When I opened the drum several times a day, the big pieces came out clear and well. Maybe being a Christian was doing the same thing.

"Now over forty years later, I still see that little shed where I worked by myself, the door with its broken windows patched up. It was a strange encounter between an Eternal Spirit, and a mortal being. Slowly, ever so slowly, I seemed to hear in perfect Dutch, which I will translate for you, 'If anyone would come after me, let that one deny oneself, and take up the cross and follow me wherever I go.' It was somewhere in the Gospels, but most of all it was in this utterly hopeless life in the Tsumori camp. Even in this concentration camp, ultimately I was a free man. I was free to reject the 'nonsense' of a God who cares. A God who was in people in this camp in my fellow Japanese laborers, yes, even in the guards. I could also try it again and again. It was in those moments of starting again behind that mystery man the Christ.

"Suddenly I heard the screaming voice of a guard, but he was not yet in sight. I wanted to take the scrap iron cross home to my barracks, but there was only one way they might not search me. If I was lucky. It was in my boot on whose tip it had landed. Arriving at the camp, they indeed skipped my group in searching for contraband. When I took the rags off my foot, it was quite bloody, so was the little cross; but I could wash it off. Even now when I look at that piece of iron scrap, which accompanied me all over the world, and I wore every time I addressed the many groups I was invited to speak to, it calls me back to the freedom Christ gives all of us. I have clutched it in difficult moments, was asked over and over again where I bought it. I will never know what it did for others, with whom I have shared its story. The dream that I was a free man, the moment I found it, slowly became a reality.

"Christmas 1944 came into sight, the third Christmas in the camps. We had planned ahead of time with the Americans, with the English who had come to Tsumori in 1944, with Roman Catholics and Protestants, with churchgoers and non-churchgoers. It had been a chilly autumn, and a cold winter was in sight. Our average weight had gone down to 120 pounds, our resistance feeble. In November, I was again in the sick bay with pneumonia.

"Dr. Ort put me in the large sick bay which indicated that this sickness was not critical. This time it was a welcome break. Once my fever returned to normal [that was 102, for at 100 one was sent to work in the factories again] I had a chance to meet several Americans I did not know yet. The marines who worked in the same factory had become good buddies, and we had many chats about life in the States. For some reason most of them were from Texas, a state I remembered from Java when the Major had sent me to make contact with the American Colonel of a regiment of American artillery soldiers who had just arrived.

"When I was at the schoolhouse where the Americans were stationed, I met a lanky young man with his legs propped on a school desk. I assumed that he was a private, and we talked for a few moments. He was most easy go-ing. I asked if he was one of the Americans, and he nodded and said in a kind of English which was hard to follow, 'Yep, kind of an American, but more than that I am a Texan.' This meant nothing to me at the time. Then he talked at length about Texas, which did not help me either. Slowly I became aware that Texas was a state which considered itself, more or less, as belonging to the United States. When I finally asked to see the colonel, he smiled and said that he was sitting in front of me! He was it. But we got along well, as I remained the liaison between our two regiments.

"In the camps, on the whole, the Yankees and the Dutch got along splen-didly, though most Dutch also made friends with the limeys, as they were called. The second evening we met Americans who had been caught when Wake Island fell. One of them stopped near me and asked if I had salt. He offered me a sweater. I had no idea how much salt to offer him and made a bid. He looked at me, and shook his head, and told me that I was offering far too much. Salt was in short supply. He took half of what I offered, and I got a much-needed sweater. Church Varney and I became close friends.

"He had a common interest in geography, and we smuggled an empty cement bag into the camp. Many evenings, for months on end, we worked to develop a map of the United States. When it was finished, I was able to hide it. The Japanese were paranoid with respect to maps. They never found our map, and later on it covered my wall for decades. People were amazed at how Chuck, who at the time had a high school diploma, was able from memory to draw states, mountains, rivers, cities, and coastlines with near perfection. Chuck was later to become a professor of geography at the University of Wisconsin.

"We were severely deprived of food during the summer and fall of 1944. Still the fall was a more relaxed time that enabled me to rest up be-fore we entered that last very bad winter of 1944/1945. The food situation became increasingly desperate, however. The little bread we had received was cancelled. The fish soup at the factory had less and less fish heads. The Japanese civilians seemed to have less rice in their wooden boxes. Men fainted at work, and in the camp. One night when we had gathered in our barracks, a man said, 'You can pray for food can't you.' This was a dubious matter. Would God direct the Japanese to increase our food when the Japa-nese themselves had less to eat? One did not discuss this issue even when our weight decreased to an average of 110 pounds.

"So we prayed for food. In a few days the other men who closed the day with prayer did too. Nothing seemed to change. I remember laying on my back one night staring in the darkness. I had just filled my stom-ach with water to still the hunger pain. I pictured the feeding of the five

thousand. Was this a parable written down for the early church to empha-
size Christ's power, or did it really happen? I had never thought about the
possibility, and somewhere in me I had to believe it; I had to for all of us
in that corner; all with a hunger about which we strangely enough never
talked much. I had to believe in miracles; not because it was written in the
Bible alone, but because we were so desperately in need of one, so I prayed,
convinced it would happen!

"It was November 27, again my wife's birthday, the third one I would
miss. It was a beautiful day with deep blue skies. There was an air raid
siren to which we paid no attention. There were many air raid drills. Suddenly, the guards came running toward us, screaming, hitting a few, and
driving us to the main road back to the camp. There was a general con-
sternation, as nobody expected an air attack. Then the man in front of me
suddenly stopped, and I bumped into him. He slowly raised his arm, and
his trembling hand to the sky. The whole group of men, even the Japanese
looked up. In the deep blue sky were huge planes, perhaps sixty. We could
faintly see the stars of the American Air Force, and suddenly there was the
shouting of hurrahs, and then the guards started hitting us with their guns
and got us going again.

"We had to run because the planes circled. There were no Japanese
fighter planes anywhere around. We had largely reached the Tsumori
camp when the dull thuds of falling bombs were heard; but always at a
great distance. We did not even try to take shelter. We peered through the
doors, but did not see the planes again. A year before on November 27,
our prison ships were bombed but we had escaped. Again today, on my
wife's birthday, we escaped.

"This was the great turning point of the war. Finally, after all those
years of waiting, we had seen the American planes. There was a stirring
sensation; we had seen them with our own eyes, and all the information
from the secret radio seemed loudly confirmed. We thought it might all be
over by Christmas, or at least by spring. So many died before it was finally
over, among them some of my best friends.

"The camp kept praying for food. We saw people in the camp church
that never before came near it. It was not just the hunger, it was a belief,
maybe primitive in some, maybe deep in others, that something would
come in, maybe at Christmas. Christmas a year back had marked our en-
try into this hellish place. The weeks passed, the sick died faster. The fairly
healthy got sick, and the bombing became more intensive.

"Then the miracle happened! The day before Christmas, when we returned from the factory, we sensed a mood change. The officers stood outside and waved. The kitchen crew was outside. We ran to the barracks, and

there, at each man's place, was a square box with a red cross printed on top. Some tore it open; others stared for a while. Then came the moment of see-ing all that had come: butter, bread, razor blades, cheese. We were, as always, sitting on the floor with all the gifts around us. Some tore the cover off the Nestlé bars and ate, but slowly. It was concentrated, and each little square had the nourishment of three bars of chocolate.

"Eating together there was an out pouring of gratitude to God, and also to the Swedish merchant marine who had anchored and deposited the food. They had seen to it that it had reached the camps in Osaka. I thought again of my wife and child. The baby would now have been three years old. I had not been able to be at one of her birthdays. In a bittersweet daydream that she was yet alive, I imagined myself saving a candy bar for her. It made no sense.

"Christmas 1944, the third in the camps, we celebrated together with our Roman Catholic friends and with the Americans and English. We were also joined by humanists, such as a botany teacher who became a friend of mine, and the many agnostics among us. For it meant more and more that there is a Spirit in this world attempting the impossible, at least from a world-ly perspective. It is not crucial to define that Spirit narrowly as working only through Christians or certain Christians. The caring was crucial wherever it came from. For me, it was an outpouring of the Spirit.

"Christmas 1944 did not have the horror of 1943. In retrospect, I perceived that after an entire year in the camp, with high wire fences, tow-ers with machine guns, there had come an adjustment humans are able to achieve. There was camaraderie, the daily life in the factories. I have often been far more lonely in the postwar years than in the camps. We were not hungry alone, nobody died alone, except when death came too fast. When one was down, another noticed. Though we could write cards to our family once in a great while, they never reached them. They only reached us when a wife or child had died. One day, a man just stood frozen. He kept say-ing, 'But my children, but my children.' There was no mention in the card, written by another woman. She was only allowed to write about death." Jop seemed to pause here. The sad wistful smile on his face made Don think of the two old photos that sat at one end of the middle shelf behind Jop's chair. One was a picture of Jop and the pretty dark-haired young woman sitting on a coach Don now knew was Irene, her legs across his lap. The other a picture of Jop, and the same young woman holding a baby sitting together on the front steps of a building.

Don felt an overwhelming desire to ask Jop what had happened to Irene and Renee. He hesitated a moment partly because he didn't want to break the protocol, in place, that once the question for the session was asked, Don did not interrupt, or at least did so seldomly. Don knew that to do so could disturb the natural flow of Jop's story and might derail it. Don was also worried about coming off as insensitive, in any way, by how he asked the question. Perhaps Jop would share this information in the last interview when the camp was finally liberated. Still an appropriate context had arisen, and what if Jop chose to avoid the subject. Don asked the question with as gentle and as respectful a tone and as indirectly as he could to give Jop space to deflect the question if for whatever reason he wanted to do this.

"Jop, I noticed a couple of older photos on the shelf behind you, are they of Irene, you, and Renee?" Don asked. Jop looked directly at Don and smiled in a knowing way that indicated that he knew this question or topic would have to come up sooner or later. "Don, this is the one subject I still have trouble speaking about. I too received a card one day. It was during the late winter of 1944. The card gave me the news I had most dreaded to hear, that my wife and child had both passed over that winter. I later learned that my baby had died first, and after that, that my wife had given up on life. The news devastated me and challenged my faith to its core. Only the loving support of friends within the Christian camp church kept me from giving up as well. At that time when I felt farthest from God, I really was the closest, for that is when I needed God most. The revelation of the iron cross had brought me to the brink of a decision, of a leap of faith. I had lost everything but my faith, and now I needed to decide whether to throw that away as well. My decision to trust God not only with the incredible pain, but anger I felt, did not make this pain go away, or even ease it right away. In fact for a time I railed at God. I had not so much made the decision for faith, as to stay turned toward God. You might say I got in God's face, as they say today. I directed all my anger at God and accused God of utterly deserting me, despite all my openness to God and to those who guided me toward God in the camps. I was not consciously quoting Psalm 22, or trying to imitate Christ on the cross here, I was really feeling utterly abandoned by the God whose love I had sought and had thought I had experienced. I said other things to God at the time, and for some time after, that I would be ashamed to share with anyone. I have come to accept that I either needed to say these things, at the time, or I would turn my back on God. Somehow, though my heart was utterly broken in a thousand pieces, Paul's words from 2 Corinthians 12:9 echoed in my head, 'My grace is sufficient for you, for my power is made perfect in weakness.'

"It was in the end not the words in themselves, on biblical authority alone, that made any difference. It was the outpouring of love from friends and fellow Christians, and the growing experience over time, that if the God I had thought I knew in Jesus Christ was really there. These experiences enabled me to slowly trust that God could not only handle whatever I said in the outpourings of anger and grief but hold me and love me through them. My experience of God's grace, in that cast-off iron cross, not only put before me a faith decision, it offered me, if not confirmation, a strong suspicion that God's grace might be sufficient for me. In a way that I could not yet grasp, or fully appreciate, I dared to hope that that grace would one day be sufficient to bear up and bind up all the broken pieces of my heart with his loving hands.

"I also had a vision, as I held that iron cross in my hands, of the suffering Christ with both my wife and daughter as they crossed into the light of the next reality in God's love. I am still healing these many years later from their loss but I know when we will meet again. I remarried, as you know, soon after I came to this country. My children are now grown with families of their own, but we are a close family, and Marie and I often have grandchildren running through the house reminding us of the many blessing God has bestowed on us. The only thing I know for sure—and there are many questions I still have for God, that arose from this life tragedy and my camp experiences—is that God's love is the strongest force in this universe, and that its bonds extend from this world into the next and back. That same love, in the form of Christ's grace, not only has the power to forgive sins, but to bind up the broken hearted."

Don had been listening intently, and trying to absorb something of the depth of Jop's loss and grief, while at the same time appreciating, and hoping he might someday too experience more fully the deep healing potential of God's grace. Jop shifted in his seat, and took a deep breath, and then returning to his narrative he attempted to pick up where he had left off, or at least close to it. "One big sailor from Ijmuiden who lived in our barracks was one of the few men who looked superb. He was never sick, never had colds, and with a big smile gave everyone he met a lift. We would sit and talk. He would tell me of his hometown, long walks along the North Sea canal, the ships he watched coming in and out, which led him to enlist in the Dutch Navy. One night when I was visiting the sick in the death sick bay, I saw a man near death. He looked vaguely familiar. The rattling sound which came from his chest indicated he was dying of pneumonia. It was only a few weeks after Christmas. I sat down with him, but he was already in a coma. In a short span of weeks he had been reduced into an emaciated figure. I thought of his family in Ijmuiden, who he had been sure he would see again. On what did it depend to survive? What did one live for to come through this camp? Beaulieu was unmarried, and the cheer of everyone he met. I knew my reason to live through, which had been at first only my wife and child, then them together with my faith and Christian relationships. Now the mustard seed of what was left of that faith had to carry me forward alone.

"The question of suffering was not solved by Job. The Creator Spirit, who formed women and men could not wish disease upon them. That Spirit did not create suffering, but was in all hours of human suffering, if only humans would share that presence in their own lives as Beaulieu had done. We did not talk about death often, but it was clear that many thought about it. The uncanny thing was that some wiry men in their fifties were seldom ill. Those under twenty seemed to die first, followed by the group between thirty-five and fifty. Dr. Ort said that those between twenty and forty had the best chance to pull through. Exceptions clouded the issue. My own first bout with double pneumonia taught me that.

"The winter of 1945 trailed on and on. The one moment of the week we looked forward to happened on Fridays, and that was steaming bath. It had been weekly, then it became twice a month, and in 1945's winter, only every now and then. It was in a shed next to the death bay. The American marines kidded that if you caught a cold taking a bath, you could simply go next door to die.

"The first time I saw it, it looked like a surrealistic painting. Steaming hot water, the whole shed filled with steam, clothes hanging on hooks, the little windows all filled with moisture. Closely shaved heads, emaciated faces, bobbing in the fog of filthy water, showed expressions of sheer bliss. There was place for thirty men at a time, though being in very warm water was an experience that changed a human body from a constantly cold state of temperature to one that approached normalcy. There was an easy coming and going from the water. At times we showered, ran to the barracks, and fell into a deep sleep.

"As the winter wore on, the day bombings became night bombings. Each night the sky over Osaka was lit up in a different place. The harbor was gradually destroyed, but our factory escaped a direct hit. One night a nearby rubber factory caught fire, and the foul smell hung for days over the camp. The only drawback to the nightly bombing was that we had already worked ten hours during the day.

"Work at the factory was monotonous. I was still inside the plant drilling small holes in cast iron plates. I had no idea of its purpose until Danny Whipple, and American marine, tutored me. It was for the engine room of a ship, and by drilling one more hole to the right, the plate was rendered useless, as it would not correspond with the next plate. They were masters in sabotaging, and we were fast learners. We were never caught. I worked on a German-made machine; next to us were for exact copies made by the Japanese in the prewar years. Next to me worked a middle-aged Japanese man. One morning I asked the 'hanchau' [civilian supervisor] where Nakata-san was, and the hanchau, with a sad smile, told me that Nakata-san had been killed in the bombings of the previous night.

"We now had to rise at 4:30 a.m. in the cold snowy night to go to the factory. The work hours were lengthened to twelve hours. The Japanese civilians we worked with often increasingly repeated the term 'senso Yeroshik emai,' which again means 'war is no good.' What bound us together was the horror of war. I never found out what their attitude toward the war had been in December 1940. Many educated Japanese, including Admiral Yamamoto, had tried to convince the Tojo regime that war with America would not be winnable. I think that many of the common people, who lost their sons all over the Far East, were not excited about the war either.

"Early March 1945, during a rest period, a guard suddenly jumped up and ran out of the building. We wondered for a moment, and then noticed the swaying of a lamp. We had become accustomed to tremors almost weekly, but these were minor earthquakes. We were hardly outside when the building collapsed. We had trouble staying on our feet. It was over in seconds. The instinct of the guard had kept us out of harm's way. Danger had made us respond with counter decisions. Later that afternoon there was another minor tremor.

"In the winter the lice and fleas found a warming spot under our clothes. We wore newspapers over our undershirts. Our clothing took on a grayness. We seldom washed them in winter. Worn sweaters covered the newspapers. Around little fires, at rest periods in the factories, we took them off, and while killing crawling lice, and jumping fleas, we talked about the war. At night the explosions seemed to come closer and closer to the Tsumori camp. We had been ordered to dig fox holes for the Japanese. We also dug them for ourselves, near the main entrance of the barracks. At times, the noiselessness of the current bombing, and the wildfires at the nearby horizon, made us hug the earth outside. An expert told us that the noiseless bombs must be incendiary missiles. There was no ear-shattering boom when they landed.

"On March 12, a clear sky hovered over us. I remembered how clear the skies over Java had been before the war. I remembered cool nights in Modjo Kerto in sleeping bags with my then-pregnant wife. I remembered too how active our unborn baby was. My grief had ebbed just enough for me to treasure, however bittersweetly, these memories. We turned in early, in the camp, because with clear skies, the Americans might fly over earlier than one o'clock in the morning. They did, indeed. A Japanese guard barked a warning at the entrance door. Already alert, we heard the planes over us. We were standing around, when an object came through a roof, and landed in a sand pile near our barracks. In the dim light of the moon we stared at it through the window. Its octagonal form, like a huge pencil, lying there as still as if it had never moved. Then the piercing shout of our missile expert to 'get the hell out of the barracks' and we ran. It was a dud, it never exploded. Outside the camp the incendiary bombs fell, and the sky's darkness was lit by wooden homes burning.

"Then it happened. One of the bombs hit the first barracks where the Americans were housed. Within seconds we were running toward that barracks; men came running out, one was a living torch. Others threw blankets on him. The drills had trained us, and we stood in line passing water buckets. I saw some Americans on the roof, and miraculously the fire was put out. We saw badly burned men, when the initial shock had worn off. The camp was in an amazing motion of working together. Dr. Ort and the other physicians used whatever medication they had to help the wounded. Then, as drawn by a huge magnet, we went to the gates. The shouting of the guards had been stilled. There were no guards anywhere. We walked out of the gates for a moment trying to comprehend what was happening. They had gone; they had run, including the commanding officer. We returned to our barracks, escaping was futile; too many had tried, were immediately recognized and executed.

"The next morning there was an unusual roll call. The men in all barracks slept far beyond the 4:30 a.m. get-up time. At daylight we stood in the snow, in front of the barracks. There was the usual little platform indicating we were in for a speech. At times a high officer, generally an old man, would come and address us in broken English, mainly repeating what they all said: 'Work is good for you, we treat you well if you work well.'

"This time our Japanese camp commander climbed on the platform. We rarely ever saw him. Scarface was his deputy, a mean, always-shouting man with an immense scar from his one ear to his chin. The camp commander seemed happy to leave all the work to Scarface. This time he talked to us. He was very satisfied and praised us for putting out the fire at the barracks. He and the guards had been putting out fires elsewhere. Someone next to me hissed, 'He's lying through his teeth.'

"We were not sure if they had run away in panic. The fact was that no guard had been found for a long time. It was clearly a disgrace to be assigned to a concentration camp, and they took it out on the prisoners. The only exception had been the camp commander at Java Jaarmarkt camp, who had called me to his office. The Japanese officer continued to tell us that we were good, and that he was rewarding us. At that time a truck drove up dragging a dead horse with a rope around its neck. We stared at the animal and noticed that parts of its hind legs were missing. It was quite bloody and was probably killed in the bombing the previous night. It was ours, and for the first time a cheer went up.

"The commander descended his platform, the guards left; the horse was dragged to the kitchen. The other bonus was that we did not have to work that day. I have no idea how the kitchen crew prepared the horse, but at meal time there was extra rice, and horse meat. Later we found out the Japanese would renege on this promise. When the meal was ready, they came to take the best meat to their own quarters. Still, we could not believe our good luck. We guessed that the Japanese were trying to save face, and the whole comedy was part of that effort.

"In the spring of 1945, the Church Under the Cross had many new confessing members, and was more alive than ever. Our average weight was down to 110 pounds. The Japanese weighed us at regular intervals, and Dr. Ort guessed that it was another approach to undermine emotional strength. On Easter of 1945 a strange event took place. It was almost as if God infused in the Japanese what I just mentioned above. We never knew who initiated it, but one morning the entire camp was headed outside to a large meadow across the road. There was a platform with a crucifix, candles, and a kneeling bench. Two of our men there served as altar assistants. We later learned that the Japanese had staged this to impress a delegate from the pope who was coming to see how the POWs were being treated.

"In April, the dietetic problems had grown unbearable. We were mainly fed crude rice, milled in ways that would cause some serious intestinal problems. We all suffered. Diarrhea was the least of the intestinal problems. My diarrhea lasted until the war was over. The only medicine Dr. Ort could offer was charcoal, from the little fires in the center of the barrack. Dysentery was a far worse disease, as it was caused by bacilli. The worst problem for many was beriberi, caused by neuritis, with severe burning in one's legs. It also causes systemic edema. Some of the men had testicles the size of soccer balls. The doctors worked long hours to save lives, and to prevent the fluid from reaching the heart. Beriberi began with swollen ankles, and calves, and often ended in death.

"In April, Dr. Ort sent me to the larger sick bay with beriberi. The swelling in my ankles prevented me from putting on my old shoes. Many men would just cut the upper parts of their boots, but in wintertime this would cause frostbite. My calves were so swollen I could create deep pits by pushing my finger down. At night it was almost impossible to sleep. The neuritis kept our legs in constant motion. I do not remember what treatment I was given, but eventually it eased up and I returned to work.

"One night a guard came in with a big grin on his face and said, 'Bad news, you all, Roosevelt is dead.' We did not know much about the American president, but the marines were stunned, and turned in somber silence. The guard kept grinning. He said: 'Now you lost war.' The secret radio also reported that the new president was one Harry Truman. That night I was visited by a friend, named Paul Driessen, in the large sick bay. An American came in and told of a new president from Missouri. Neither Truman nor Missouri meant anything to us, but there was merriment among the Yankees. They kept shaking their heads saying, 'God help the States, with a man from Missouri as president.' One night after studying American literature with Warren Minton, I left the barracks to be stopped by a guard. In the grass was a smoking cigarette stub. He began to yell at me. I explained that I did not smoke, but he kept pointing at the stub. Warren heard the shouting and joined us, telling the guard that, indeed, I did not smoke. Just then two other Americans came around the corner with another guard. They had been caught smoking in a forbidden area.

"There we stood, the four of us and Scarface, the sergeant major who ruled the camp. He worked himself into a crazy frenzy. As with most of the soldiers, he was a man from the rural districts. He had joined the army and made it to sergeant major. His facial wound probably caused mental problems. Instead of being returned to the front, he was assigned to our camp. This was a deep humiliation for any Japanese soldier, rooted in a belief in the sun goddess, from whom even the most humble Japanese descended. Education played no role in the mysticism of the Japanese. They believed each tale and legend, willing to die for it. They were most willing to kill us too for that faith.

"There was a full moon that night, and somehow Scarface and his people were more likely to kill us during such a night. He turned to Warren and ordered him to beat the two Americans. He ordered me to leave. Warren told him that in Western military tradition they did not hit men for trespassing. Scarface kept screaming at him, but Warren remained cool, and refused to hit his men. The inevitable happened, Warren was hit with the stick Scarface always carried with him. There was no use trying to cover one's face, because the beating would turn more cruel. Blood came down Warren's face, from his nose to one ear. He stood there without flinching. Finally Scarface stopped, glared, and walked away. I came outside, and the three of us helped Warren to his box. On May 15, the Tsumori camp was closed. Our factory finally had been bombed out, and we were sent to Northern Japan. Thirty percent of our group who had landed there in 1943 had died. They were left there in urns. The next camp I was transported to would be the last one I was in before the end of the war."

Jop paused and shifted in his chair, and then leaned forward. "Don," he said, "I have shared more with you in this session than any other. In fact we have run over time by nearly an hour. That is a long time to sit and listen, Don, and you have done so without interruption or complaint. Thank you for sitting so patiently and letting me share experiences that must have been hard to listen to at times." Don lowered his head for a moment and then looked up and, shaking his head, he said, "Jop, I think you are the one who deserves all the thanks; first for sharing what had to be some of the most painful experiences of your life. Second for allowing me to come into your home, as we both know, in an effort to help me, and you have. I still have much to process but there is much in what you shared that I resonated with, and that helped me to get in touch with the pain and suffering in own life. So, Jop, thank you." "Well," Jop replied, "maybe so, but being able to tell this story perhaps one last time, and at length, has meant a lot to me as well." Jop then smiled and stood up, and in the down-to-earth manner Don had grown so accustomed to, said, "Well either way, I think that is enough for today." Yet again Jop walked Don to the door and saw him off.

Liberation

This time Don did not reflect as much on the way home. He felt over-whelmed and moved by all that Jop had shared and needed a break before revisiting the interview by listening to the recordings. He planned to do this at some point during the week. Don knew his next interview with Jop would be his last, and this made him sad. He felt a strong bond with Jop now, a relationship had developed and Don did not want it to end. The week seemed to go by more quickly than usual. Time spent with Cindy, and Tom in the cafeteria, again added some respite to an otherwise tedious week of intense study. It had only been a month and yet Don had grown to trust Cindy more than anyone else, almost as much as his mother. He couldn't explain it, but somehow in such a short time they had made a connection that had always taken a much longer time with someone he had just met. He had shared with Cindy about the interviews he was doing with Jop, and how and why they had been set up. Cindy had given him a long searching look before responding, "You know I do believe we all have guardian angels, I just don't believe all of them are from up above. I think God puts people in our path, human guardian angels, that guide us, point us in the right direction at criti-cal times. I think Jop might be one of those. Sometime I will share with you about some of the guardian angels that have crossed paths with me in my life." Both had been sitting at the time. Don looked at Cindy and smiled. "Thank you for understanding, and by the way, I am beginning to believe in those kind of people too, whether you call them human guardian angels, spiritual guides, or something else. What they all have in common, I now think, is that God's hand is working behind the scenes placing them on our paths through life." Don had then broken the seriousness of the moment by saying that if he kept sharing like this during their sessions there would no longer be time for meditation. She laughingly agreed, and they had settled down to meditate. Secretly Don wondered if Cindy too was not one of his spiritual guides. It had also occurred to him that, at times, people could be led to meet on their life paths who could be spiritual guides to one another.

The following Tuesday Don found himself sitting across from Jop for the final interview. He had picked up the envelope with the final question from his mailbox. As usual he had read the question to himself upon opening the envelope. "Can you share with me something about your experiences leading up to your liberation as a POW?" Now Don found himself sitting across from Jop. They had mostly finished their coffee break, and taking one last sip from his mug before setting it down, Jop had said, "Don, I believe you have one more question to ask me." His tone as usual was warm and friendly, while at the same time being down to earth, and to the point.

"I believe I left off telling you that the Tsumori camp had been closed after our factory had been destroyed by the bombings. We were then sent to northern Japan. Somewhere in the north we were split into two groups. Both groups were put in camps near each other. The name of our camp was Nagaoka. I would be in Nagaoka from May 16 to September 9 of 1945, when we were liberated.

"In the new camp we started the church the first day. Kortweg became our moderator. Kortweg had never really relished speaking at our services, Joost however, had developed into our best speaker. None of us really had ever been prepared to speak in church, even a camp church. We only had our Bibles. I generally used a parable, and retold it in the context of our lives and times in the concentration camp. Often I mentioned my mother, a gentle figure in daily life, but the strong spiritual leader of our family. I knew that along with my father, they had prayed daily for my small family, and the distance of thousands of miles was closed. They of course did not know of my loss of Irene and Renee.

"Somewhere in the north we were split into two groups. Both groups worked in small family factories, almost a stone's throw from the camps. Ours was a carbide and carbon factory, with fumes all around us. For the first time we worked in three shifts, each one eight hours, around the clock. Dr. Ort ordered us to wear rags around our faces, to prevent the smoke from entering our lungs. The Japanese civilians wore face masks, covering the nose and mouth. All civilians wore this protection during winter.

"This time Paul Driessen and I shared bunks side by side. They were two high, as in most camps, and near a window, which gave a view over the fence. Next to us was Leo Vroman, my good Jewish friend, who had designed the paper we gave to those who joined the camp church. It was Christ under a cross, not on it, bending down to help. Kortweg asked us to serve Holy Communion, and baptize if necessary. I remember when I served communion for the first time, there was an uneasiness about me until the chaplain said, 'It's just another meal, with God as our guest.'

"We did not use the exact words; we just broke the rice and poured the water in army cups. We used a short prayer, we did not have the elaborate service of the Reformed Church. In our prayers we had a prolonged silence, with the worship leader suggesting names; we came so close then to those we loved so dearly, and had not seen in so long, or would not see again. One day the elder leading worship interjected, "God, we pray for our Japanese guards and civilians, good and bad." Some years back this would not have been accepted, but since we entered Japan, it did not make a difference for whom we prayed.

"Work was hard; tuberculosis now had become a common illness because of the carbon fumes which drifted through the factory. Food was so insufficient that we were fed potato leaves, which have a most bitter taste. Now the first men weighed less than one hundred pounds. Dr. Ort teased me that I was a heavy weight, because of my heavy bone structure. Our main problem was diarrhea. Many a night, upon coming home from the factory, we did not make it to the bathroom, and had to wash our underclothes. We only had one set of everything, and in the summer our undershorts dried fast. We had not seen soap for over a year, and the water was cold. But we kidded just the same. I had found a piece of a broken mirror and tried to shave at times. We had, once a month, one razor blade for a hundred men. Our faces looked scrubby and grey. When I looked into that little triangle of a mirror, I stared into a face I did not know. Other faces looked the same, but I had never thought my face looked like that of the others: eyes rather deep in their sockets, thin cheeks and big ears sticking out. Cold water and lack of soap never got us clean. The warm bath only warmed us, never cleaned us. In this camp there was no such luxury.

"I let Paul look in the mirror piece, and we both said that if we survived, we would need time to get back in shape. We survived, and by the time I landed in Singapore, there was no trace of what I had looked like in the camps. That was good, for it was finally behind us. Dr. Ort had made a great discovery in finding wild spinach, which the Japanese cut down as weeds and burned. We ate it for three months, no salt and it tasted terrible, but it was loaded with vitamins. It saved many a life.

"The church council met often to discuss the needs of the camp. Kortweg had a holistic view of the situation. We looked at the religious, the emotional, the mental, and the physical needs, and set into motion all kinds of recreational enterprises. The kitchen now had a man named Labrie at its head, and we could trust the men there. They often made food from all kinds of scrap. One night we had blood cakes. The rumor was that a train with wounded Japanese had passed by, and the blood that dripped in containers was given to the camp. Nobody believed it, but the

story kept circulating. It never took our appetite away. Another time Labrie found bags with locusts, heaven knew from where, and had them fried
with grease the Japanese used to clean the guns. The locusts stuck to our
teeth, but it filled us well.

"The first service in Nagaoka was led by me. It was not a new experience, but it was a new camp. It was different. It was small, to begin with Dr.
Ort was the only officer now. The plant was nearby, the civilians were as in
Osaka, and the guards seemed easier, also younger. The Japanese commander walked around with a long whip, but never seemed to hit anyone. We were
all exhausted, and the work load eased correspondingly. The Americans had
taken the secret camp radio, and we were totally cut off from the outside
world. There was a young medic, Sasaki-san, who spoke some English and
worked with Dr. Ort. Not even the Japanese had much medicine anymore.
And then planes, which the guards had said would never come this far north
in Japan, well they came! The bomb from one of the planes came a little too
close, and the pressure threw me against a wall, and I broke part of a tooth.
Nowhere else would anyone have given it a thought, but Sasaki-san was allowed to take me to the dentist in the little town.

"Here the mood was different. We walked together through the streets.
Sasaki-san asked about my family and told me that he was a student at the
Imperial University in Tokyo. He pointed to a little church as we passed and
wanted to know how many gods we had. I was nonplussed, but he insisted we
had more than one god. He had seen one group praying in a corner, another
elsewhere at camp. I realized that the Roman Catholics, though they came to
our service, prayed the Rosary. But I was at a loss how to explain that. Then I
thought about Zen Buddhism and Confucianism, but I wasn't quite sure if he
understood it. We did not talk about the war, except that he was the first one
who said that we might go home soon. I shrugged my shoulders, just another
rumor, though now it came from the other side.

"Near the dentist's office I stopped in my tracks. There was in the front
of the house a small amphitheater of shelves, about five feet high. It had all
kinds of flowers, some made of paper others natural; in front, on her knees,
a woman dressed in her good and traditional Japanese clothing was sob-
bing, so utterly devastated by grief that her whole body was shaking. Having
worked with Japanese civilians for more than a year and a half, I only knew
of their self-control, their keeping a straight face. This woman did nothing
of the kind. I looked at Sasaki-san, and he pointed over her shoulder to the
central shelf. In the midst of natural flowers there was a picture of a Japanese
soldier, ever so young. Her son had been killed in action. For a moment she
looked up and saw me. She seemed to stare for a moment, but never betrayed

any sense of anger at seeing a white man whose army had killed her son. She once again rearranged a flower or two and sobbed quietly.

"I saw the young Dutch and Americans, who had died without reason. With medicine, they could have lived. I remember at the Katabang Kali bridge in Surabaya, when we were shot at by a machine gun from a Waringin tree. Our howitzer people shot point blank at the tree, and when it had been blown apart we cheered, not knowing how many Japanese had been killed. I remember reading after the war that when the Japanese equestrian champion of the 1936 Olympic games in Berlin, Germany, was told that they had lost a few men in the fighting on Tarawa, he said, 'Each of them is an irreparable loss to their family.' To this Japanese woman, it was such a loss. To the wife of Pieter Volten it was a loss. To the parents and sisters of Dennis Moppet it was irreparable loss. After the bombers came, I asked Sasaki-san to see the dentist again. He said, 'Street is gone, dentist is dead.' I thought of my wife and daughter.

"So came July. I had a kidney infection and got a shot from Dr. Ort. In early August there was a subtle change in the air. Did it have to do with beautiful summer in rural Japan? Nearby was a river, lazily winding its way to an unknown sea. There was an abundance of flowers along the river. We saw children swimming, and older folks sitting and watching them. It was like the twilight of an era, though we did not know why. We thought about the coming winter, now in northern Japan, it would be so much colder than Osaka. We did not talk about the war ending, I do not know why. We just didn't. Maybe it was too tempting, and too impossible, that this concentration camp life could soon end. In the meantime we prayed for peace. We lost a few good men, but far fewer than the previous summer in Osaka.

"The camp church now played a major role in all phases of camp life. We organized recreational evenings, lectures, courses. Whatever helped men survive in that camp was related to other men, and the One who created people. Weight went steadily down. The lowest probably was Leo Vroman, who was now seventy pounds. Leo lived, though he was never big, and his system adjusted to less and less food. It was not that more people came to the services on Sunday, but we had ceased to be just a Sunday church. We discussed how much time Jesus spent in the synagogue, and how much walking the roads of Palestine (teaching, listening, healing, telling jokes, going to weddings, and dinners). It was maybe 5 percent to 95 percent in ratio we concluded.

"We did most of this work because we had to prepare the people for the hard winter of 1945–1946. New members wanted to enter the camp church. All the others baptized, but I refrained. I did begin to enjoy serving communion, because I knew that in the early church, it was not a rite to be observed, but a family meal in the fellowship of their Lord Christ. This aspect never left me, and is still with me, when I celebrate the Communion today. And I would never understand the reluctance of the church, after the war, to let communion be celebrated by both pastors and laity. I knew we were all laity when we had camp Communions. It was not a crisis situation, we felt. Maybe the church in the camps was more reminiscent of the church in the book of Acts; of the young church in action, than of the stilted church outside the camps, in countries the world over. Except in Asia and Africa, where the newness of it all, and its being a minority, just like in the camps, draws people more to be a new humanity than in European and American churches.

"In early August the beatings by the guards, which had slacked off anyhow, stopped altogether. They entered our building without guns. Several of them were students like Sakaki-san. They came to barter. We wondered why. Whatever we had was old and worn, if not rags. The blankets were Japanese issued, one to a man. They wanted them badly. We kept saying that we needed them for the coming winter, and they repeated that by then we would be home. Nothing was exchanged or sold. We did not trust any soldier, not even these young men, all of whom spoke English.

"It was August 27. Paul and I, who were on the same shift, didn't have to go out till midnight, so we were sunning ourselves on the second floor of the barracks. Subsequent events happened that are engraved in my mind. First, we had seen the afternoon shift leave at mid-afternoon. In the warm sun we had taken off our shirts and were busy killing lice and fleas in our shirts. Then I happened to look up and notice a Japanese soldier on a bike approaching the main gate. He was immediately admitted, and ran to the camp commander's office. Nothing unusual thus far, and I would have forgotten it, if a moment later the commander had not come outside his office, barked an order to the guards at the gate, and one of them ran like mad to the nearby factory.

"The second event: the afternoon/evening shift returned. They were not excited. The machines often broke down, and shifts returned. The camp commander barked another order to a soldier who ran at top speed to Dr. Ort's office. This time we became mildly interested and put our shirts down. Finally, the soldier accompanied Dr. Ort to the Japanese commander's office. It seemed like an old movie, replayed. Often Dr. Ort was called to the office, generally to be berated for one thing or another. This time the Japanese officer came outside. Dr. Ort was just about to make the required bow, when the other bowed deeply before Dr. Ort. We yelled for others to come and see this phenomenon.

"It was like an operetta. We expected Dr. Ort to make a bow and both to start dancing, but the commander prevented our physician from bowing, and they shook hands.

"I can still hear the deafening silence all around us. We knew something of tremendous importance to all of us went on there, the two men talking. We did not want to believe that the war was over. It could not be so suddenly after nearly four years . . . it simply was out of the question. Yet deep in my guts I knew that it was true, that we were about to have freedom. Dr. Ort turned around when he saw the crowds of men up in the sleeping area. He stopped when his eyes met ours, and this unusually unflappable man shouted at the top of his lungs: "All men out, immediately!" We stood outside, wondering and yet knowing. The Japanese guards were at the gate. At other times they would have stormed down and beaten us back. They had already known what we surmised. Everyone knew for months that the Japanese resistance against American air attacks had almost ceased to exist. When the city of Nagaoka had been destroyed, in early August, no anti-aircraft guns had been heard.

"Dr. Ort, in a few words, said something like the following: 'Men, the war is over. The Japanese commander told us the emperor, out of the goodness of his heart, has called the war off.' He stopped, and suddenly ripples of laughter went through the ranks, concluding in a contemptuous roar of laughter. Dr. Ort waved his hand and said, 'The fact is that the Americans have beaten the hell out of them. We are free, can you believe it? We are free! In time we will go home and see our families again.'

"We stood silently for a moment, with mixed feelings, not able to digest it all, thinking about those that did not make it. I thought particularly of my wife and daughter. Then Dr. Ort's voice sounded again as if in afterthought 'I am no military officer, just a doctor, but I always wanted to give an order and here it is: As the Japanese commander is now under my command, neither he nor any other soldier will be attacked by anyone. I know this is tempting, but if you do, you will be court-martialed. We are not the beasts they have been all these long years!' Then he dismissed us. I guess he knew some of the hotheads had been talking of tearing the Japs apart, if they had a chance. We were all too weary, and knew each other well enough in this small camp.

"In seconds it was flowing through the crowd. It was then that we truly realized we were free again, that the nightmare of sickness, death by accidents, ships torpedoed, suicides, beatings, exhaustion, and starvation had ended. Then I became aware that my eyes were strangely covered with a film of moisture. I rubbed them dry and saw one after another . . . men all doing the same. Kortweg raised his voice and announced, 'The camp church will celebrate tonight at 7:30, we will give thanks to God.'

"The first change we noticed: the kitchen crew with Labrie went to the Japanese commander's office, and demanded access to the Japanese food supplies. He got the key immediately. The real surprise was that those supplies were very low. The civilian population had been starving, but now we knew that the army had little more. Kortweg held an unforgettable service of thanksgiving. Nearly the entire camp was present. As a church council we went to the sick bay, mainly filled with beriberi patients. One young soldier, swollen monstrously with water, smiled faintly. Dr. Ort had told those sick that medicine should arrive soon. No one knew how or when. The next morning the young soldier died. He had survived the war, one day beyond the end, until August 28. It was perhaps one of the saddest services. We stood around his mortal remains, covered with his torn blanket. All the others had died when the war was in process; but he passed over the line, like a long-distance runner, collapsing and seeing the victory slipping away. He was the last one to die, barely twenty years old.

"That same day we heard a plane come over flying rather low. We ran outside and it must have seen us. It tipped its wings, greeting us. Then it dropped a parcel on a small parachute. It landed exactly in the center of the field. The pilot had found the camp, because all morning Japanese soldiers had been painting, with white colors, large POW signs on all the roofs. This was routine under the Geneva Convention Rules of Prisoners of War, but the Japanese never adhered to the convention's requirements; this was one reason so many POWs drowned when their unmarked ships were torpedoed by American submarines. We had received a small parcel that contained current copies of *Life* magazine, and a letter. While Dr. Ort was reading the letter, we poured over the magazine copies. They were read to pieces, we even found pictures of liberated Holland. Then Dr. Ort cursed loudly, 'Those filthy bastards!' He had just read that the actual surrender of the war was August 15, and we were only informed August 27, twelve days later. We were a camp in northern Japan, and maybe the camp commander was not known to the Allies until now. But the Japanese knew, and they had just let us rot there a bit longer and let the young soldier die. Dr. Ort carefully documented this for the war crimes courts, which had already asked all European and American camp commanders to detail all crimes committed against the POWs.

"The letter read by Dr. Ort requested that a large white cross cover a nearby meadow. The next day food, clothing, and medicine would be dropped. The end said, 'You will soon go home, fellows. Thanks for sticking it out so many years. We admire you!' Our brave countrymen and the Allied forces had done the fighting and lost thousands of people. We thought their sacrifice was far greater than ours. The next day we stayed at the edge of the field as the bomb doors began to open. Parachutes opened and drums began to come down. We ran back when some parachutes did not open. We collected the loose articles from the broken drums.

Suddenly there were pieces of a Hershey chocolate bar. We tasted them cautiously. Then we rushed back to camp. A man next to me kept saying: 'real chocolate, real chocolate.'

"What does one remember of those days? The drums were opened, and an unending stream of almost forgotten things came out; they were put on long tables. There were clothes in all sizes, shoes, underwear, army jackets, one I still have today, socks, hankies, and other apparel. Medicine, which Dr. Ort and medic Verhoff sorted and handed out immediately to the beriberi and dysentery patients, the two diseases which never left us at camp.

"After the evening meal we were all ordered to get vitamin tablets. In a few days the entire building was scented by the capsules. All these years later when I smell a vitamin capsule, I have a flashback. I immediately see the upstairs of our barrack, the long tables with medicine, and receiving daily what was needed to help us over our basic physical deficiencies. Mine was diarrhea, which had been my most unwelcome companion for months. It was cured in a week's time. The head of our kitchen, Labrie, made us a queen's meal: soup, potatoes, steak, pudding, coffee with cream. But all to be eaten in small portions, by order of Dr. Ort. Even then, several men threw up that evening; overeating was a danger. Before we ate, Kortweg stood and waved his hand, saying something like: 'Whatever our religious ways of thinking are, don't you think we should be silent now? Even if only to give thanks to the pilot, who made it possible to give us this first nourishing meal in years?' I still see all the heads bowed, with the food's now unfamiliar aromas drifting around. Then we ate.

"At ten o'clock that night Labrie came out of the kitchen, ringing a bell. He had picked it up in the Japanese office. Steaming pans of hot chocolate, sliced bread, and plates with butter were carried out. We were spellbound, it was like home. Home in Holland, on a cold day. Home where mother had hot cocoa for us after skating. The bread tasted like pound cake. At first we didn't use butter; it was just the taste of good bread so well made that we savored it little by little.

"So went the first evenings after the war was over. We wandered around the burned downtown of Nagaoka. We saw women and children, but few men. People were cooking meals over little makeshift stoves. We had an abundance of food now, and the church council talked about it. After only a few days, food was already being discarded. We suggested to Dr. Ort that all leftovers would be put in pans outside. We would invite the town's people to share it with us.

"The final worship service was held on Sunday, September 2, 1945. It was my turn to lead the hour of worship. Most of the camp was there. In the week to come we would leave for Tokyo. I do not have any notes of that hour and do not remember which Bible story I used. It was the last service of the Church Under the Cross and, on impulse, I asked each of my church council members to take part. In the last row I saw Sasaki-san. He had been accepted by our men, for he had gone out of his way to help Dr. Ort with whatever medicine he could find. Kortweg led us again in singing. Our handwritten hymn sheets were almost worn out; Verhoff read from his Bible, something to do with healing. He had been a friend to us, a friend far more than a medic. Labrie ran in from the kitchen, and thanked God for food that had come to us those last few weeks. Groen, our Jewish friend, who had given so many groups a Jewish insight to the Bible, read one of his favorite texts, from what we call the Old Testament, on Israel leaving Egypt. I am sure that I touched on the basic tenet of the 'Church Under the Cross,' that all of us had been ministers to one another. This was now a deep-rooted conviction.

"We had two years without chaplains and the church had flourished beyond all expectations. We thanked God for the faithfulness of the men. They had worked so hard in ministering to others. Then there were those who had not understood the spiritual aspects of this world until today. Sacrifices from our beaten-down men gave a glimpse of the earth-living Christ, the image of the Creator-Spirit. Some had grasped Christ's hand, in a real leap of faith. Many in their own ways, as Pieter Volten had taught us so urgently, had shared that Christ, as a way of living with the Spirit within, which they could share with others.

"There was the Church Under the Cross, the seed of the ecumenical movement, in which people with great theological differences had lived. We worked and worshipped together. It had been difficult at first, especially in my own mind. But we had grown, each on his own journey. After all these years, I still miss the close fellowship of the Church Under the Cross in the Japanese concentration camps. The times were so different then. Maybe it was easier in the camps to live the life of God's Christ. Maybe our relationships were closer. We depended so much on one another, the strong helping the growing.

"My own gratitude reaches out to so many of my fellow prisoners. Slowly I have turned from a superficial acceptance of the church and God, to a coming to my senses. Something that began in the camps, but then put me on a journey, and a relationship, that still continues today. Nothing came easily. There had been rocky roads, the falling short of commitments, and many moody moments. I was often judgmental of those I did not like. My friends stood by me; Dennis Moppet, Pieter Volten, Siestse Van Dyke, Warren Minton, Chuck Varney, even Goosens whose religious rigidity—while at times an obstacle, at other times could, because of its rock-solid nature also be inspiring—and my friends outside the church, Leo Vroman, Paul Driessen, and too many others to mention.

"There were miles to go after the war, when my little world was not what I had dreamt about. Without those years, which some have called 'lost years,' I might not have had the courage to go on in life. During the war, we saw God's gracious care for us. The darkest moments of the hungry winter of 1944–1945 in Osaka, when the Red Cross boxes had come. As Joost Wentink wrote in closing his report: 'God was in ons midden, God was tegenwordig,' God was in our midst, God was ever present!"

Jop stopped talking and sat back and looked affectionately at Don. "Well Don, that's about it. I thank you again for sitting through these sessions. I can't say I have ever shared this much of my POW experiences, in this much detail, and I was concerned that it might prove to be too much for you. You shared that you found your interviews with me interesting. You also indicated that you resonated with some of my experiences. I am glad for both of these things. It seems John knew what he was doing, and perhaps God was working through John when he set up these interviews.

"There is one more thing I want to say: you have heard my story, but I have not heard yours. If you would like to come back and share something of your life with me you are welcome to do this at any time. Please know I do not expect this and will understand if you choose not to." Don had been afraid that when the sessions with Jop ended he would not have an excuse, given the formal way their relationship had been set up, to maintain a relationship with Jop. He felt a bond with Jop now, who he had come to see almost as a father, or grandfather figure. He realized, given the dysfunction in his family background, that this relationship might fill a negative void he felt in this relational part of his life, and he did not want to let go of it. "Jop, I would love to stop by from time to time. I would be glad to share something of why I think Dr. McCall set our sessions up, but I also would just like to visit with you and Marie informally if that is okay." Don hoped he had not overstepped. "Marie and I would like that very much," Jop said, to Don's relief. "I also wouldn't mind hearing about what they're teaching you at that seminary. I have heard that these days there is not always much of an emphasis on the spiritual." Don smiled, "That has been my experience, but I think under Dr. McCall's leadership that may gradually change."

Jop walked Don to the door and shook his hand with an affectionate firmness that seemed to indicate he also felt a bond with Don. On his walk back to the seminary Don did not try to reflect on what Jop had shared in this last interview, or in the previous ones. He felt mentally drained, and yet at the same time a certain peace had settled on him. Don knew that all he heard from Jop, which he would revisit by listening to the tapes, had germinated something in him. He would take some time, perhaps even later that day, to process the mix of emotions and thoughts that the last couple sessions in particular had stirred within him.

Later that evening after dinner as Don was walking back from the cafeteria to his dorm room he found himself in a more reflective mood. Three themes immediately came to mind from his interviews with Jop: one was the incredible way in which the men had lived out their faith by ministering to each other selflessly, depending on each other for survival through the sharing of Christian love. The second was that the God we know in Jesus Christ was not a distant God, but one who came down off the cross and suffered with us. The third theme was that the God Jop and so many experienced in the camps wasn't just a God that suffered passively with us, but offered us, often through relationship, a divine otherworldly gift of transformative healing and empowering love. Their experience of God was of one who, in Christ, not only suffered on the cross, but had won an ultimate victory over sin and death on that cross. A victory all who chose to make that first shaky leap of faith into the loving grace of Abba's arms can experience. What brought the three themes full circle was that love and grace could most commonly be found, given the social creatures God created us to be, in the love and grace Christians shared with each other.

Don knew as he tried to recap these major points in his head that he was in danger once again of overanalyzing and intellectualizing what he had learned from Jop. He knew that the experiential side of his faith was still weak, and that he had much work to do here. He also knew he still had questions, and that doubts remained within him. Don had no illusions about whether any church could be perfect, Christ would not have died on the cross if that was the case. What he doubted was whether any church could be a place where sharing Christian love, among forgiven and forgiving Christians, was the norm. Could it even be a reality? These doubts had been with Don since his early teen years. He had witnessed political tensions in his home church, where a clique unwilling to reconcile with the pastor had divided the church and driven the pastor out. Don's deeper doubts, of course, stemmed from the accident. They had to do with his inability to reconcile the injustice of such a senseless tragedy God had allowed and his faith. Don's inability to resolve this tension had led him to doubt severely that anyone's faith could survive such life circumstances. Still these doubts, which he had before he had met Jop and which continually threatened to extinguish his faith, had now been confronted by the undeniable counterevidence of Jop's incredible Christian witness of his camp experiences.

It was a beautiful summer moonlit night, and Don chose not to return to his room, but to take an extended walk around the campus. He had decided, as he reflected further in light of Jop's witness, to allow himself to think more about where he was at, both emotionally and theologically, with these doubts in light of Jop's witness, and perhaps in the process to open himself up to God.

Don reflected on the suffering and loss Jop had experienced in the camps. He had lost everything and yet here was an individual with as deep and richly lived a faith life as anyone he knew. How could Jop have gone through all he had, in the hell hole of the prison camps, and still end up believing in a loving God who wanted him to share that love with others. It seemed an impossibility, but the living proof had been sitting across from him earlier that day. No doubt the Christian love and camaraderie in the camps had helped keep his faith alive, as had having that faith stripped bare of nearly all its institutional trappings. This had allowed Jop, and others, to open themselves to an experience of faith.

This was becoming increasingly difficult in many institutionalized mainline churches in the West. Don recalled Goosen's attempt to impose a form of rigid institutional Christianity on the camp church. He had tried to do this during the 1944–1945 years in the camps when the men were starving and barely hanging on. That had indeed seemed obscene to Don. He began to think again about the institutional idolatry which could devolve into a worship of turf, the church building and finances. We live in a time, Don thought, where secular culture now competes with the church, where the family and community support for the church has begun to break down, where the modern scientific worldview, itself entrenching, and no longer content to take a live-and-let-live stance toward religious faith now proselytizes its faith in materialism.

Don, once again, began to see a parallel between the physically starving souls of the camps encountering a Goosens, and spiritually starving souls seeking out a faith community to nurture them only to have one or another form of institutional Christianity imposed on them instead. No wonder an increasing number of the casualties—of the harried, informationally overloaded, graceless times we live in—see the institutional church as the last place they would want to go to seek spiritual refuge, and sanctuary. Don recalled a C. S. Lewis quote that seemed particularly relevant to his current musings: "If you put second things first you will lose both the first and second things." Don was well aware that too many institutionalized churches had become known for demanding conformity to institutional tradition, and antiquated social tradition, sometimes along with rigid Christian doctrine, as the litmus tests for belonging. So-called Christian love, in the form of acceptance, if present at all, was too often tied to a strict adherence to one or more of the above.

Having grown up in a conservative Christian tradition Don also knew well how provincial, closed-minded understandings of faith could color and distort the otherwise vital spiritual life of a church. Love the sinner hate the sin in such churches too often was expressed as a love of judging the sinner and hating any association with them. He worried that churches, at both the liberal and conservative extremes, were creating bubbles of conformity that chilled out anyone who didn't fit the mold. Don knew he was being overly judgmental and painting different Christian traditions with too broad a brush. Still with many different Christian traditions in the West in rapid decline he knew that while we live in culturally challenging times for the church, it was what was going on inside them that was the greatest threat to their survival. After all, in addition to other places in the world—such as parts of Africa, Asian, and South America, where churches thrived—there were still churches in many Christian traditions in the West and the United States that had managed not only to stay spiritually vital, but to attract many new folk truly seeking a living faith community. Part of the reason Don had not considered ministry seriously was his fear that such churches might be few and far between, and he had no interest in preserving an institution or running a social club.

Despite all the doubts that had been fostered in Don, from his readings, research, and life experiences, there again was Jop's witness that in the worst life circumstances, or perhaps partly because of them, a living, loving Christian faith and community could not only exist but thrive. Don turned over in his mind three of the most pervasive themes from his interviews with Jop. He summed them up in his head differently and more succinctly, hoping to gain greater insight into their meaning and relevance for his own life: living the Christian faith passionately by sharing the love of Christ, the Christ that suffers with us, and who often expresses the power of his healing, transformative, and loving grace through relationship. He was struck by the cyclical nature of that love, which through the conduit of human interrelationship finds both its source and goal in God's grace. Such a seemingly simple dynamic, Don thought, but the nature of its flow, or spiritual force, has profound implications for the Christian life. It also offers a stark contrast to more stagnant understandings of the Christian life.

This led Don to reflect on one special expression of this sharing, all the spiritual guides that had nurtured Jop's faith and emotional well-being, and that of others. This in turn caused Don to utter a prayer of thanks to God for the spiritual guides he had been blessed with since attending the seminary. As counterintuitive as it sounded to him, had Jop too not found what happiness, meaning, and purpose he could by losing himself in helping others in the camps? Don could not foresee how a revitalized Christian faith might reemerge in the West, but faith as movement, a force, a verb that lost itself in helping others in God's loving grace had to be essential to this. Don recalled the iron cross, and was reminded that experiences of God's grace could work through other mediums, including the natural world and the miraculous. His reflections on these themes, rather than satisfying some intellectual need to summarize his interviews with Jop, seemed to call out for an experience of faith that would affirm them.

As Don recounted insights gained from his interviews with Jop he was completing a second walk around the outskirts of the campus. The sidewalks on which he had been walking took him through the residential neighbor-hoods that surrounded the seminary. However valuable these insights and his reflections on them might be, Don wanted to get out of his head. He also knew he must set aside for the time being his deep concerns about the church. He had the more pressing matter of his own relationship with God to address first. Don's plight was deeply personal, at stake was his faith and a personal relationship with God in Jesus Christ. Don was growing tired of walking and decided to cross over onto the center of the campus. He found himself on the sidewalk next to the seminary chapel, and as he came around to the front of it, he decided to sit on its front steps.

So central to Jop's faith experience in the camps, the iron cross again came to mind for Don. This had not only been a deeply personal spiritual experience, and an extraordinary one, it had been a pivotal one for Jop as well. It was a moment where the growing critical mass of his camp experi-ences had resulted in a spiritual transformative experience. It was the one where Jop had been cleaning iron tools in a barrel with scraps of iron. Jop's anger and frustration over the loss of close friends and the wasted years in the camps had led him in a moment of utter despair and anger to kick the pile of assorted shapes and sizes of scrap iron. Don then recalled how that kick had resulted in those pieces flying in all directions; how one, in the exact shape of a cross, had landed on his foot; how Jop had hidden it in his boot despite the risk of being caught.

Then Don remembered something else, something Jop had said as he held that scrap iron cross in the crook of his hand, that, as if for the first time he felt free; that no matter what circumstances we find ourselves in life, or how horrific they might be, we always have a choice. That choice, or leap might not change the harsh reality of our situation, but it can change the way we look at it, react to it, and cope with it. For Jop this choice had made all the difference. Jop had clearly been led to this choice, both by God, and the Holy Spirit working through others. The choice had been between faith in the transformative love of God in Christ, or the chaotic, destructive barbarity all around him. Jop saw this choice as one that had precipitated a change in him from the inside out. Jop had been on the path to that choice, and had been deeply intrigued, and guided by men in the camps who had already made that choice. In his experience with the iron cross Jop came face-to-face with God and had chosen not to turn back or away. An aimless spiritual journey had found a destination, or been led to one.

Don knew all too well that he could make the other choice, and he knew where that led. He had seen his father make it. Don recalled that his mother had shared with him that when she and his dad were first married he had professed a simple but genuine faith. She had also shared that as the years went by, and he began to feel ground down by demons from his childhood, depression, and declining self-worth he had abandoned that faith and chosen the bottle as his ultimate source of comfort and means of coping. The self-centered, abusive, and rudderless existence that followed had not only reduced Jim to a shell of a human being but made those closest to him casualties as well. Don could see now that his decision to go to seminary had not been a clear choice to seek a personal relationship with God, but merely a more neutral choice to not go down a path that he knew all too well led somewhere he did not want to go. His inability to choose a relationship with God had been impeded by the deep questions he had about suffering and loss in the wake of the accident. The anger that the injustice and suffering of the accident had aroused within him, while protecting him from feeling the raw pain of his grief, had also impeded such a choice. Still his choice to not go down the path his father had, had set Don on the path that led to where he now was. He may not have chosen God, but God had chosen him, and had been able to turn a more positive, but still aimless path, into one that led straight to him.

Even now, though, Don was left pondering why God allowed so much suffering in life? He had learned some of the intellectual theological/philosophical answers to this question. Much suffering is caused by free will, and the sinful tendencies of human beings, which in Christian doctrine is attributed to some theological understanding of original sin. Evil as an entity that attempts to corrupt human nature and free will was another traditional Christian doctrine Don had long been aware of. He was also familiar with the theological argument that if God interfered too often with free will, or the inherent anarchy in nature, the delicate balance that ensured a free creation would be upset. In college Don had learned of Leibniz's rational argument that God had created the best of all possible worlds. He had also been introduced to philosopher J. L. Mackie's argument that if God is omnipotent, omniscient, and omnipresent God must know about evil and suffering and be capable of preventing it. God's moral perfection would be the motivation to do so. Mackie's conclusion was, since God and evil and suffering are incompatible, then the existence of God is not logical. The philosopher Alvin Plantinga countered, and Mackie conceded to his argument, that God's three ultimate attributes are not contradictory with evil. Mackie, Plantinga points out, has premises that are not implicit in his argument and need to be included. A defender of atheism Mackie was also skeptical of both free will and objective moral values. Plantinga then adds his own two additional premises to strengthen his own argument that God and evil and suffering can coexist. First, logically, even God cannot do anything he/she wants. God cannot create beings, such as humans, give them free will, and then not allow them to exercise that free will in choosing evil with the suffering that results. Plantinga, additionally, argued that the moral value of free will more than compensates for God's permitting of evil and suffering.

While such arguments might provide some intellectual satisfaction, none of these arguments and others he had come across in light of the tragedy Don had experienced in his life had satisfied him in the end. What all these arguments too often had in common was that they tried to answer the most powerful subjective negative experiences a person can have with external intellectual arguments. Our emotions and our intellect offer two qualitatively different experiences, Don thought to himself. They speak two different languages. Reason often tries to reduce even healthy emotional responses to expressions of secondary importance and input to itself, rather than letting both inform each other. Spiritual experience, though potentially offering a holistic experience of self, and unity with God, and others, often transcends language's ability to describe or narrowly prescribe.

We can know things about ourselves and God through faith experiences that are real and ring true in ways that transcend our intellectual and verbal abilities to articulate them. If there is a God, and through Christ's Spirit that God consciousness intersects, or perhaps even expands, our conscious experience, it is completely understandable that our brain and mind in concert with our emotions, in retrospect, would have trouble articulating this experience. Still this would in no way make that experience less real or true. Don knew, however, that even though such an argument alluded to and affirmed the reality of a particular kind of faith experience, it was yet one more intellectual argument. The only way faith arguments, even this one, could be helpful to him, Don intuited, is if they in some way resonated with or were grounded in a faith experience. This had not yet been the case with him.

Don thought about his own experience. He thought of his mother and sister dying almost instantly in the car accident from the reckless choice of a young man, driving too fast, to run a stop sign. For a long time Don had felt a rage and hatred toward that young man. Before all the emotions this memory triggered could be aroused, Don remembered something else Jop had shared; his realization that no matter how someone had died, the suffering Christ, the one that had come down off the cross, was there with them. He enveloped them, all those who accepted his unconditional restorative love and took them to the next reality.

But what about those left behind, those tasked with living on, those who must suffer further. The answer that came to Don was not theological or intellectual. It came in the form of a person, Jop De Vries, in the life experiences he shared both before the cast iron cross, and in the stumbling steps Jop took after his faith leap, where he still had to confront the devastating loss of his wife and daughter. His had not been a leap toward rational certainty but toward letting God affirm his faith, in daily life in the face of injustice, loss and pain, doubt, and questions yet to be answered. His had not been the leap of a blindly surrendered will to a distant God who we know little about, and who might lead us down paths of masochistic self-denial. Rather Jop's leap had been toward a God whose guiding will, for those who surrendered their lives to it, was to share the love that Christ had first shared with us in our everyday lives. It had been a leap uncluttered of the many institutional and scriptural distortions of faith that so easily can discourage one from making that leap. Jop had come to understand that God's saving love in Christ is the highest peak of Scripture and the faith, and it is from this elevated awareness that one must interpret and understand all of Scripture and the faith. By his witness and example Jop had uncluttered Don's path to see the clear choice, or leap, he had to make. Don had doubted that God's love could handle, much less heal, the hurt and anger that had come to define him. Despite his intellectual appreciation of the radical choice a genuine and passionate faith demanded, Don had not trusted God enough to make that leap; to surrender himself warts and all to God's saving grace.

Jop was the living proof that such a surrender, despite great suffering, was possible. His life had been renewed and restored not in spite of his suffering but through it. He had found new meaning and purpose in the love of Christ shared through others, and directly, at just the right moment, in his experience with the iron cross. Jop had risked surrendering all his pain and suffering to God in the moment before he kicked the scrap iron pile and had experienced the full reality and truth of God's saving grace. The miracle in the end had not been the cross, which was merely a signpost. It had been that when Jop was at his weakest point in the most dire life circumstances, rife with sin and death, that the power of God's love could still win out. A point God had led him to through experiences that along the way had shaped and nurtured his growing spiritual awareness. Jop, like so many others in the camps, had decided to choose faith in the midst of suffering, and it transformed the way they related to, handled, and saw the world around them. Instead of hopelessness they saw opportunity; instead of an enemy, a common humanity; instead of cowed humiliation in the face of barbaric cruelty they saw the humble resoluteness of faith; in place of vindictive hatred, forbearance and eventually a forgiveness that leaves justice in God's hands.

In Don's case his anger and rage had protected him for a long time from feeling the raw grief and pain he tried to suppress within, but that anger at the same time had prevented him from processing his pain and beginning to heal. For Don, following Job's example would mean trusting that God's healing love and grace could handle all the underlying feelings of vulnerability, weakness, humiliation, shame, and raw grief. Many of these feelings stemmed from the accident. Some had their origins further back, as with the bullying Don experienced during his middle school years. Could God handle this list? Everything his father had taught him told him this would make him weaker not stronger. But Don knew what his father had become, the very epitome of a pathetic weakling, a shell of a man. He also knew that kind of strength was built on sand. It had not given his father any real peace, self-esteem, or sense of fulfillment.

In pondering what he might have to surrender to God, Don suddenly felt a little of the raw pain his anger had deflected his attention from for so long. Having lost those who loved him most he had felt that he had no one left that truly loved him. Another deeper pain then stabbed at his heart there had been nothing he had been able to do to protect his mother and sister, to prevent this senseless tragedy. In the face of his father's lack of control Don had tried to compensate by staying in control. But the accident had torn away from him that which he valued the most, and he had had no control over it. Tears welled up in Don's eyes, he felt his heart beginning to break. The pain Don was now feeling was bubbling up from the deepest level. He knew it could be as dangerous to stay mired in it as it had been to deny it. Don knew something else, that he had been on the road to becoming an endless spiritual seeker who never made a choice, even if that choice was solely one of opening himself up to God's love in Christ. God had brought him to this place and time to make that choice. He felt himself at the very brink of a chasm. The chasm representing all the doubts and questions with which he had struggled for so long. He was not sure he had the courage to leap over that chasm to get to the other side where he hoped God waited with open and loving arms.

It was a warm, moonlit summer night and as Don sat there on the chapel steps he felt a gentle breeze blowing in his face. Despite his awakening grief there was a feeling of release from suppressed emotions that had bubbled up in such destructive ways. There was also something special about this night. Despite the waves of sorrow that had begun to come over him there was an ambience about the night that suggested an otherworldly consolation. He settled back on his forearms and looked up at the moonlit sky. Perhaps the stars did not shine in the spectacular abundance they had in Java so many years before, but it was still a beautiful night. Don knew God was not some distant, aloof God of the heavens alone. Still, the night sky somehow inspired him to start praying. "Lord, I am in so much pain. I miss my mother and sister so much. I hold so much anger inside. I now have some idea, actually it's more of a feeling, of what's underneath that anger, Lord. I feel like such a failure, my mother and sister would be so ashamed. My anger has only left me feeling humiliated and ashamed and feeling like an outcast, like I don't belong anywhere. It has only deepened my sense of worthlessness. Lord, to surrender that anger to you means feeling the deeper pain I fear so much, the helplessness and vulnerability, the feeling that I am weak, and broken, and that I am alone in the world and unloved, not worth anything, since there is no one left that loves me, and the raw grief I still can't put into words over losing my mother and sister. There it is, Lord, the raw honest truth, as much as I understand it myself. So are you there, God? Does your truth work?" Don had said words like this before in anger challenging God. This time he said them differently, imploringly, with an increasing openness and willingness to trust. Tears had welled up in his eyes as he bared his heart and soul to God in prayer.

It was probably his imagination, but as clouds parted, the moonlight suddenly seemed to shine on the chapel steps and on him. In its light Don suddenly experienced both peace and a life-affirming hope. As he waited for some kind of answer he gradually became aware that the experience he was having could not be adequately articulated with words. There was a growing sense that he was loved unconditionally by someone, something much greater than himself that at the same time was within him. As the feeling enveloped him and all that he was, he began to have another experience. Don, for the first time, accepted himself for who he really was. The moonlight, shinning down on him, became a visible sign of the divine grace and love he felt was enveloping him.

Don knew that somehow, between the prayer and the experience of God's love, he had already made the choice, he had leaped the chasm, and even in making the leap he had not been alone. He hadn't made the choice verbally or as a thought, but he had made it nonetheless. He knew this was a shaky first step and that he might regress. There would be other leaps of faith over chasms of pain and doubt, but something had changed with this leap. He had opened himself to the power of God's healing love and surrendered his will to the divine author of that sacrificial love. There was a something

qualitatively different too about this experience. He had somehow left behind his insatiable desire to prove and justify his faith rationally. What he had
just experienced could not be explained empirically. It was not anything that
arose from a materialistic cause, but it had seemed as real, more real, than any
experience he had had within physical reality.

Don, recalling Jop's witness, knew that he would need a faith community where he could experience the sharing of Christian love. But none of
that mattered to him now or worried him. What he had just experienced had
worked, it had rung true, and he knew he would never be the same knowing
what he now knew. Forever cancelling out his father's stepping back and letting him fall, God had caught him, just as he had caught Jop. In his weakness
Don had experienced the power God's love had to take the broken pieces of
who he was and bind them back together through his love and grace, and in
that wholeness, he felt stronger than he ever had before.

Don later came to realize that such a leap could happen very differently for different people. For many it would happen within the heart of a
faith community alive with the Holy Spirit and fully capable of sharing the
accepting, forgiving, reconciling love of Jesus Christ. For many traditional
Christians this could take the form of a very gradual surrender involving
a series of small leaps that at some point would culminate in a holistic experience of God's healing, transformative love. What all these experiences
had in common, for Don, was an individual's decision, or leap, to open
themselves prayerfully, in hope and trust, to the transformative healing
love of Jesus Christ. A transformative healing that revealed a faith that
worked and that could be lived.

Don now knew that those who claim to be Christians but have never
made such a decision often confuse a living faith with one of two things,
or both: the worship of the institutional church for the transcendent living
God we know in Jesus Christ, and/or an aimless spiritual journey for one
that seeks a relationship with that God. The former is a form of religious
idolatry, the latter an excuse for never having to open oneself to an experience of the Spirit that might afford a divinely guided purpose and fulfillment. Never deciding could be particularly insidious, Don had found,
where an exclusive obsession with rational and intellectual justifications
for the faith had replaced any openness to the possibility of a transcendent
faith experience. What both impediments to making a leap had in common was how easily they could deceive the Christian into substituting
religious forms for the transformative power of a true faith experience in
God's saving and healing grace in Christ. What these two, and all forms
of faith indecision, share in common is the individual's reluctance to

surrender themselves holistically, at some critical juncture, or over time to that same transformative grace.

There is often, as well, an unwillingness to prayerfully seek the power of God's saving love not only to catch us once we've leaped the chasm, but in helping to bring us up to and over all the things the chasm represents: a bottomless pit of shame, guilt, doubts, fears, false fulfillments, and addictions. False pride in the form of a go-it-alone attitude and a need for self-control often masks a deep insecurity of trusting others, God included, much like his father, Don thought. It came to Don once more that his experience that night had not proven God's existence and nature intellectually or rationally. It had revealed God to Don in a way that was deeper, more profound, and experiential. The closest Don could come, and it was inadequate to describe the depth of love he had felt, was the way a small child who has just fallen feels when held in the arms of its mother. For the first time Don felt no need to rationally analyze his experience. He now knew that while human reason might be able to get you part of the way to a relationship with God in Christ, it could never get you all the way there. In his experience of feeling totally loved and accepted by God Don felt the burden of his anger at others begin to slip away. In the weeks and months to come Don found the bitterness and anger he had felt toward so many: his father, the dean, his roommate, even the young man who had killed his mother and sister, dissipating. Don had come to understand that what bound all God's children together was the need for such a love, as well as the wayward suffering of all those who will not journey toward its source. Don liked the theologian Paul Tillich's definition of sin, which was not a list of transgressions, but the state of being separated from God's love where our human imperfections cannot be informed, reformed, and transformed.

The worst of the worst, Don had realized, was not out of reach of the saving love of God. Nor could the best of the best, who too fell victim to sin, and were even more prone to self-righteousness, come any closer to the infinitely greater love of God. There is a spark of the Divine within us all, Don now knew. We all have an animating light within that was created good in God's sight. For those truly repentant and receptive to God's saving grace no sinner's rap sheet is beyond the transformative refiner's fire of that love. These were understandings that only rang true for Don because of the transcendent, transformative nature of his own experience, because he had experienced the reality of such a love.

The morning after Don's experience on the chapel steps, as usual, he left for breakfast early to meditate with Cindy. As he walked into the student lounge, Cindy greeted him with a happy, but surprised look. "Something seems different about you, Don," she said. "I took a shower this morning," he said in a teasing way. "I am not sure I can explain it but you seem to have a lighter step, like some great burden has been lifted," Cindy persisted in saying. Don became more serious, and in a calm, quiet voice said, "Something happened last night, I had an experience of a spiritual kind that I can't fully explain and that I am still processing. One thing I know for sure was that it was real." "You don't have to share what happened with me right now, but it sounds like it was a good experience," Cindy replied. "It was beyond good, Cindy, and I do want to share it with you soon. What I can tell you now is that I have reached a turning point in my life spiritually," Don said, wanting to pick a time with no other agenda to share this experience with Cindy. "Don," Cindy replied in a caring but insistent tone, "can you be more specific? I don't know what you're talking about." "I can and I will, but can I tell you about it over dinner tonight?" Don gulped as he realized how impulsive he had just been, and the risk he had just taken. Cindy turned her head and looked directly into Don's eyes. She did so searchingly, with a shy, smiling expression. Then suddenly in a more confident tone and manner she answered him, "I thought you'd never ask."

www.ingramcontent.com/pod-product-compliance
Lightning Source LLC
Chambersburg PA
CBHW050406030726
47503CB00006B/2046